D0914376

DEATH
ON A
CELLULAR LEVEL

A Low Country Mystery

Other books by Vicky Hunnings:

The Low Country Mystery Series
The Bride Wore Blood

Lee Ann,
Hope you enjoy my new book and that
all your phone calls are good news.
Vicky Hunnings
10/1/03

DEATH
ON A
CELLULAR
LEVEL

•

Vicky Hunnings

AVALON BOOKS
NEW YORK

PRINTED IN THE UNITED STATES OF AMERICA
ON ACID-FREE PAPER
BY HADDON CRAFTSMEN, BLOOMSBURG, PENNSYLVANIA

For Dad,
who never doubted

Acknowledgments

I would like to express my appreciation to the following individuals who were kind enough to share their expertise with me while I was researching this novel: Eric Krieger, Captain of Division #10 of the Coast Guard Auxiliary on Hilton Head Island; Sean McDonald, Chief Petty Officer of Coast Guard Station Tybee; Mike Vick, helicopter pilot and rescue diver; Bill Schilling, charter boat captain; and Hospital Corpsman First Class Kevin Frank, who gave up a Sunday afternoon with his family to give me a tour of the Angel One Helicopter. Sadly, on March 9, 2002, Kevin lost his life when Angel One developed mechanical problems and crashed into the Atlantic Ocean off the coast of Georgia while attempting to rescue two civilian defense contract workers whose helicopter had crashed in the same area.

Special thanks go to the very talented members of my writers' critique group, Peg Cronin, Kathy Wall and Linda McCabe, who have been good friends as well as mentors. Without you guys I wouldn't be writing.

I would also like to thank my father, Robert Rouse, my sister, Debra Rouse, and my son, Brad Hunnings, who continue to encourage me.

Thanks to friends extraordinaire, Pat and Harry Skevington, who will read anything I send their way, usually more than once, and never complain, and to Helen Evans, who graciously takes time away from her art to help me put the finishing touches on my manuscript.

I am responsible for all technical errors.

Prologue

September 2, 1992

Dr. Jared Phillips closed the door softly behind the last mourner. He stood in the foyer absorbing the silence, broken only by the muted ticking of the grandfather clock in the living room. He wasn't sure how long he stood there, unable to bring himself to move.

"It's finally over," he whispered. Marshaling what little strength remained, he walked into the living room and dropped like a stone onto the blue floral sofa. He undid the knot in his tie and opened the top button of his shirt. Though he tried to fight it, his eyes were drawn, as if by a magnet, to the picture on the mantel. His lovely wife, Amelia, dressed in a black cocktail dress, her head cocked at a familiar angle, laughing, stared back at him.

He stood without being conscious of doing so, crossed the room and picked up the picture. He looked at it for a moment, then clutched it to his chest. A sob caught in his throat. "Be at peace, my darling. No more suffering."

The last two weeks had been a living nightmare. Amelia, in a coma from the tumor that had devoured her brain, had been unable to recognize him, or even squeeze his hand to communicate that she knew he was there. He had never felt so helpless. A neurologist, he should have been able to do something to save her. What a cruel God to give him the knowledge to help others, but not the ability to cure the one he loved the most.

He sank back down on the sofa and gazed into the green eyes of his beautiful 35-year-old wife. "I'm so sorry," he whispered, as tears flooded down his cheeks. "Please forgive me."

They had been together since their senior year of high school. Amelia had put her dream of being a teacher on hold to work at a variety of jobs, while he made his way through medical school, internship, and residency. Only in the past year, since Jared had opened his office, had they begun to talk of starting a family. Oh how he wished they hadn't waited.

Jared wasn't sure how long he sat, remembering, before the absolute stillness became more than he could bear. He flipped on a light, picked up the remote control, and hit the power button. He needed something to fill the silence. He didn't surf the channels. It didn't really matter what was on, as long as it was noise.

The program that flooded the room was "Sixty Minutes," and Mike Wallace was interviewing a physician. Jared found himself paying closer attention.

The doctor was discussing the increased incidence of testicular cancer being detected in state troopers who used radar guns. Almost all of the policemen he'd interviewed said they rested the device between their legs when it was not in use. The physician went on to hypothesize a correlation between cancer and the radio frequency, non-ionizing radiation that the guns emitted when held close to the body. He pleaded for the troopers to place the guns on the passenger seats of their autos when not in use, until further studies could be done.

Jared found it interesting, as any physician would, but didn't think any more about it as the program broke for a commercial.

That night, lying alone in his king-size bed, he hung in that state between consciousness and sleep. But words kept floating through his mind: Radio frequency, non-ionizing radiation. He was trying to remember something, but it was just outside his grasp. Then visions of his wife darted through his mind. Amelia tending her flower garden, stripping layers of paint off an old trunk she had found at a garage sale. Bringing him coffee while he shaved, and talking for hours on her cell phone with her real estate clients.

His last thought, as he finally drifted off to sleep, was cell phones and non-ionizing radiation. Could there possibly be a connection?

Chapter One

February 10, 1995 Wall Street Journal

IMMUNE SYSTEM ATTACKED
BY MOBILE PHONES

Dr. Jared Phillips, a much-respected neurologist, spoke at the American Medical Association convention in Miami, Florida yesterday. He announced that he is launching a campaign to require that health warnings be attached to mobile phones. Dr. Phillips' studies have already linked headaches, memory loss, loss of concentration, and many more damaging side effects to the use of mobile phones.

His latest research suggests that microwaves generated by mobile phones may damage the ability of white blood cells in the body to fight off infection and disease. Dr. Phillips claims our immune system is partially controlled by electromagnetic fields emitted by the body. He believes the radiation discharged by mobile phones damages these magnetic fields and keeps the immune system from functioning properly.

Dr. Phillips stated there is no danger in using cell phones for two or three minutes at a time. But people who leave them on, even on standby for 20 minutes or more, could be harming their immune system.

He is forwarding his results to the Journal of the American Medical Association for publication, and plans to co-operate with other scientists trying to replicate his findings.

A spokesman for the National Radiological Board said, "We have no comment to make at this time. If his work is published in a scientific journal, our board will review it."

Dr. Phillips became interested in studying the immune system's response to radiation emitted by mobile phones after his 35-year-old wife died from a rare brain tumor, a neurocytoma, in 1992. Mrs. Phillips used her cell phone approximately six to eight hours a day. He has filed a lawsuit against the mobile phone manufacturer.

Vincent Laslow, CEO of Wireless Communications Inc., noticed his hands were shaking as he picked up his coffee mug. "Oh crap!" he muttered. His phone buzzed before he could get the coffee cup to his mouth. He picked up the receiver, "Yes, Margaret."

"Randall Palmer, CEO of Palmer Communications, is on line one."

"Put him through."

Vincent listened for a minute, and then muttered, "Yeah, I just read it."

"We're going to have to present a united front on this and squelch the rumors before they get out of hand," Randall said.

"I agree. What do you think we should do?"

"Well, I think we need to get all of the CEOs of the major manufacturers together and plan a strategy. You know the press is going to be calling all of us for comments, and we want to be saying the same thing."

"I'll contact Walter Bergman, Dave Oliver, and Grayce Smithfield. Let's try to schedule a conference call for tomorrow evening around seven," Vincent said.

"I'll get in touch with Alan Sullivan, Drew Fulton, and Robert Kraus. That should cover the major players. So how big a hit do you think our stocks will take when the market opens today?" Randall asked.

"More than I want to think about. Hopefully this'll fade fast."

"Don't count on it. Tomorrow at seven then," Randall said.

Vincent had just hung up the phone when Margaret buzzed again. "A reporter from *USA Today* on line two, sir."

"Tell him I have no comment, and tell any other reporters who call the same thing. And get me Walter Bergman on the phone. When I'm done talking to him I'll want to speak with Dave Oliver and Grayce Smithfield."

"Yes, sir."

The rest of the day was a disaster. The stock prices of all the leading manufacturers of cell phones dropped nearly 30 percent. By four o'clock, when the market closed, Vincent Laslow's company was worth six billion dollars less than it had been just a few hours before. He pulled a fifth of Jack Daniels from his desk drawer, and drank straight from the bottle.

Margaret buzzed him. "Randall Palmer on line one."

"God, I'm glad today's over. Looks like your stock got creamed, too," Palmer said.

"That's an understatement. Did you get hold of the other CEOs?"

"Yeah, that's really why I'm calling. Alan Sullivan was okay with the conference call, but Fulton and Kraus think we should meet in person. They don't feel secure talking over the phone."

"That's interesting. Dave Oliver said the same thing."

"Drew suggested we all meet two days from now in Vegas. Said we could all stay in different hotels and just meet up somewhere. He thinks it's a big enough town to get lost in."

"Let me look at my schedule." Vincent flipped the pages of his appointment book. "I'll have to do some rearranging, but I can probably swing it. I'll call the other guys I talked to this morning and see what they think. I'll call you back shortly, or in the morning, if I can't reach them right away."

"Okay. I'll make a list of hotels and figure out who will stay where and try to line up a meeting place. You have a hotel preference?"

"Nah. Anyplace is okay with me, as long as it has a bar."

Two days later, eight powerful men who controlled the world of wireless communications sat around the conference table in an attorney's office in Las Vegas.

"Let's call this meeting to order and get started," Randall Palmer bellowed. "You know why we're here. We need to agree on how we're going to respond to the article that was in the *Wall Street Journal*. I've made a copy of it for everyone. Those of you from Europe may not have seen it. Take one and pass them on."

"Who the hell is Dr. Jared Phillips anyway?" asked Walter Bergman of BGA Communications, whose headquarters was in France.

"A neurologist who thinks his wife's brain tumor was caused by her cell phone," Vincent Laslow answered.

"Won't people just think he's a zealot?" Grayce Smithfield, CEO of Rondale, asked.

Dave Oliver studied the article then replied, "Let's hope that's what people surmise. But still, we need to find out more about his research."

"How many of us have been contacted by the press for a statement?" asked Alan Sullivan, of Lawrence Telecom. All but one person raised their hands. Robert Kraus, who had flown in from Germany for the meeting, was the only one without his hand in the air.

Vincent Laslow spoke up. "I had seven different reporters contact me. We can't ignore the issue and just hope it'll go away. All of our stocks were decimated. I think we have to make some kind of a statement to reassure the public that our phones are safe. It'll carry a lot more weight if we all say about the same thing."

"Well, it all went away a few years ago when there was that speculation about radar guns cops used causing testicular cancer. What makes you think it won't all just blow over again?" Drew Fulton asked.

"Because it appears, this time, that Dr. Phillips may have scientific data to back up his claims," Palmer answered quickly.

For a moment, no one spoke. Finally, Robert Kraus turned to Palmer and said, "My company, as well as several others represented in this room, I'm sure, have had concerns about the effects of the radiation emitted by our phones. We have chosen to ignore some of the data our research and development departments have shared with us. If it becomes common knowledge about some of the side effects we have speculated about, then we could be the next industry at risk for multiple litigation, just like the tobacco companies are now. If that happens, our stock prices will hit rock bottom, and some of us will not survive. It may be in our mutual interest to consider funding an independent researcher to find out for sure exactly what we're dealing with."

"I like that idea," Grayce Smithfield said with a hint of excitement in his voice. "We could tell the press that we want to make sure the public is safe, so we are conducting our own research. We could make it a long study, maybe three to five years or so. That way, if we find after a couple of years that there really is a problem, we can correct it in our phones before the results of the study are released to the public."

"We would appear to be *proactive* instead of *reactive*," Walter Bergman added, nodding his head and gesturing with his hands.

"It would have to be an impartial researcher we could be assured would keep the results strictly confidential," Dave Oliver replied.

"Do you think we should find someone in the U.S. or in Europe?" Alan Sullivan asked.

"First of all, I think we need to vote on whether this is the way we want to proceed," Randall Palmer interrupted.

"After all, we're talking about expending a lot of money to fund a lengthy research project."

"But in the long run, it will be cheaper than each of us trying to go it alone," Vincent Laslow chimed in.

They discussed the pros and cons for over an hour before voting. When they finally did, it was unanimous.

"Now that we've agreed on that, let's form a committee to come up with a list of names of researchers who would be able to conduct the study. Do I have any volunteers?" Randall Palmer asked.

Walter Bergman spoke up. "If Robert will help me, we can check all over Europe." Kraus nodded affirmatively.

"Then let's have two from the U.S. on the committee as well. Vince, what about you and Dave?"

Vincent looked over at Oliver with a questioning look. "Sure," Dave answered.

"Okay. We're moving right along. If the press contacts us, we can tell them we are going to launch a study to determine if there are any harmful side effects from the use of cell phones. Agreed?" Palmer asked.

"Agreed," several voices answered in unison.

"Then why don't we plan to reconvene here six weeks from today and review the names the committee has come up with?" Palmer said, surveying the faces of his cohorts.

"That should be enough time," Robert Kraus chimed in.

"I suggest, before you leave town, that you go ahead and make a reservation at your hotel for six weeks from now. Consider this meeting adjourned." Randall Palmer pushed his chair back. "I don't know about anyone else in this room, but I'm headed to the craps table. Anyone care to join me?"

Chapter Two

Dusk was rapidly approaching as Dr. Anthony Kline gazed out the window of his study in his oceanfront home in Port Royal Plantation. October on Hilton Head Island, South Carolina, was his favorite month. Most of the tourists, humidity, and unbearable traffic were gone for another year. The sun would be setting soon, and the sky was streaked with various shades of orange and purple. Seagulls glided effortlessly across the beach.

Cecilia Campbell, his research assistant, sat in front of her computer feeding data into the machine from the stack of faxes she had received from the 50 researchers all across the United States and Europe who were participating in the study they were conducting.

Dr. Kline returned to his desk to review the results on his screen. "I don't think our employers are going to like the way things are turning out. Dr. Vespey's study on the changes in the immune system function is especially damaging, and Dr. Margot's study shows a significant increase in malignant tumors."

"Well, if you don't like those, then you're really not going to like Kee's results of single and double strand DNA breaks in rat brain cells," Cece said, continuing to pound the keys.

10

"I see what you mean. And Dr. Bellows' results I'm reviewing now show changes in the hippocampus of the brain. Not only that, but EEG brain waves are altered with exposure to cell phone signals. Damn, I don't think I'll ever use a cell phone again for longer than two minutes at a time," Kline said, removing his glasses and rubbing his eyes.

"Me either. I even told my brother to cool it with his."

"As soon as you've finished, back up all the data to a couple of disks and take them with you. I want you to run by the bank on Monday before you come in, and rent a safe deposit box for them. I don't want to lose any of this if the electricity goes off, or the computer crashes."

"Will do."

"So, Cece, what did you decide to wear to the Halloween party tonight?"

"The costume shop hardly had anything left, so I bought a long black wig and I'm going as Cher."

"Cher?"

"Yeah, I dug an old pair of black hip huggers out of my closet and a pink bandeau top. Combined with some huge funky earrings and long beads, it should work."

Dr. Kline regarded Cece's tall, willowy figure, and decided she could probably pull it off.

"What about you, doing anything?" she asked.

"No, I'm too old for all that."

"So you're going to pass out the treats, huh?"

"That won't take long. We don't usually have more than a couple of door-ringers. Last year we had none. Not many kids live on the street, mostly just retired folks."

"That's no fun."

"You can party for the both of us."

Cece finished backing up all the data off both computers and slipped the disks into her purse. "Well, I'm out of here. See you Monday," she said, digging in her purse for her car keys.

"Have a good weekend."

"You too. Playing golf tomorrow?"

"Play *at* it you mean, don't you? Yeah, I'll get in eighteen holes."

"Ruth playing with you?"

"No, she's got a tennis match in the morning. I'm going with Sammy, my dentist buddy."

"Well, have a good time."

After Cece left, Tony Kline walked to the kitchen and fixed two drinks with Captain Morgan Spiced Rum, which his wife, Ruth, said tasted like a vanilla coke. He carried them into the living room, handed her one, and sank down next to her on the peach floral sofa.

She was reading a book on quilting, which was her latest passion. She had even attended several quilting seminars, in different parts of the country, over the past six months. Ruth didn't seem to be as content with the idyllic island life as he was. She was more a "big city" person.

"What's for dinner?" he asked.

Ruth looked up from her book. "I don't feel like cooking, so what do you think about ordering a pizza or getting Chinese takeout?"

"Pizza sounds kind of good."

"Okay. As soon as I finish my drink, I'll call it in. I need to get a few things at the grocery store, then I'll pick up the pizza on my way home."

"Sounds like a plan."

"I fixed a bowl of candy and set it on the credenza by the front door in case you have any trick or treaters while I'm gone."

Tony picked up the remote control for the TV and surfed until he found CNBC. He wanted to see how his stocks had done today, and try to figure out what the hell the market would do on Monday. He'd really gotten into it since he had opened an Ameritrade account. At only $10 a trade, he could afford to do a little playing around.

Ruth shook her head and headed to the kitchen to order the pizza. The stock market didn't interest her at all. She phoned in their order, picked up her purse and keys, and called into the living room. "I'll be back in about forty-five minutes with food."

"Can't be soon enough. I'm starved."

"Well don't be nibbling while I'm gone," she said as she walked toward the front door.

A few minutes later, while Tony stood at the kitchen counter fixing himself another drink, he heard the doorbell. "Oh, a goblin, no doubt."

He picked up the bowl of candy off the credenza and pulled open the front door.

A person, covered from head to toe in a black wetsuit with a mask, regulator, and a mouthpiece hanging at his chin, stood on his doorstep. *What are they feeding kids these days? He's taller than I am.*

"Scuba Man, huh," he said offering the bowl of candy. "Where's your trick or treat bag?"

"No treats, just tricks," the figure said, opening a fanny pack at his waist.

Tony's eyes opened wide in fear and his mouth formed a silent O when he saw the gun.

Ruth hit the remote control and pulled her Mercedes into the garage. She grabbed her purse and the pizza, and hurried in the kitchen door. "Tony, I'm back. I've got a few bags of groceries I need to bring in, then we'll be ready to eat."

Tony didn't answer, but she heard the TV and figured he was engrossed in something. She returned to the garage, brought in the groceries and set them on the counter—eggs, milk, and cheese into the fridge, the rest into the pantry.

Pulling out two plates she placed several pieces of pizza on each. "Do you need something to drink?" she yelled to Tony.

When he didn't answer, she grabbed two cans of Coor's Lite out of the refrigerator and put them in the crook of her arm, then picked up the plates and a handful of napkins. "What are you so engrossed in?" she asked as she walked into the living room.

But the room was empty. *He must be in the bathroom.* She set everything down on the glass-topped coffee table. CNN blared away on the TV. Ruth popped open both cans of beer and took a big bite of pizza. *Um, that's good.* She wiped the string of cheese off her chin.

A couple of minutes later, when Tony still hadn't returned, Ruth stood up and started toward the bathroom in search of him. "Tony, the pizza's getting cold," she yelled.

Ruth heard the doorbell and changed direction and headed toward the foyer. She froze when she saw Tony sprawled on the floor, the candy bowl shattered and little boxes of Mild Duds and miniature Snickers bars scattered all over the floor. The doorbell rang again as she let out a loud scream. She raced to the front door and flung it open. "Help me. My husband has collapsed," she yelled to the miniature Beauty and The Beast that stood on her doorstep. Her neighbor, James Redding, from two houses over, came bounding out of the bushes. "James, its Tony. Call 911."

James raced toward the kitchen as Ruth rushed over and knelt at her husband's side. "Tony, Tony!" she screamed, shaking him. There was no response.

"911, what is your emergency?"

"My neighbor, Dr. Kline, has collapsed. Send an ambulance!"

"Is the address 560 North Port Royal Drive?"

"Yes. Hurry, please!"

"What is your name?"

"James Redding."

"Mr. Redding, is your neighbor having any trouble breathing?"

"I don't know. He's unconscious."

"I'll stay on the line. I've already dispatched an ambulance. Go check and see if Mr. Kline is breathing and come back and tell me."

James threw the phone on the counter and ran into the foyer. He instructed his children to sit down in the living room where they couldn't see what was going on. Then he knelt down next to Ruth and looked for the rise and fall of

Dr. Kline's chest. Nothing. Ruth leaned over and put her cheek just under his nose. "He's not breathing and I can't feel a pulse," she said softly, as tears streamed down her cheeks. "I'll start CPR."

James hurried back to the phone. "He's not breathing. His wife is doing CPR. Help us, please!" he pleaded

Ruth cleared Tony's airway, pinched his nose, and blew three times into his mouth. Then she moved around to his side and placed her hands tentatively on his chest and pushed.

It was much harder than she remembered on that doll, Annie, in the class she had taken several years ago. *Why do I remember the doll's name?*

She and James continued CPR until they finally heard a siren. James rushed to the front door and ran to the end of the driveway, frantically waving his arms and shouting, "Here, here."

The ambulance came to a screeching halt and two paramedics jumped out, each carrying a large blue bag.

"His wife is doing CPR, but he's still unconscious."

The paramedics ran inside and asked Ruth to step back, and immediately began to assess their patient. "No pulse, no breathing," the younger one said quickly to his partner. James went to be with his children.

The second paramedic noticed a small hole and what looked like a powder burn in the left chest area of Tony's shirt. "Looks like a possible GSW. Let's roll him over for a minute."

They ran their hands over his back, but couldn't find an exit wound.

They turned Tony back to the position he had been in when they arrived. The older of the two, Bert, according to the name on his uniform, raised Tony's eyelid. His pupil was fixed and dilated.

"Why aren't you doing anything?" Ruth screamed. "Help him!"

The younger paramedic rose and took Ruth's arm, moving her into the dining room. "Ma'am. There's nothing we can do. He's already gone."

"Gone? You mean he's dead?" she screamed.

"Yes ma'am. He's been shot."

"Shot? No, you must be mistaken," she said, shaking her head back and forth. "Nooooo!"

"Ma'am, just have a seat here at the table," he said, taking her arm and forcing her down into the chair.

Bert walked into the kitchen and picked up the dangling phone. "Hello."

"This is the 911 operator. Who is this?"

"Paramedic Bert Sellers. Please dispatch the police and coroner to this address immediately. We have a GSW and he's DOA. Happy Halloween."

Chapter Three

An hour later, crime scene tape strung all along the front lawn, the driveway full of police cars and the coroner's wagon, a cluster of people stood across the street on the bike path.

Goblins, witches, Power Rangers, princesses and ballerinas were peppered throughout the crowd.

Detective William Morgan, known as Shark because of his love of shark fishing, and his partner, Dell Hassler, death investigators for the Beaufort County Sheriff's Department, worked the crime scene inside.

Anna Connors, the only female coroner in South Carolina, completed her examination of the body. "Single gunshot wound to the chest, point blank range, probably a small caliber weapon like a .22," she said to the detectives.

"Looks like he opened the door, expecting trick or treaters, and was shot," Dell said.

"Hell of a trick, if you ask me," Shark said, pulling out his camera. He began to snap pictures from several different angles.

"What a perfect way to shoot someone. Walk right up to the door in a mask and bam! I bet you don't find any physical evidence," Connors said, looking around.

"I think you're probably right," Shark said, nodding his head.

"So what's the line on this guy anyway?" the coroner asked.

"His wife said he was a doctor and doing research. That's all we know so far. We haven't really interviewed her yet. She's pretty much a basket case. It didn't help any when we asked to do a paraffin test on her hands to see if there was any gunshot residue."

"And?" she said, turning to Shark with her eyebrows raised.

"Negative," he replied.

"I'm pretty much finished here. Is it okay for the guys to load up the body and transport it to Charleston?" Connors asked.

"Yeah, I've got enough pictures," Shark said, stuffing his camera back in his bag.

"How long before you figure we'll get an autopsy report?" Dell asked.

"Depends on how many bodies are ahead of yours in the big city, I guess. Probably a couple of days, not that it's going to tell you much. Kind of reminds me of the Marcus DeSilva case, gunshot wound to the heart and no physical evidence," she said, referring to a crime scene they had worked the previous year.

"At least, this time, we know who the target was," Dell said.

"You thought you knew the last time too, but you were wrong. October seems to be the month for murder on Hilton Head."

"Remind me to take my vacation next October, Dell," Shark said, remembering the DeSilva case. He glanced over at her to see if Anna's mention of it had brought back unpleasant memories. He had almost lost his partner on that one.

Dell avoided his eyes and continued writing in her notebook. She refused to think back on that time, but the memories were never very far away.

"Well, I'm out of here," Connors said, lifting her bag and turning toward the door.

"So do you think the widow has sufficiently calmed down so we can ask her some questions?" Dell asked, turning to Shark.

"There's only one way to find out." Shark turned and stepped into the hallway, Dell close on his heels.

Ruth Kline, a petite blond, sat staring off into space. Several crumpled tissues were strewn on the coffee table in front of her, and she clutched another in her right hand.

"Excuse me, Mrs. Kline, but we need to ask you a few questions," Shark said, as he sat down on the sofa next to her and Dell in a matching wing chair next to the couch.

"I told the officers everything," she said, trying to suppress a sob.

"I know, but we need to find out as much as we can about your husband. First of all, do you know anyone who would want to kill him?" Shark asked softly.

"No. Tony was a good man. He didn't have any enemies."

"You said your husband did research. What kind?" Dell inquired.

Ruth blew her nose loudly before answering. "He is, I mean was, an independent researcher. Companies hired him to do a variety of studies."

"What was he currently working on?" Dell asked, pen in hand.

"Something to do with the amount of radiation cell phones emit, and the side effects that could cause. Really, that's about all I know," she said, reaching for the glass of water on the coffee table.

"Who hired him to do the study?" Shark asked.

"A bunch of companies who manufacture mobile phones."

"And was that the only study he was currently working on?"

"Yes, he and Cece had been working on it exclusively the past three years."

"Cece?"

"Cecilia Campbell, his research assistant."

"Where did they do this research?" Shark asked.

Ruth wiped away the tears that streamed down her face and dabbed at her eyes. "They didn't really do the research themselves. They hired doctors all across the United States and Europe to do the studies. They just compiled the results. They worked here, in his office."

Shark glanced over at Dell. She stood and quietly slipped into the hallway. It didn't take her long to find the workplace. She sat down in front of the first computer she came to. Computers were like best friends to her. They shared everything they knew in the hands of the right person, and she was that person.

Back in the living room, Shark continued. "Who did your husband report his findings to?"

"I'm not sure. The study was for five years, so it wasn't complete yet. I don't know if he had to send reports periodically, or planned to wait until the final results were in."

"Do you know where Cecilia Campbell lives?" Shark asked.

"Here in the plantation, on Tabby Road. She lives with her aunt."

"Do you know the address?"

Ruth paused for a moment. "I'm not sure, but it's the third house on the left, a brown two-story."

Shark asked Ruth to repeat what had happened earlier and wrote down the times and details, but she really had little to offer.

"If only I'd found him sooner. Maybe it wouldn't have been too late. I mean, I put away the groceries and fixed the plates of pizza before I even started looking for him. I just can't believe this."

Shark tried to reassure her that it probably wouldn't have made any difference. "Do you have family or someone we can call for you?"

"We never had any kids. I couldn't. Would you call Reverend Wheeler, my minister?"

"Of course. I'll have one of the officers contact him immediately."

When Shark was finished with the widow, he walked back to the doctor's office. He was surprised to find Dell going through the drawers of a file cabinet. He couldn't believe she wasn't working her magic with the computers.

"Done with the PCs already?" he asked.

"Didn't even get to start," she said disgustedly. "The hard drives have been wiped clean, probably with a magnet."

Eyes wide with surprise, Shark turned to look. "There's *nothing* left on them?"

"Nada! But at least we know the perp came in the house. Maybe we'll find some physical evidence."

"That would be nice. But did you have to say perp? Makes you sound like a rookie. Anyway, maybe his assistant can tell us what was on the computers."

"Better yet, let's hope she has some backup disks."

"What else have you found?" Shark asked.

"A lot of records of personal stuff. Bank statements, copies of tax returns, investment portfolio, stuff like that. But nothing related to his current research."

"So, the murderer destroys the computers and maybe takes some records with him. He did spend a little time in here."

"There's some sand in front of the desk and file cabinets," Dell said, pointing to the floor.

"Well, this is an oceanfront house," Shark said, peeking out the dark window toward the beach.

For the next two hours Shark and Dell combed through all the files, fruitlessly. By 11 o'clock they felt they would glean nothing further from the crime scene.

"Don't you think it's odd that Mrs. Kline didn't notice the gunshot wound in her husband's chest when she started CPR?" Dell asked.

"Not necessarily. She was probably in shock by then, and the entrance wound was small. Now, if he'd been shot with a .45, there would have been no way she could have missed it, but with a .22, it's not that hard to imagine. Let's go by Cecilia Campbell's house since she lives here in the plantation," Shark said, closing the last file drawer.

"Might as well." Dell groaned and heaved her tired body out of the desk chair. "Who needs sleep anyway? Josh is getting used to going to bed alone."

"Hell, you've only been married four months. He can't be going to bed alone that often. Honeymoon over already?"

"No. It just seems between this job and his in Charleston, one of us is always gone."

"I thought he was in California."

"He got home last night."

"That's what he gets for being such a hot-shot architect. Just as long as you guys don't up and move to the west coast or someplace like that. I would hate to have to break in a new partner."

They offered Ruth Kline their condolences, then walked into the moonlit night. They could hear the roar of the surf. "I would love to be able to hear that sound everyday," Shark said, as he climbed into the car and buckled his seat-belt.

"I know what you mean. But on a cop's salary that's like wishing for the moon. I bet there's not a single oceanfront home in this whole plantation for less than a million."

"I have a feeling that two mil is more like it. Anyway, let's see if Campbell is home."

Five minutes later they pulled into the circular drive in front of the brown two-story. There were no lights on.

"I'll try the bell in case she turned in early," Dell said, opening the passenger door. She walked up the wooden front steps and rang the bell. When there was no answer she leaned on it again for about 15 seconds. Still, nothing.

"Guess it'll have to wait until tomorrow," Dell said, slipping her shoes off and propping her feet up on the dashboard. "Maybe if we drive like a bat out of hell all the way to Beaufort, Josh won't be *too tired* by the time I get there."

"Let's make a quick stop at the guard gate and pick up a copy of the list of visitor passes that were called in this evening. I promise I'll have you home by midnight."

"Damn, I guess that means I have to put my shoes back on."

"Nah, you can wait in the car. I'll run in and get it."

Forty-five minutes later Shark dropped Dell off at her house on Lady's Island, then drove on to Pleasant Farms, the subdivision where he lived.

Shark threw his keys in the basket he kept right by the front door and called to the silent house. "I'm home." *Maybe I should get some kind of a pet. Then at least someone would care if I got home or not.* Shark headed straight for the refrigerator and pulled out a beer. He stood in his silent kitchen, the only light that of the dim refrigerator bulb, and chugged half of the brew before he closed the door. In the darkness he could hear the slow dripping of the faucet. He had meant to pick up a new washer for it today, but he had forgotten.

He thought about Ruth Kline. She would have to get used to the silence, like he had since his wife had died. It was one of the toughest things. He willed his tired legs to carry him toward the bedroom.

He dropped his clothes next to the bed. You could do that when you lived alone. What he wouldn't give to hear Laura yell at him to put his clothes into the hamper.

Shark stood in the shower, and let the hot water loosen the tight muscles in his neck. He thought of Jazz, but decided it was too late to call her.

Dell had introduced him to Josh's sister the previous Christmas. She was an attorney in Charleston, and they had been an item ever since. Recently divorced when they met, she wanted to take it slow. He was ready to take the plunge. He wanted to start a family, something he and Laura had never had an opportunity to do. Being a widower for four years was plenty long enough. He hated coming home to an empty house and bed every night.

Chapter Four

Cecilia Campbell, Cece to her friends, still dressed in her Cher costume, stumbled out to her Honda Civic del Sol around eight o'clock Saturday morning. *Hell of a party.* She buckled her seatbelt and started the engine. Her head was pounding, and her mouth tasted like a desert. She had fallen asleep on Damon's couch at four o'clock, the party still in full swing. Glancing in the rearview mirror, she straightened her wig, which was a little askew, and turned up the volume on the radio. Her clothes reeked of cigarette smoke and she noticed a large dark stain on her pink bandeau top. She grabbed the elastic and stared down at her ample breasts. *No sign of injury, so it must be wine.* Visions of a tub overflowing with bubbles and smelling of lilacs spurred her into action. She pulled out into the heavy traffic on William Hilton Parkway and was trying to decide whether to stop and buy a cappuccino at the Starvin' Marvin convenience store, when the news came on.

"Last night, Dr. Anthony Kline, noted researcher, was shot to death in his home in Port Royal Plantation. No arrests have been made at this time. Police are asking anyone with information to please contact the Beaufort County Sheriff's office.

"Beaufort County School Superintendent . . ."

"Noooooo!" Cece screamed, her eyes wide in disbelief.

Her left hand flew to her mouth. And then her whole body began to shake.

The car drifted slowly to the right, as her mind tried to filter the unbelievable announcement she'd heard. The front tire drifted off the edge of the pavement spitting up small pieces of gravel. The man in the car behind her began to lay on his horn, probably fearing she was falling asleep. Cece was jerked back to reality, as cars raced past in the left-hand lane. Tears clouded her vision and she tried to choke back her sobs. She flipped on her right turn signal, and barely managed to pull into the parking lot of Long-horn Steak House. Cece straddled two parking spots and cut the engine. Surely she must be dreaming. This had to be a nightmare. She pinched her arm hard, and then began to sob uncontrollably. *It can't be Tony. There has to be some kind of mistake.* She groped for a tissue in her purse. *Why would anyone kill Tony? Ruth must be devastated.*

Cece fought to get herself under control, still not sure she really believed what she had heard. Finally she wiped her eyes, blew her nose again, and restarted her vehicle. She turned on the car heater, even though it was probably close to 60 outside. But she felt chilled to the bone. *I'll go talk to Ruth and find out what happened.*

In record time Cece pulled into the entrance of Port Royal Plantation and was waved through the guard gate when the officer saw the blue resident sticker on her wind-shield. She ignored the plantation speed limit of 35 mph and was at Tony's in a matter of minutes—and knew there had been no mistake when she saw the yellow crime scene tape and two officers methodically searching the yard.

Pulling her car into the empty lot alongside two police cars, she just sat there for a moment trying to compose herself before she spoke with Ruth. She closed her eyes and took a deep breath, then exhaled through her mouth, like she did when she was running. She repeated the ex-ercise several times, wanting to postpone the inevitable. Finally, willing her legs to work, she walked slowly toward the yellow tape. It felt as if she was dragging a concrete block around each ankle. When she reached it, she paused, as if touching it was some kind of crime or something, then ducked under and ran to the front door. She stood on the porch for a moment, her hands clenched in tight fists, then reached out and jabbed the doorbell insistently.

Too soon, a man dressed in a black suit answered the door. "Can I help you?" he inquired, surveying her from head to toe, a deep frown wrinkling his forehead.

"Is Ruth here? I'm Cecilia Campbell, Tony's research assistant. I was on the way home from an all-night Halloween party when I heard the news on the radio. Is Ruth all right? Do they know who shot Tony? What happened?"

The man raised his hand like a traffic cop. "Slow down. I'm Reverend Wheeler, Ruth's pastor. Please come in," he said, motioning her inside. Cece stopped, foot in midair, when she saw the chalk outline on the floor of the foyer. She lowered her foot and remained standing on the porch. She covered her mouth with her hand, afraid she would cry out.

The reverend, very aware of what had stopped her in her tracks, motioned for her to step to her right just inside the door. "I'm sorry you had to see that. Ruth is doing okay physically. Emotionally she's a wreck, as you would imagine. She's the one who discovered the body."

"Oh, how terrible. Do you think I could talk to her for just a minute?" Cece asked, trying to choke back her tears, her eyes drawn back to the outline.

"I'll see if she's up to seeing anyone." The words were hardly out of his mouth when Ruth, dressed in a paisley kimono, walked out of the kitchen, both hands wrapped around a large steaming black Barnes and Noble mug. When she saw Cece, she cried out, dropped the cup, then slumped to the floor.

"Oh my God," Cece cried, as they rushed to her side and bent over her. "Is she all right?"

Reverend Wheeler knelt down and wrapped his fingers around her wrist and felt for a pulse. "I think she's just fainted. She'll probably be okay in a minute. Perhaps you should go."

"Are you sure we shouldn't call an ambulance or 911?"

"I was a medic in the army years ago. See, she's already starting to come around a little."

"Can you just tell me what happened?" Cece whispered

"I really don't know much. Apparently Ruth went out to pick up a pizza and when she came home she found her husband dead in the foyer. He'd been shot."

"I just can't believe this. Who would want to kill Tony?"

Ruth began to moan, and the minister patted her hand. He whispered, "Apparently the police think it may have something to do with the work he was doing. Both computers in the office were tampered with. Since you're his assistant, I'm sure the police will want to talk to you as soon as possible. Maybe I should tell the officers outside that you're here."

"Wait! Let me run home and get out of this awful costume. I'll take a shower and then come right back."

"Okay. I'll tell them you'll return shortly."

"Thanks," Cece whispered, standing and moving toward the door. "Tell Ruth I'm really sorry. I'll be back in a few minutes."

Cece's mind was a blur as she turned onto Tabby Road. Suddenly her progress was halted by two fire trucks and a couple of police cars blocking the way. She pulled over and parked, then hurried out of the car. Immediately she smelled smoke.

A crowd of people filled the street. Cece passed a couple of her neighbors, but she didn't really know them well, and they didn't recognize her in her costume.

"Excuse me," she said, working her way through the crowd. When she finally elbowed her way through the throng of onlookers, she couldn't believe her eyes. The only thing left of her aunt's house was a pile of smoldering rubble, and concrete blocks that had held up the foundation. She stood frozen to the spot. "Aunt Sophie," she whispered.

"They've found two bodies," she heard someone in the

crowd say. "The police think it may be related to that murder last night."

Sophie was her mother's younger sister. Cece remembered how her mother, who had struggled with her weight her entire life, had often kidded Sophie that she must really be the milkman's daughter, as tall and svelte as she was. Always impeccably dressed, it would have taken a mild hurricane to blow a strand of hair out of place in her highlighted coiffure. Divorced after 32 years of marriage, and alone for several years after, she had recently started dating a nice man, Carl, whom she had met playing bridge. Cece knew, as sure as the sun would come up tomorrow, that the other body found in the house must have been his. She desperately hoped they hadn't suffered, that the smoke had overcome them in their sleep, before the flames had ravaged their bodies.

Now, Cece would never get the opportunity to thank Aunt Sophie for opening up her home and heart to her after her fiancé, Mark, had been killed in an automobile accident just 12 days before their wedding. What a terrible time that had been. Having just graduated from college, and feeling her whole life was just about to start, she had been devastated. Cece wasn't sure how she had survived it. And if it hadn't been for Aunt Sophie, literally taking her by the hand and bringing her home to Hilton Head, she might not have. She had left her mother to contact all the wedding guests, return the beautiful presents, and cancel all the arrangements.

It was her aunt who had told her about the blurb in *The Trident*, the monthly newsletter for the plantation, regarding a doctor seeking a research assistant. Since her college degree was in biology, her aunt had twisted her arm to answer the ad.

"One of the ladies who lived here worked for the man who was murdered last night," another onlooker stated.

A cold chill crept up Cece's spine. She wasn't sure how long she stood there, paralyzed. Then, head down, she began to edge her way back through the crowd. *Oh my God, oh my God. I've got to get out of here.*

As she pawed her way back towards her car, averting her eyes when she recognized a couple of people who lived on the street, she heard someone say. "They think it was arson. Apparently the fire started about four o'clock this morning. Those poor women who lived there! Who would do such a thing?"

When Cece finally reached the edge of the crowd, she made herself walk to the car; not run, which was her first instinct.

She quickly made her way to the plantation exit. *This can't be happening. Please God let me wake up from this nightmare.* She slapped her cheek, but this was no dream.

Cece pulled onto William Hilton Parkway and headed north for the bridge off the island. *My God! What should I do? Where should I go? Should I call the police? Did someone try to kill me too? What's happening? My God, Aunt Sophie, I'm sorry. I've got to get somewhere safe, where I can think things through.*

A nice looking man about six-foot tall, dressed in beige cargo shorts and a white T-shirt, parked his red 10-speed bicycle at the end of Tabby Road. He politely made his way to the front of the crowd, where he could see the results of his night's work. *Perfect.* Trying not to smile, he turned to the elderly man standing on his right and asked, "Anyone hurt?"

"They found two bodies. Probably the two women who lived there."

"What a tragedy," he said, shaking his head.

The man slipped back through the crowd, retrieved his bike, and rode away. When he reached the stop sign on Oak Creek, he couldn't help turning, not in the direction of the back entrance to the plantation, but in the direction of 560 North Port Royal Drive.

Five minutes later he rode by on the bike path, directly across the street from the house, and smiled when he saw two deputies combing the lawn with plastic bags in their hands.

You can look all you want, but you won't find anything— not even a hair. The wet suit covered me from head to toe.

As he rode on toward the back gate he couldn't help but think of the $250,000 that was about to be added to his bank account in the Turks and Caicos.

After exiting the plantation through the back gate, which had no security officer, he stopped at a pay phone outside the Amoco station. He dropped in some coins and dialed the number from memory. When the answering machine picked up he left a cryptic message. "I took out both loads of laundry, and the washing machine is broken beyond repair."

He remounted his bike and continued on to Shelter Cove, where in addition to shops and restaurants, luxury condominiums overlooked a beautiful harbor. He rode his bike down the ramp to his large fishing boat. He stored the collapsible bicycle on board, grabbed a beer, then flicked on the marine radio and listened to the tide schedule and forecast. Conditions sounded great. He was torn between pulling anchor and heading on back to Fort Lauderdale, or trying his hand fishing the local waters for a day or two. By the time he had finished his beer, he had started rigging his poles for a little bottom fishing. He grabbed his chart and began to search for the fishing reef, Fish America. At dinner last night he had heard a couple of guys at the next table talking about it.

Cece didn't even remember the drive to Savannah, and was surprised to find herself grabbing a ticket from the machine at the entrance to the long-term parking lot at Savannah International Airport. She found a space at the far edge of the tract and cut the engine. She folded her arms on the steering wheel and rested her head on them. *Now what? Did someone really try to murder me too, like they did Tony, to keep the study results quiet? Was this all happening because of the interim report we sent to Randall*

Palmer two weeks ago? Who else would care about the results? Too many questions and not any answers.

How long before whoever killed Tony discovers I didn't die in the fire? The police will know right away since I stopped to see Ruth. But it may be a day or so before the murderer finds out. Frantically, Cece grabbed her purse and dumped the contents on the passenger seat. She breathed a sigh of relief when she saw the backup disks. *Should I contact the police and turn them over to them? Would I be safe then?* Cece had no idea how long she sat there trying to figure out what would be the best course of action, but her brain wasn't working too well. Then it dawned on her. *Not hardly, because I still know what's on them. Maybe the police could protect me, put me in the Witness Protection Program, or something.*

But Cece's one encounter with the police in the small town in Indiana where she grew up had left her with a healthy skepticism of anyone in uniform. She thought back to the time she had reported that one of their officers had stopped her one evening on her way home from work and given her a warning about watching her speed. He had come on to her and asked her out. When she refused, he had followed her home; and continued to do so each night after work, for several weeks. When she had finally gotten up enough nerve to report it, the officer she talked to said she should be thrilled that the police were doing such a fine job of protecting its citizens. But he wasn't too happy when Cece pointed out that the officer was leaving his jurisdiction and following her into another county, down a tiny country road, and sitting at the end of her driveway until she went inside and locked her door. It was several months before she read in the newspaper that the officer had been discharged from the force—after 13 women had complained. Maybe if she could just get someplace safe to think for a day or two she could convince herself to trust the police.

Cece's head was itching, so she pulled off the wig. A minute later she whipped it back on, and looked over her shoulder. Maybe whoever killed Tony already knew she didn't die in the fire and had followed her. He probably knew what kind of car she drove, and maybe even had a picture of her. Hopefully, in the Cher wig he wouldn't recognize her, but he would the car.

Cece quickly stuffed everything back into her purse and opened the glove box to see if she had anything she could use for a weapon. She shrieked with delight as she grabbed the little spray of nerve paralyzer, with a pink whistle attached, that she had bought from the sheriff's department after attending a class on "Don't Be A Rape Victim." *Wonder if this stuff is still any good? It's been in here for at least two years.*

Cece rummaged between the tapes and the three pairs of sunglasses, but found nothing more dangerous than a box of Tic Tac. But she did have a screwdriver and a flashlight in the trunk! She pulled the release and jumped out of the car.

When it popped open she was surprised to see her gym bag. She had forgotten about it since she hadn't worked out in a while. It held not only her workout clothes, but a couple of changes of clothing, in addition to all the toiletries and stuff to get ready for work. She had gone through a phase of getting up early and driving to Gold's Gym to work out early in the morning. That had lasted about two weeks. *At least I can get out of my Cher clothes.* She added the screwdriver and flashlight to the bag and closed the trunk.

Cece, her eyes to the ground, made herself stride sedately to the terminal, where she could become part of the crowd. She hesitated just outside the entrance where several taxis were parked waiting for fares. *I don't know how much money I have in my purse, but I know it's not a lot. I can take a courtesy van to the Hyatt Hotel on River Street and catch a city bus there—to where, I don't know.* She stepped on the black pad, and the pneumatic doors swung open wide.

Frequently looking over her shoulder, she hurried

through the terminal and took the stairs down to the bottom level. She knew the courtesy vehicles left from the baggage claim area.

Once she was seated in the van, she sighed with relief. *So far, so good, but now what?* She glanced around to make sure no one was paying any special attention to her, then opened her purse and tried to surreptitiously count her money. She had a total of $72.36. *Wait! What about your "mad" money?*

Cece rifled to the bottom of her purse and took out the plastic folder with her car and medical insurance information. Behind her medical card was a $20 bill—cab fare in case she ever got in a bind. *So, ninety-two-dollars and thirty-six cents.* She had her checkbook and ATM card, but decided she probably shouldn't use them. On TV, and in the movies, the bad guys always seemed to be able to find people as soon as they wrote a check or used their credit cards. Maybe that wasn't true in real life, but she couldn't afford to take any chances.

So where can I go that will be safe and not cost me anything? God, Mom, help me out here! Cece wasn't in the habit of talking to her dead mother, except in dire emergencies—and this certainly seemed to qualify.

She thought back to those unpleasant days the previous year in Indiana when her mother lay in a coma, her spine and brain ravished from malignant melanoma. The endless days, sitting in the critical care waiting room, praying that her mother's strong heart would finally give up and end her suffering. The many nights she and her father had spent stretched out on the couches in the waiting room, trying to catch a few hours of sleep. Drinking endless cups of coffee along with other strangers, who were also maintaining "the death watch."

That's it! Who would think to look for me in a hospital? Thank you, Mom! I'll have to get a message to Dad somehow that I'm okay.

Cece exited the van at the Hyatt Hotel on Bay Street, walked over to the bus stop and sank down on the bench.

Fifteen minutes later a bus approached for Abercorn/Shopping Centers. She knew Chandler Hospital was only a couple of blocks from Abercorn. She hadn't decided whether to go to Memorial Medical Center, St. Joseph's Hospital, or Chandler, all in different parts of the city. The decision had been made for her.

Chapter Five

Cece slung the gym bag over her shoulder and strode purposefully toward the main entrance of Chandler Hospital. The modern looking multi-storied facility reminded her of the medical center where her mother had been a patient. As she approached the highly polished wood counter at the information desk she asked, "Can you tell me what floor the critical care waiting room is on please?"

The silver-haired lady looked up at her and smiled, then the smile froze on her face as her eyes took in Cece's getup. "Uh, third floor. Just walk down this hall and the elevators are on your right."

"Thank you."

When the elevator came, Cece joined a black orderly, dressed in scrubs, accompanying a teenage boy seated in a wheelchair. The young man wore a yellow Walkman. His eyes were closed, and he was snapping his fingers to his private concert.

The elevator quickly reached the third floor and Cece stepped into a hushed corridor. As she made her way slowly down the hall, she was struck by the fact that she didn't see any patient rooms. A little further down, she noticed a set of swinging doors with a large sign announcing "Critical Care Unit." Cece could see a nurse's station on the other side of the glass. Just before the doors, on the right, was a large waiting room. Tentatively, Cece stuck her head inside and noted four couches and multiple chairs scattered about. In the center of the room was a small wooden desk with a telephone. To her right, two older men and a woman sat engrossed in front of a television that played softly. At the opposite end of the room, six people, a variety of ages, huddled in a group. A middle-aged woman cried softly while a young man patted her on the shoulder and whispered into her ear.

Cece wandered to the middle of the room and sat down on one of the empty couches. The other inhabitants sprinkled around the room looked at her curiously. *Damn! I've got to get out of this costume before they expect Sonny to show up.*

Quickly, she picked up her gym bag and went in search of the nearest ladies room. Once locked inside, she yanked off the wig and scratched her head. She stripped out of her Cher clothes, and pulled a towel and washcloth out of her bag and scrubbed her face, as well as other essential areas. The smell of the harsh bactericidal soap assailed her nostrils. What she longed for was a long hot shower or a huge tub filled with lavender-scented bubbles. Having neither, she took a deep breath and pulled on a pair of jeans and a red T-shirt. Next, she awkwardly doused her head under the faucet and grabbed her shampoo.

Toweling her hair dry, she longed for a blow dryer. She hadn't needed to carry one since there had been one at the gym. Grateful for a short haircut at least, she worked some gel through her auburn hair and tried to style it a little with her fingers. Her beautician had told her the "wet look" was in, but Cece didn't really like it. She pulled out her floral zip makeup case, then paused. Putting makeup on her freshly scrubbed face didn't appeal to her. Even though the rest of her still felt grimy, her face was the one thing that felt clean.

Well this should be a good disguise—no makeup and hair that looks like hell. She stuffed the Cher costume and makeup case into her gym bag and returned to the waiting room.

* * *

Detective Morgan's cell phone rang as he and Dell were talking to the arson investigator at the crime scene on Tabby Road.

"Shark, this is Deputy Sayles. While I was out searching the premises, you're not going to believe who showed up here Cecilia Campbell."

"What? Is she still there?"

Sayles told him about Reverend Wheeler's encounter with Ms. Campbell.

"Let me get this straight. She said she was going home to shower and change clothes, then she would contact us? Damn! She probably came here, saw her house burned to a crisp and got scared. If she contacts Mrs. Kline, or shows up there again, let me know. How was she dressed, and how long ago did she leave?"

"Hold on a minute and I'll ask the preacher."

Shark chewed on his fingernails while he waited impatiently.

"It's been about a little over an hour and she was dressed like Cher."

"Cher?"

"That's what the reverend said. She told him she had been to an all-night party and heard the news about Dr. Kline on the radio this morning."

"Well, she shouldn't be hard to spot if she's still here. Thanks."

Shark turned to the arson investigator, Russ Halloway, and said, "Cecilia Campbell is *not* one of your victims. She showed up at Kline's house a little while ago."

"Where is she now?" Dell asked. Shark told her what little he knew. The detectives fanned out and started searching.

A few minutes later they met at the back of the crowd. "Several people remembered seeing someone dressed like Cher, but I didn't find her. How about you?" Dell asked.

"Two people saw her a while ago. She's flown the coop."

"Maybe she'll contact us," Dell said, hopefully.

"That would certainly be the smartest thing for her to do. Once she tells us what she knows, she should no longer be a target."

"Let's hope she's bright enough to figure that out."

"If our guy thinks she died in the fire, it may buy her a little time."

"But not much," Dell said, nodding her head in agreement.

Cece sat in the critical care waiting room and leafed through a three-month old dog-eared copy of *Family Circle*. It didn't really matter since she wasn't reading, her mind in overdrive. *Should I contact the police? Who killed Tony? Who's trying to kill me? Oh God, I don't know what to do.*

The longer she thought, the more confused and frightened she became.

About six o'clock, a harried looking man in his early 30s carrying a Pizza Hut box in one hand and a laptop computer in the other, entered the waiting room. He placed the pizza box on a coffee table and sat down on a nearby chair next to an older woman who had been knitting ever since Cece had arrived. The cheesy aroma from the box quickly filled the air and made Cece salivate. The man leaned down and spoke briefly to the woman. A couple of minutes later, she gathered up her yarn and left.

The man pulled off his necktie, rolled up the sleeves on his blue dress shirt, then opened the pizza box. Smells so delicious they almost made Cece faint, wafted throughout the room. She hadn't eaten anything all day, unless you counted about 10 cups of black mud that the hospital passed off as coffee, which was supplied in the waiting room. Cece knew she would have to get something to eat soon, but wanted to conserve her limited funds as long as possible.

Her eyes kept straying to the man as he devoured piece after piece of what looked to be a meat lover's pizza, the stringy mozzarella as enticing as liquid gold. Just when she thought she couldn't stand the hunger pains any longer and would have to find the cafeteria, he approached her with the closed pizza box clutched in his right hand.

"Hi! Would you like to have these last couple of slices of pizza? I can't eat any more. I'll be forced to throw them away if you say no. And I feel guilty every time I throw food away—the old lecture from childhood about all the people in the world going hungry. Did you get that lecture too, when you were a kid?"

"Didn't everyone?" Cece said, smiling up at him. She forced herself not to grab the box, but instead, sedately put out her hand and took it from him slowly. "Thanks. This smells great, and I haven't eaten yet."

He chuckled. "I thought that might be the case. Every time I took a bite I thought I could see you looking my way. And your attention seemed to be focused more on the pizza than on my handsome face. Only kidding, I'm Brad Johnson. My father's been here for two days. I don't think I've seen you before."

"No. My grandmother just came in today. Do you mind if I go ahead and eat this while it's still hot?"

"Not at all. It's never as good when it gets cold. So what happened to your grandmother?" he asked, then sat down in the chair next to her.

"She had a stroke," Cece improvised, licking pizza sauce off her fingers. "This is wonderful. What about your father?" she asked, wanting to change the subject.

Brad Johnson hurried over and picked up a couple of leftover napkins. Then walked back and handed them to Cece. "He had an aneurysm rupture in his brain. He's been in a coma ever since."

"I'm sorry. Is there any kind of brain surgery or something they can do?"

"No. They did a CAT scan and said the damage was too extensive, and that there's no hope." Brad took a deep breath and looked down at the floor. "It's really hard on my mom. It's just a matter of time. They said it could be tonight, or not for several days." Looking back up at Cece, his left hand picking at a small scab on his right arm, he said, "I finally convinced her to go home and try to get some rest. I told her I'd stay through the night. What about you? Are you staying all night too?"

"Yes, I'm the only family she has."

Smiling at her he said, "I don't think I caught your name."

Cece quickly looked away. "Grace Parker." *How quickly lying becomes second nature.*

"Nice to meet you. Grace is a nice name. Are you named after your grandmother?"

"Grace is her middle name." *Can we stop with the twenty questions here?*

"I figured it must be something like that. Don't hear it too often these days. Well, I'll let you enjoy the rest of the pizza in peace."

Thankful to be done with the interrogation, Cece finished off the pizza in what had to be record time. "That was great. Thanks again," she called over to Brad.

He waved and went back to typing on his laptop.

Cece picked up an *Architectural Digest,* the only thing on the table she hadn't already leafed through.

Every two hours a nurse came to the door of the room and announced visiting hours, which lasted only 10 minutes. Cece hid in the bathroom the first time, and just walked around the hall the next time, thankful that Brad's father's room was right next to the nurse's station. She could continue on past, and he would never see that she really hadn't gone into any of the rooms.

By 9:30, Cece was still staring off into space trying to figure out how she could get a message to her father without anyone being able to trace it. She was afraid to call, in case his line was tapped—or did that happen only in the movies? But she felt she had a right to feel truly paranoid at the moment. She didn't want the police to contact her father and tell him she had died in the fire. That would surely give him a heart attack. The mail was definitely too slow. She still hadn't figured out what to do when Brad walked over to her.

"Can I ask a favor?"

"Sure, anybody who gives me pizza is definitely entitled to a favor."

"I just finished this real estate appraisal that's due tomorrow, and I need to run by and drop this disk in the mail slot. Would you mind babysitting my computer while I'm gone? Shouldn't take more than twenty minutes or so."

"Not at all. I'll just sit over there next to it and make sure no one with sticky fingers comes by."

"Thanks. I appreciate it."

Cece picked up her purse and gym bag and plopped down on the couch in front of the computer, which was sitting on the coffee table. She picked up a two-month-old copy of *People* magazine and began to flip the pages. "Take your time. I'm not going anywhere."

"Like I said, I shouldn't be gone very long."

Cece waited for a full five minutes after Brad left, then looked over her shoulder furtively. No one seemed to be paying any particular attention to her. She leaned over and looked at the computer screen.

Yes! He has AOL.

Cece moved the laptop over to the phone on the desk and connected to it. She quickly typed in her password and logged on. As soon as she was connected she clicked on Write Mail. She typed in her father's e-mail address and a short message.

Dad,

Regardless of what you may hear, I'm fine. Tony was murdered last night and both our computers were destroyed. The police seem to think that the work Tony and I had been doing may be the reason he was murdered. Also, Aunt Sophie's house burned down as well. Two bodies were recovered from inside. I fear it was Sophie and her boyfriend. Since I think my life may be in danger, I've left the island. I don't think it is a good idea to tell you where I am. That way, if anyone asks, you can honestly say you don't know. But I'm

*safe for the time being. I'll try and e-mail you again
in a few days.*
   Love,
   Island Girl

Cece hit the Send button and once it told her the message
had been transmitted, she clicked on Mail Center again. She
brought up Sent Mail and deleted her transmission and
went back to the sign-on screen and removed Guest from
the log-on line. That way there would be no record that she
had used the computer. *Thank you God for providing this
means to communicate with Dad.*

Cece exited AOL, disconnected the phone line and resumed leafing through her magazine. That's how Brad
found her a few minutes later.

Brad slumped down on the couch next to her. "Thanks
again for watching my stuff. How was your grandmother
last visiting time? Any change?"

"About the same. How about your father?"

"No change. He's not getting any nourishment or anything. That's what he requested in his living will, so I don't
think he can last too much longer." Brad looked away as
tears began to well up in his eyes.

After the 11 o'clock visiting time, the occupants of the
waiting room thinned out until only Brad, Cece, and another couple were left. Brad turned off the TV and dimmed
the lights on their end of the waiting room. Then he strode
purposefully out the door.

A couple of minutes later he returned carrying two pillows and two blankets. He handed one of each to Cece. "I
talked the nurses out of these. I'm going to try and get
some shuteye. I have to work tomorrow. Looks like you're
ready to drop too."

"Thanks. It's definitely been a long day," Cece said, trying to stifle a yawn. Now that the adrenaline rush had dissipated, she felt as if she had done hard physical labor for
three days straight.

Brad kicked off his shoes and lay down on the couch. In less than five minutes he was snoring loudly.

Cece fluffed up the pillow, then stretched out on the couch, placing her purse halfway under her on the inside of the couch. She left her gym bag on the floor, but looped her right arm through the handle. She couldn't afford to lose either one. She pulled the soft blanket up to her neck.

Cece tried to clear the day's events out of her mind and go to sleep. But her brain, which had been on over-drive the entire day, took a long time to slow down. Finally she drifted off, wondering what tomorrow would bring.

Shark ran his hand over the stubble on his face and looked up at the clock. It was a few minutes before mid-night. He yawned, stretched his arms over his head and turned his neck left to right trying to work out the kinks. He glanced over at Dell. She was glued to the computer screen. He knew that once she got started she went into a Zen-like state and could work without food, or even a bath-room break it seemed, for hours at a time. He had refilled her coffee cup every time he had his, and she hadn't even noticed.

Shark cleared his throat. "I hate to interrupt, but my brain's about numb. I'm ready to call it a day."

"Just give me a couple more minutes."

Shark stood up and gathered the pizza box, napkins, and soda cans off his desk and flung them into the trash.

"Hey, was there anything left in there?" Dell asked, her eyes never leaving the screen.

"Just a couple of packets of those hot red peppers you always deface your slices with."

"Don't throw those away! Sometimes they forget to stick them in the box. Pull those out and I'll squirrel them away for the next time that happens."

"I don't know why you want to ruin a good pizza with that crap," Shark said as he reached into the trash.

Dell turned off her machine and caught the two small packs that Shark had retrieved and flung in her direction.

She opened her top right hand drawer and dropped them inside.

"Ready?" he asked.

"I've got to pee first."

"No wonder with all that coffee you drank. Hurry up so we can hit the road."

Once they were headed off the island, Shark asked, "So what kept you glued to the computer for so long?"

"I was trying to get some background on the group that hired Dr. Kline, and on our victims."

"I would ask you to tell me what you found, but I think you better wait until tomorrow. I'm so damned tired I doubt I would remember in the morning."

"I know what you mean. Three homicides, can you believe it? We go for months without any, then bang—three in one night."

"October is definitely not our month. Let's just skip it next year—plan on taking a vacation or something."

"Sure. You think the sheriff is going to let both of his death investigators just take off at the same time? Not likely."

Dell turned her head and stared out the window.

Shark could have bit his tongue for mentioning October. They had been working the Marcus DeSilva murder this time last year. Not his finest hour. He had become infatuated with the beautiful widow, Marissa, and not only put his career on the line, but just as important, had almost lost the respect of his partner. He had worked hard to try and rebuild it. And Dell had almost lost her life.

Dell still hadn't said anything. "What you thinking about?" he asked.

"Nothing."

"Nothing, my ass. I'm sorry I mentioned October. I know that has to bring back bad memories for you."

"Don't worry about it. It happened. It's over. End of discussion."

But Shark knew it would never be over. He had been on the other end of a bullet before, and it's not something you ever forget. He wondered if Dell still had nightmares about it, but knew not to ask.

"Talked to Jazz?" Dell asked, wanting to change the subject.

"No. It was too late to call her last night."

"Are you two ever going to get married?"

"That's the sixty-four thousand dollar question. She keeps saying she's not ready yet. That she hasn't been divorced that long and doesn't want to make another mistake."

"Why don't you just cut to the chase and buy her an engagement ring for Christmas? That kind of puts her on the spot, don't you think?"

Shark thought about that for a minute. "But isn't that forcing her to make a decision one way or the other? What if I don't like her answer?"

"At least you would know."

"Maybe it's better if I just keep building my case that she can't get along without me."

"I guess you know what's best," Dell said as they pulled up in front of her house. Josh had left the porch light on for her.

"About nine or so okay in the morning?"

"Let's see, it's almost one now. That leaves six hours for sleep, an hour and a half for sex, and a half hour to get ready. That should work."

Shark chuckled. "An hour and a half for sex—Josh is a better man than I am!"

"You got that right," Dell said as she slammed the car door.

Chapter Six

The next morning, Bama, the nickname he'd had since his childhood in rural Alabama, sauntered down the walkway along the dock at Shelter Cove Marina. The air was a little crisp, but the sky was a picture-perfect blue. The warm rays of the sun felt good on his bare head. He loved marinas. Boats were one of the few things that interested him. One of his aspirations in life was to be able to afford a yacht like the small palaces at dock lying before him. Payment on this job would put him a little closer to being able to fulfill his dream of cruising the islands of the Caribbean all winter.

Bama approached the Hilton Head Café, and decided to sit outside. Shortly the waitress came by and offered him a cup of coffee and a menu. When she returned a few minutes later, she refilled his coffee cup and he ordered orange juice, and a ham and cheese omelet. With the waitress off on her mission, he sauntered over to the newspaper machine and pulled out a copy of *The Island Packet*. The headline announced Dr. Kline's murder. He read the story carefully, then began to read the article about the fire.

Spreading the newspaper out on the table, he turned pale a couple of minutes later when he read that the bodies they had recovered from the fire were those of a middle-aged couple.

46

Damn! Cecilia Campbell is in her late-twenties. She wasn't in the house!

He stood up so fast he almost overturned his chair, then hurried down to the pay phone by the delicatessen. He dialed the same number he'd rung yesterday. When the answering machine clicked on he said, "A minor compli cation. One pile of dirty laundry is still not clean. But don't worry, I'll take care of it right away."

Sitting back down at his table, he took a bite of his waiting omelet and wondered how he was going to find Cecilia Campbell. He read the rest of the article.

Detective Morgan requests that anyone with information about this case contact him at 689-4300.

Bama chuckled. *Thank you Detective Morgan. Now I know who's in charge, and hopefully you'll lead me to Campbell.* After checking the marine forecast, he folded up the paper, threw it on the empty chair, and speared the last piece of cantaloupe on his plate.

Cece woke abruptly the next morning at six when a nurse walked into the lounge and announced visiting hours. At first she was disoriented, but then realized where she was. Suddenly, she was grief-stricken thinking of Sophie and Tony, and all the fear from yesterday washed over her. She sat on the edge of the couch, her head in her hands.

A rumpled Brad Johnson neatly folded his blanket and carefully placed it on top of the pillow. "Did you get any sleep?" he asked glancing at Cece.

"A little. How about you?"

As he ran his hand through his sleep-tousled hair he said, "I can sack out anywhere. That's about the only useful thing I learned in the military. But I found myself waking up frequently. And that damn intercom paging someone every few minutes didn't help. As soon as I see Dad I'm going to run by the house and shower and change. Then I'm headed to the office. Mom should be here shortly. Will I see you tonight?"

"Maybe. I'm not sure."

"Well, have a good day," he said, then hurried out of the lounge and turned in the direction of his father's room.

Cece grabbed her purse and gym bag and hobbled stiffly into the ladies room. She washed her hands and stared at her reflection in the mirror. She had dark circles under her eyes. *I look like hell.* She splashed warm water over her face and brushed her teeth, applied a minimum of makeup and ran a brush through her limp hair. At least she looked a little better than she had. With a final glance at her appearance, she gathered up her things and made her way out into the corridor. *Okay, now what?*

Her grumbling stomach decided her first priorities were food and coffee. But could she somehow get breakfast without having to pay for it?

Cece smiled as she remembered the hurricane evacuation last fall. After being trapped for hours on the interstate in bumper to bumper traffic, when she had finally been able to get off at an exit in Metter, Georgia, she had fainted while standing in line at the McDonald's. The staff had been very solicitous; they had even given her a free hamburger, orange juice, and an apple pie. But faking unconsciousness seemed a little drastic. She'd save that as a last resort.

Where else have I gotten free food? And then it hit her. Quickly gathering her things, Cece hurried down to the nurse's station. "Excuse me, is there a Robert's Inn in town?" she asked the unit clerk. She had often wondered when she traveled, as she had sat enjoying complimentary rolls, fruit, and cereal, what would keep the homeless from just wondering in off the street and helping themselves?

"I'm not sure. But here's a phone book if you want to check."

Cece could hear the whooshing sound of a respirator, and the beeping of a heart monitor. The sounds brought back memories of her mother.

She turned to the Yellow Pages and checked under motels. She ran her finger down the listings and found a Robert's Inn on Stevenson Street. "Thanks," she said, handing back the phone book.

In the lounge, she grabbed a cup of what the hospital was trying to pass off as coffee and hurried to the elevator.

Exiting the front of the hospital, she noticed the sun wasn't quite up yet, but it was light enough to locate the bus stop at the corner of the block.

A few minutes later, Cece squared her shoulders, threw open the door to the inn, and tried to look as if she belonged there. Immediately she saw a room off to the left of the lobby where people were eating. Furtively looking over to see if anyone was watching, she quickly headed in that direction.

Dropping her bag onto a chair at an empty table, she grabbed a tray and began to fill it with goodies.

No one seemed to pay any special attention to her as she inhaled everything on her tray. Hunger pains finally satiated, she leaned back and leisurely drank a second cup of Earl Grey tea. What a nice break from the strong coffee at the hospital. *So now what?*

Cece sat debating whether she should call the police and turn over the disks. One minute she'd convince herself that once she did, she wouldn't be a target anymore. But then she'd wonder if they were the only things keeping her alive. Even if she turned them over, she'd still know what was on them. Killing Tony and destroying their computers hadn't been enough—they would have to kill her too. After all, they hadn't hesitated to kill Aunt Sophie and Carl. Who were these madmen who were capable of such dastardly acts?

Confused, and still not sure what she was going to do, Cece stood and casually sauntered over to an empty table and picked up *The Savannah Morning News*. There was an article about Tony's murder on the front page. She poured over it, but found no answers. The story about the fire was on page three. She read the article carefully as tears threatened to spill onto her cheeks, and when she came to the last paragraph she filed away Detective Morgan's name and phone number. She'd think about calling him when she got back to the hospital. Glancing up from the paper, Cece realized she was the last person left in the breakfast room. Sneaking a glance over to the front desk, she saw the two clerks in deep conversation. Trusting her luck, she hurried over to the breakfast bar where she wrapped two blueberry and one banana nut muffin in napkins and quickly squirreled them away in her gym bag. Making sure the clerks were still absorbed in their conversation, she added three containers of orange juice, two pastries and three boxes of Kellogg's Frosted Flakes to her bag. Feeling extremely guilty, she left quickly by the side door into the parking lot. *I'll send them a donation when this is all over.*

Bama called a cab from the same pay phone he'd used earlier and had it drop him off mid-island at the Hilton Head Diner. From there he called Enterprise Rent-A-Car. A few minutes later they picked him up in front of the diner in a dark-blue Taurus, then returned to their office on Pope Avenue so he could fill out the rental contract. He gave them one of his fake driver's licenses and a phony credit card.

Once in the car, Bama drove back to the diner and used the pay phone again.

"Beaufort County Sheriff's Department, how may I help you?" a pleasant female voice asked.

"Detective Morgan, please."

"One moment."

"This is Morgan."

"I know who set that fire in Port Royal Plantation. Meet me at the Hilton Head Diner and I'll tell you what I know."

"Who is this? Why can't you come to the station?" Morgan demanded.

"I'm too afraid."

"Okay, I'll meet you at the diner. How will I recognize you?"

"I've got on a white Cincinnati Reds T-shirt and a matching ball cap."

"I'll be there in ten minutes."

Bama returned to the Taurus and fiddled with a small piece of equipment lying on the passenger seat.

Eight minutes later, an unmarked tan Pontiac roared to a stop. A man and woman jumped out quickly, and he didn't have to see their badges to know they were cops.

While the two hurried inside, Bama casually palmed the piece of equipment on the seat and opened the car door. He glanced around the parking lot to see if anyone was watching, then sauntered over and walked between the Pontiac and a silver Mercedes. Stooping down to tie his shoe, he reached up and stuck the transmitter inside the left front wheel well of the Pontiac. He stood slowly, snapped his fingers as if he'd forgotten something, and returned to his car.

Thirty minutes later, the two detectives returned to their vehicle and roared away. Bama followed, pulling out into traffic a few cars behind them.

Shark and Dell returned to the office while Bama pulled into the parking lot of the Huddle House Restaurant, which was just in front of the sheriff department's satellite office. Parking under a large oak tree dripping with Spanish moss, he opened his window, prepared to wait for as long as it took to see if they would lead him to Cecilia Campbell, or see if she'd show up to talk to them. He had had plenty of practice in the art of waiting. As a small child, not yet able to talk, his mother had left him for hours at a time locked in a closet, while she went out and partied. When he got a little older, she would hide him there and threaten to beat him if he made a sound while she entertained her host of male friends. And much of his time behind bars had been spent in solitary confinement. Bama settled in and watched as the detectives seemed to be arguing as they stormed inside.

"What a waste of time," Shark said, holding the office door open for Dell.

"Why would someone call and say they have info and not show up?" she asked.

"Either they got cold feet, or it was a crank call," Shark said disgustedly. He dropped down in his chair. "So you're going to work on the list of people who called in visitor passes Halloween night?"

"Yeah, I've got thirty names. Plus I need to check the list against the residents who called in the pass to see if I can find one that doesn't match."

"Port Royal Plantation has the reputation of being one of the toughest plantations on the island to get into, since all the tourist related things are outside the gates. How else could someone have gotten in?" Shark asked.

Dell thought for a moment. "Well, you could ride a bike through the back gate and eventually the bike path would take you into the residents' area. You're supposed to have a sticker on your bike, but the bike patrol is only on from Memorial Day to Labor Day."

"Or you could just drive to the Westin and walk down the beach. It's not very far," Shark said. "I'll give them a call and see if anyone checked out suddenly last night."

"Someone could come in by boat, park close to the shore and wade in."

"There are lots of sandbars in that area of the beach, but that's a possibility," Shark said. "Let's ask Ruth and the neighbors if they remember any boats anchoring close to the shore that night," Shark said, making a note on his list. "Any other ways you can think of?"

"Well, we've covered by land and by sea, what about by air?" Dell asked. Shark rolled his eyes. "I think the neighbors would remember seeing someone parachuting in, don't you?"

"Well, they do a lot of parasailing in Port Royal Sound," Dell said defensively. "So okay, maybe it's a stupid idea."

Before Shark could say anything the phone rang on his desk. Picking it up, he listened for a minute, then hung up and turned to Dell. "They found Cecilia Campbell's car at the Savannah airport. Damn it, she could be anywhere by now."

"Maybe Mrs. Kline can tell us where she's from and if her parents are still alive."

Cece exited the bus and walked for several blocks in each direction all around the hospital. At some point on her bus ride back from the Robert's Inn, she had decided to contact Detective Morgan. Now, Cece was trying to pick out a safe place where they could meet, and at the same time ensure the detective wouldn't figure out where she was hiding out. Finally, she decided on the McDonald's just a few blocks down on Derenne Avenue. She'd turn over the disks and then disappear for awhile.

Cece felt sure Tony had been killed because of the information in her purse. Once the police had the disks, and the information became public, maybe she wouldn't be at risk anymore. She thought she knew who was responsible for Tony's death. Maybe not directly, but it had to be someone from the committee who had hired them to do the research. Cece knew the information she was carrying could destroy the whole wireless sector. Okay, maybe not destroy, since she couldn't see people giving up their cell phones easily, but change the way they were manufactured.

Tony had told her the big guns already knew there were lots of major problems from the exposure to radiation. In fact, Global Link in Germany had just released a new style phone with the antenna pointing away from the brain. They were also pushing handless headsets, where the phone clipped onto a belt and the antenna was nowhere near the head. They couldn't say why they had done it, or it would open them up to major litigation on their older models, but they were obviously trying to prevent future legal problems. All the manufacturers had been running scared since Lloyd's of London had canceled their insurance policies, citing the potential for litigation similar to that of asbestos and tobacco. That had really gotten their attention.

Cece couldn't really envision Randall Palmer, the person they reported to directly, dirtying his manicured hands to shoot Tony, but she could envision the committee hiring someone to do their dirty work.

Cece glanced over her shoulder and hurried toward the entrance to the hospital. She felt too exposed outside.

Ruth Kline answered the door and ushered the detectives in. She motioned for them to sit at the dining room table, and a neighbor friend of hers served them coffee and a plate of banana bread.

"Have you found out who killed my husband?" she asked.

"Not yet. Have you heard anything more from Cecilia Campbell?" Shark asked.

"No, I'm afraid not. I hope Cece's okay."

"We found her car at the Savannah airport. We're checking to see if she boarded a plane. Do you know if her parents are still alive, and if so, where they live?" Shark asked.

"I know her mother died last year, but I'm not sure about her father."

"We'll do some checking when we get back to the office," Shark said as he made a quick scribble in his notebook.

"Mrs. Kline, we need to ask you some additional questions about your husband's research. He must have had someone he reported to, maybe the head of the committee that hired him. Can you remember him mentioning anyone's name?" Dell asked.

"Oh, he talked about different doctors all across the country who were involved in running the different studies, but I didn't pay much attention to the names. I do remember hearing him mention sending some reports to a Mr. Palmer a few weeks ago. I may be able to find his phone number on Tony's Rolodex if you think it would help."

"Thank you, I'd like to talk to Mr. Palmer," Shark said. "Do you remember any other names?"

"Tony just referred to them as the movers and shakers

in the wireless industry. Cece would probably know their names, or what companies they were with."

"Did Miss Campbell ever do any work at home on her computer?" Dell asked.

"I don't think so, but I couldn't say for sure."

"Do you know if your husband had any backup disks for the data on the computers in his office?" Dell asked.

"I think Cece used to do that periodically."

"We didn't find any disks when we went through your husband's office. Do you have any idea where they might be?" Shark asked.

"No, I'm sorry, I don't."

"Would you mind if we searched the rest of the house?" Dell asked.

"Not at all. Anything that may help. I'll see if I can find Mr. Palmer's number while you're doing that," she said, standing up and putting the coffee cups back on the tray.

Shark and Dell searched methodically for almost two hours, but came up empty-handed. "Mrs. Kline, do you and your husband have a safe deposit box?" Shark asked.

"Yes, at Wachovia Bank."

"If we accompany you there, would you open it and see if there are any disks inside?" Dell asked.

"Of course," she answered without hesitation. "Why don't you just follow me to the bank. I have to go on to the funeral home to discuss the arrangements afterwards."

When they entered Wachovia, Ruth Kline walked directly to the customer service desk and asked to get into her box. The middle-aged lady behind the desk opened a drawer, pulled out a ring of keys, and rose.

Shark and Dell waited in chairs just outside the vault door. A few minutes later the widow returned and said softly, "Nothing but our personal documents, mortgage papers, copies of wills, and stuff like that."

"Well, thank you for looking," Shark said, rising from his chair.

As they crept through the Wendy's drive-thru line on

their way back to the office, Dell asked, "You're awfully quiet. What are you thinking?"

"I'm wondering how cooperative Randall Palmer is going to be, and I wish Campbell would contact us. I don't think anything is going to be easy about this case. How about you? Any female vibes telling you who our murderer is?"

Dell waited while Shark gave their order, then said, "Didn't you think the widow was pretty put together for someone who so recently found her husband murdered on the foyer floor?"

Shark pulled out his wallet before he answered. "That's a hard call. Some people are hysterical for days, others seem to function fairly normally and grieve in private."

As Shark pulled up to the pick-up window Dell said, "Don't forget to ask for lots of ketchup."

Bama had tailed the detectives to Port Royal Plantation, but failing to get past the guard gate, he had pulled into the clubhouse parking lot, where he had waited impatiently until they came out.

Following them to the bank, he was relieved to see the lady, probably Kline's widow, walk out empty-handed from the vault. He put the binoculars back on the seat and smiled.

Three cars behind them at Wendy's, he followed the duo back to their office. Bama swung into the Huddle House parking lot again and got comfortable under his favorite tree. He finished off his double cheeseburger and fries, then pulled an electronic poker game out of his bag and began to stab the buttons.

Chapter Seven

Tossing the empty container of orange juice and the paper from a blueberry muffin into the trash, Cece wiped her hands on her jeans. She glanced at her watch. Almost one o'clock. She made her way to the elevator and rode down to the lobby, where she strode purposefully toward a bank of pay phones and pulled some change out of her purse.

Dropping the coins into the phone, she dialed carefully.

"Beaufort County Sheriff's Department, how may I help you?"

"Detective Morgan, please."

"One moment."

"This is Morgan."

Cece paused, took a deep breath then said, "This is Cecilia Campbell."

"Are you okay? Where are you?" Shark waved his hand at Dell to pick up on the line.

"I'm okay."

"Where are you?" Shark asked again.

"It doesn't matter where I am. I have some information I need to give you. I think it's related to Tony's death."

"Do you want to bring it here, or do you want us to meet you somewhere?"

"Who's we?"

"Just me and my partner."

"Why not just you?"

"Because I don't go anywhere without my partner to watch my back. She's okay. Where do you want to meet?"

"At the McDonald's in Savannah, the one on Derenne, just past Paulsen, in two hours."

"How will we know you?"

"I'll be carrying a black bag that says Gold's Gym on the side. What about you?"

"I've got a scar running down the side of my face and my partner has red hair. We'll both be carrying a copy of the *Island Packet*. Shouldn't be too many people in Savannah carrying a Hilton Head newspaper."

"Okay."

"We'll see you at three. Be careful."

"So she's still in Savannah," Dell said hanging up the phone. "Thank goodness she called us. Do you figure the information she referred to are the computer disks?"

"Hopefully. Pull a picture of her off the DMV records," Shark said, chewing on the tip of his pen. "While you're doing that I'm going to give Randall Palmer a call."

Shark flipped the pages in his notebook, then dialed the number Mrs. Kline had given him.

"Palmer Communications. How can I direct your call?"

"This is Detective Morgan of the Beaufort County Sheriff's Department on Hilton Head Island in South Carolina. I need to speak to Randall Palmer."

"Mr. Palmer is out of the office and will not return until tomorrow morning."

"Then I need his home phone number."

"I'm sorry, we don't give out personal numbers."

Exasperated, Shark said. "Look, this is in reference to a homicide, so cut the bull and just give me the number."

"I'm sorry. But it won't do you any good. He's in Las Vegas and won't be returning until late tonight."

"Damn! Well make sure he calls me first thing in the morning." Shark rattled off his phone number.

"I'll give him the message."

Dell threw a grainy photo of Cecilia Campbell onto his desk. "Better than nothing I guess," Shark said peering at it closely. "I'll tell the sheriff where we're headed. Then let's hit the road. I don't want to get tied up in traffic and be late."

"I'm going to make a quick trip to the ladies room while you're talking to the sheriff, then grab a diet soda out of the fridge to drink on the way. Do you want something?"

"No, I'll just have some of yours."

Dell groaned. "I figured if it was diet soda, you wouldn't want to share since you always say it tastes like piss."

Shark patted his waistline. "I've got to watch my figure since I have a girlfriend now."

At 2:30, Cece hesitated at the hospital entrance and peered outside. People rushed in and out, but no one seemed particularly interested in her. Gathering her courage, she took a deep breath, then stepped on the black pad and walked outside, the gym bag slung over her shoulder. The bright sun made her squint as she looked up at the cloudless blue sky. It felt good to be outside. The downside was she felt she had a large target, with a bull's eye in bright yellow, plastered to her back.

Cece glanced over her shoulder every few steps as her eyes scanned the pedestrians and cars as she walked rapidly down the sidewalk. You would have thought she was watching a tennis match, her eyes sweeping the sidewalk and the street back and forth.

Her heart rate rose the closer she got to the rendezvous point. She counted her pulse for 15 seconds, then multiplied times four. It was only 120, not the 200 it felt like pounding in her ears. Only one block to go. Glancing at her watch, she saw she was 15 minutes early, just like she planned. If she didn't like the looks of the detectives or the setup, she could leave without being seen.

Bama followed the detectives off the island. He shadowed them all the way to Savannah, and was surprised when they pulled into the McDonald's parking lot. *They must be meeting Campbell. Otherwise why would they be leaving their jurisdiction?* He parked in the far corner of the lot, close to the exit.

Securing the silencer on the 9mm Glock, he decided there was no way he could let her talk to the cops. He had to intercept her first. Sticking the pistol into the waistband of his pants, he pulled his T-shirt out to cover it, and put on sunglasses and an Atlanta Braves ballcap.

Campbell's vehicle shouldn't be too hard to spot. If he was lucky, he could catch her before she got out of her car. His plan was to force his way into her vehicle, abduct her, and finish his business.

Bama's eyes roamed from the cars stopped at the light on Derenne, searching for her red Honda, then quickly back to the cars pulling into the back entrance of the parking lot. Beginning to wonder if she was coming, he glanced at his watch. It was 2:45, and the cops had already been waiting 15 minutes.

As the stop light turned red on Derenne, Bama turned to check the back entrance of the lot again, and suddenly saw a young woman he thought was her. "Damn!" She was practically at the front door, and he was half a parking lot away. *She must have come on foot!* In one quick motion his gun was in his hand.

Cece looked back over her shoulder again, and stumbled on the curb. Suddenly the whole front glass of McDonald's shattered. Inside the restaurant she heard people begin to scream. She froze momentarily, then instinct took over, and she began to run.

Zig-zagging back and forth through the rear parking lot, she cut across the back of the building next door. Running blindly across Paulsen Street, she was almost hit by a silver Saturn exiting the Sun Trust Bank lot. The young lady behind the wheel laid on the horn and the brakes, silently screaming words that Cece was glad she couldn't hear. She tore down 72nd Street, not realizing it was a dead end, until she had already turned into it. Spotting several large trash containers at the end of the street and a tall chain-link fence, she could see one of the hospital's parking garages on the other side. Then she saw it, a door in the fence. Praying it wouldn't be locked, she raced toward it. Hearing a car horn blaring at the end of the street, she looked over her shoulder to see a dark blue car trying to cross traffic. Just as she reached the gate, the car came barreling toward her. She fumbled with the rusty latch, then wrenched the door open and bolted toward the emergency room entrance of the hospital.

Bama let loose a string of obscenities. He knew he'd never catch her on foot, as much of a head start as she had. Hurrying to his car, he flung open the door, and tried hard not to gun the motor as he started the engine. Sedately backing out, he tried to appear nonchalant, but he couldn't afford to lose her. He had seen her sprinting across the yard behind the next building. Pulling out the back entrance, he had glimpsed her running down a one way street, with large trash receptacles and a chain-link fence at the end. He smiled; she was trapped. While he impatiently waited to cross traffic, he could see she was almost at the fence. Darting across the busy street, he raced to the end and jumped out of the car, just in time to see her running into the emergency room entrance, a Gold's Gym bag flung over her shoulder.

McDonald's was in chaos. Multitudes of people were bleeding due to cuts from the shattered glass, while others lay on the floor crying hysterically. Mothers had thrown their bodies over their children to protect them. Fortunately, no one had been shot. One of the teenage employees had narrowly avoided being a victim as the bullet whizzed a few inches above his head and hit the large menu board.

Shark had instinctively thrown himself on top of Dell, flashing back to the time she had been shot.

"Get the hell off me and go after the shooter," she yelled at him. "I'll do what I can here." Rising quickly, she grabbed napkins to help staunch the bleeding of the injured.

Running outside, gun in hand, Shark searched for Cecilia

Campbell, to no avail. Maybe she hadn't arrived yet. He glanced at his watch, it was still only 2:50. But he knew in his gut the shot had probably been meant for her. *How had they found her?* he wondered.

Shark returned to the restaurant to assist with the injured. One young boy, about eight or nine, had a large splinter of glass sticking out of his chest. Frantically, his mother was screaming for someone to help him. Just as she reached to pull the shard out, Shark grabbed her hand. "Leave it alone until the paramedics get here. You can cause more bleeding by removing it." Finally three ambulances and several police cars arrived on the scene.

He and Dell spent the next two hours with the Savannah police before they were finally able to leave.

Cece was gasping for breath as she raced into the rear entrance of the hospital. Glancing back over her shoulder to see if she was being followed, she slammed into a short, heavyset nurse carrying a stainless steel tray of dangerous looking instruments and bloody dressings coming out of an exam room. The tray went flying. "Sorry," she muttered, barely pausing.

"Hey you, no running in the halls or I'll call security," the nurse yelled as Cece rounded the nearest corner.

Cece didn't even slow down. *Maybe I should have tried to grab some of those instruments.* She jammed the nearest elevator button over and over. She would have settled for stairs if she had seen any. Finally, after what seemed like at least 10 minutes, the elevator arrived. She punched the button for the third floor and pounded on the close door button.

As soon as the elevator opened, she made herself walk sedately to the ladies room, where she quickly closed and locked the door. Leaning her back against it, she forced herself to breathe more slowly. Her bag slid off her shoulder and dropped to the white tile floor.

How did he find me? Only Detective Morgan and his partner knew about the meeting. Are they in on it too?

Cece's back slowly slid down the door, her legs shaking so badly they couldn't support her any longer, and she collapsed onto the cold tile. She sobbed uncontrollably. *Now what am I going to do?* She drew her knees up and rested her head on them.

As soon as Bama saw Cece run into the emergency room, he backed up, and drove to the main entrance of the hospital, parking in a handicapped slot. He wanted to make sure she didn't come running out the front. After 20 minutes, he was satisfied that she must still be inside. He moved his car to another spot close by, and hurried toward the entrance.

Was the hospital just a momentary refuge, or was this where she was hiding out? Did she have a relative who was a patient? He had caught a glimpse of the bag she was carrying with Gold's Gym emblazoned on the side. That should make it easier to find her.

Bama casually approached the information desk in the lobby, and pasted on his best smile.

"Can I help you?" a white-haired lady in a pink smock asked, glancing up at the nice looking young man.

"I hope so. Can you tell me if you have a Mr. or Mrs. Campbell here? I was told my parents were in an auto accident, but I'm not sure if this is the right hospital."

"Would that admission have been today?" she asked, pushing her reading glasses up on her nose.

"No, a few days ago. I just got back in town, and there was a message on my answering machine."

"Let me check." She turned to the computer and with two fingers slowly typed in the name Campbell.

"We have a Mildred Campbell in room 403. That's the only Campbell listed."

"Well, thank you for your help. I'll try the other hospitals. Is there a men's room nearby?"

"Yes. Down the hall right across from the elevators."

"Thank you."

Bama quickly strode down the hall and pushed the up

arrow. After the lift emptied, he stepped inside and punched the button for the fourth floor.

Room 403 was just down the corridor. The door to the room stood open and an obese middle-aged female in a purple-flowered robe worked the TV remote control. He stuck his head inside.

"Hi! Is Cecilia here?"

"Cecilia?" the woman asked, her brow wrinkled in confusion.

"Yeah, Cecilia Campbell. I'm a friend of hers."

"Sorry, but I don't know anyone by that name."

"Oh, I'm terribly sorry. I must have the wrong room."

Well, it couldn't have been that easy. He smiled and backed out the door. He searched the entire floor, then stuck his head in the TV room, but didn't find her. He groaned as he realized he would have to search the entire hospital.

On the drive back from Savannah, the detectives rehashed the events of the afternoon.

"I just don't get it. Only you, Sheriff Grant and I knew about the meeting," Shark said, as he crossed the Talmadge Bridge and headed back toward Hilton Head. "And we didn't even know until two hours before the meet."

"He must have followed her," Dell said, readjusting the shoulder strap on her seat belt.

"Then why wait until she arrives at McDonald's before he tries to take her out? That's a pretty public place, don't you think? If it was me, I'd want to get any info she had first. If he'd shot her, and she had the information on her, then we would have found it when we went through her things."

"I agree. It just doesn't make sense. And we don't know for sure that she was even there. What if the shooting was totally unrelated to Campbell? Gang activity has been on the rise in Savannah over the past six months."

"That's true. And it wasn't quite three o'clock yet."

"Did you see anyone matching her description when you ran outside?" Dell asked.

"Not really. I only saw two or three cars pulling out of the lot, and a couple of teenagers on the sidewalk."

"So see, it could have been gang activity. Anyway, I know you gave the Savannah police the plate number on the last car."

"Yeah, the black Jeep Wagoner."

"What makes were the other two cars?"

"A dark-blue Taurus and a silver Honda Accord."

"Was either one a rental?"

"I don't know. I couldn't see the plates on them."

Shark struck the steering wheel with the palm of his hand. "I still think it was our guy, and not gang related."

"Well, I really do too. But you've got to consider all the possibilities. You gave the police a copy of Campbell's DMV photo. Maybe they'll find her."

"Do you think there's a rat's chance in hell she'll call us again?"

"Would you?"

"No way. I think we're going to have to approach this case from the angle of Dr. Kline's research. We need to discover what his findings were, and who would benefit from keeping that information quiet."

"Don't you think our first priority is to protect Campbell?" Dell asked.

"How can we protect her if we can't find her?"

"I don't know. I'll see what I can dig up about the radiation effects of cell phones when we get back. Boy, Sheriff Grant is sure going to be pissed when we show up without Campbell or the information."

"I'll let you tell him. He'll be so relieved you didn't get shot this time, he'll probably kiss you."

Shark became silent. His thoughts returned to that awful day, last New Year's Eve, when he had been headed to Beaufort and a call came over his radio about shots fired at a residence in Bluffton. When he had heard the address he realized Dell had gone there to check on the owner of a white Toyota truck that had been seen leaving the area after a local convenience store robbery/murder.

When he arrived, he had seen Dell lying at the foot of the front steps, unconscious. Several officers had restrained him as he attempted to go to her. He hadn't known if she was dead or alive. Those few minutes had given him several gray hairs.

His first thought, when he had heard the glass shatter today, was to protect her. Not only was she his partner, but also his best friend. She had helped him through that awful time when his wife, Laura, had died four years ago.

"Hello, Earth to Shark," Dell said. "What are you thinking about?"

"Nothing," he muttered, turning onto Highway 278.

Chapter Eight

Cece wasn't sure how long she spent on the bathroom floor. Finally pulling herself together a little, she stood on shaky legs and splashed cold water on her face. She stared into the mirror. What if he had seen her run into the hospital? Was he searching for her here right now? Maybe she should leave and go someplace else, but what if he was watching the exits? How could she disguise her appearance?

Cece opened her gym bag and pulled out a man's white shirt that came to her knees. She sometimes wore it over her leotards if she didn't want to change before she drove home. Yanking her red Salty Dog Café T-shirt over her head, she slipped the shirt on, and bunched it up and tied it in a knot at her waist. Then she spotted the Cher wig in the bottom of her bag. "Yes," she said, grabbing it and plopping it onto her head. She used her fingers to straighten out the long straight hair. *Maybe if I cut it off some it'll work.*

Cece pulled off the wig, raced down the hall to borrow a pair of scissors from the unit clerk, then returned to the bathroom. She cut off several inches and tried it on. *Needs more.* Removing it she whacked away again. After several more tries, she had cut it so it merely brushed the top of her shoulders. *That'll have to do.*

Next she pulled an eyebrow pencil out of her makeup

case and penciled in heavy arching eyebrows, and was amazed at the transformation.

Zipping up her bag, Cece grabbed her purse and stood for a moment, hand on the doorknob. Forcing herself to take a deep breath she tried to calm her racing heart, then opened the door and made herself amble casually toward the lounge.

Once inside, she stuffed her gym bag under an end table with the name turned to the wall and wandered aimlessly to the opposite end of the room before sitting down in front of the TV.

Most of the chairs in the room were taken. Cece counted nine other people, some she recognized from the day before. Each time someone new walked in, she felt her body tense and would quickly avert her eyes.

After an hour and a half, Cece was finally beginning to relax a little. She glanced up from the *Southern Living* magazine she was flipping through as yet another man entered. She didn't pay a lot of attention to him since he immediately walked over to a small group of people at the other end of the lounge. But then she heard him say, "Excuse me. Do you know if Cecilia Campbell is here? I have a message for her, but I don't really know her. She's tall with short brown hair. I was told she was dressed in jeans and a red T-shirt. Oh, and she's carrying a Gold's Gym bag."

They shook their heads. "No, sorry."

Cece's heart felt as if it had stopped beating, then lurched into overdrive like one of those bullet trains in Japan. Her stomach churned. Cece wiped her sweaty palms on her jeans, trying to hide the action behind the magazine. Her instinct was to jump up and run, but she knew that would be the worse thing she could do.

The man quickly moved onto the next clump of people clustered in the middle of the lounge. She could feel his physical presence getting closer. "Sorry, we haven't seen her either," one of the women said. Cece prayed he'd overlook the hidden gym bag.

With her eyes glued to the magazine, Cece felt him approaching. She just knew he'd be able to hear the noise of her pounding heart, deafening to her own ears. Beads of sweat ran down between her breasts. Her palms were clammy and she was chilled with fear.

"Excuse me," he said, standing just above her, his thumb and index finger massaging his right earlobe.

Surprised she could even speak, she gave him a quick glance and said, "I heard the description. Haven't seen her." She looked quickly back at the magazine.

"Well, sorry to have bothered you," he said, turning and walking away.

Cece was amazed she hadn't wet her pants, or worse. Her whole body was shaking uncontrollably. Closing her eyes, she tried to slow her breathing and get herself under control.

On her closed eyelids she could see the imprint of the man who had killed Tony and Sophie, burned down her house, and was trying to kill her. He didn't look like an assassin. She wasn't sure what she expected him to look like, maybe a biker dude or a Mafia guy, like in the movies. You could always tell just by looking at them that they were the bad guys.

Instead, this guy looked just like any other man you'd pass on the street. Now that was scary. Tall, nice haircut, washed-out denim-blue eyes, and big muscles. At least now she would be able to recognize his face.

Should she run, or was this the safest place to be now? Since he hadn't seemed to recognize her, maybe he'd go back to wherever he had come from. Fat chance. She was torn as to the best course of action.

Cece opened her eyes and was surprised to see Brad Johnson, loaded down with a briefcase, his laptop, and a bag from Captain D's Seafood. She smiled over at him. He smiled back, but didn't say anything.

"So how's your dad?" she called over to him.

He looked at her and frowned. "I'm sorry, do I know you?"

"Grace Parker. You shared your pizza with me last night."

"Gosh, is that you Grace? Sorry I didn't recognize you."

"Sometimes, when my hair is a mess, I just throw on a wig," Cece said, fiddling with the stringy black hair.

"It's the eyebrows," he said, moving his up and down. "Dad's about the same. How's your grandmother?"

"No change."

"You been here all day?"

"I went out for a little while."

"Would you watch my stuff for a minute? I need to ask the nurse something."

"Sure."

A few minutes later Brad returned. "Well, I just rented a room across the hall. The hospital has three rooms it rents out to families for ten dollars a night. I've got to finish a commercial appraisal by tomorrow, which is going to take me two or three hours. If you'll watch my stuff just a little longer, I'll run down to my car and get my printer and some paper and an overnight bag. I'll be back in just a second."

"Take your time. I'm not going anywhere."

Brad came back a few minutes later and transferred all his stuff across the hall. "Thanks for keeping an eye on everything for me. I guess I'll see you in a couple of hours when they call visiting hours. Would you knock on my door so I don't get involved working and lose track of time?"

"I can do that."

After he left, Cece pulled a box of dry cereal and the last muffin out of her bag. Then she stuffed it back under the table and walked to the opposite end of the lounge again. She wasn't really hungry, but knew she needed to eat something.

As Cece washed down her Frosted Flakes with a diet Coke, she tried to figure out what she should do. Perhaps she should move to another hospital. There were two others in the city. Or would he check them out, since he'd obviously seen her run into the emergency room here?

Since he hadn't found her, where would he go? Perhaps back to McDonald's? Or would he search the hospital again? Maybe she should call Detective Morgan and at least give him a description of the guy. Not that he looked any different from about a zillion other men in Savannah. Maybe she should call the Savannah police. How had he found her in the first place? And why wait until she was about to rendezvous with the detectives before trying to kill her? The longer she thought, the more confused she became.

Cece glanced at her watch, 8:30. They should have announced visiting hours a half-hour ago. Must mean they were having problems with one of their patients. Just then a nurse walked over to a small group of people directly across from her and spoke softly for the next 30 seconds. Two of the older women burst into tears, and the nurse led the whole group out of the room.

Tired of sitting, and feeling sorry for the loved ones who had been escorted out of the room, Cece began to pace in the hallway. A few minutes later another nurse announced visiting hours. Cece walked over and rapped three times on Brad's door. When he opened it, she told him it was time.

Brad glanced down at his watch. "They're late. I completely lost track of time. Thanks Grace."

Cece strolled down the hall with Brad until he turned into his father's room. She continued on and completed the circle around the nurse's station, then returned to the lounge.

Bama sat in the cafeteria until it closed, scrutinizing every young female who walked in. He'd searched every floor of the hospital earlier, but hadn't found who he was looking for. Now that visiting hours were over, there would be a lot fewer people milling about. If she was still here, he'd find her.

The snack bar was his first stop, but it was occupied only

by a couple of teenage boys sharing a bag of chips. From there, he made his way to the main lobby, then the emergency room waiting area, which overflowed with people of all sizes and shapes. Still not finding his prey, he cursed under his breath when he realized he would have to check every floor again. If he didn't find her, he would head back to Hilton Head. He could only hope she would be dumb enough to contact the detectives and set up another meeting.

As Bama searched the various floors, he decided he'd leave the critical care waiting room for last. It was the largest, and the only one with sofas. If she was still in the hospital and hunkering down for the night, that's where she would probably be. That's certainly what he'd do anyway. He'd love to find her fast asleep, so he could stick his gun in her ribs and hustle her out to the parking lot. Then he'd finish his business and head on down the coast tomorrow and maybe do a little fishing.

A nurse announced visiting hours again at 10:30, and Cece knocked on Brad's door. "It's time," she said, when he stuck his head out. "How's the appraisal coming?"

"Good. Another half an hour of printing should finish it up. I'll stop the printer at the end of this page, then go see dad."

"I'm gonna go on down and see grandma. Any change in your father's condition?"

"His heart rate is starting to slow down a little. Could be anytime now."

"I'm sorry."

"Thanks."

After Brad closed the door, Cece locked herself in the ladies bathroom. She reached up under the wig and scratched every part of her head. "Damn, this thing is uncomfortable," she said to the unfamiliar face in the mirror looking back at her. She washed her face and hands, careful to leave her eyebrows on, then brushed her teeth. She longed for a shower, but it would have to wait. Tomorrow she'd buy some underwear, which would take care of some of her grunginess.

The adrenaline that had pumped furiously through her system a few hours ago had now left her drained. She yawned, and felt as if she hadn't slept in days.

Returning to the lounge, Cece picked up the blanket and pillow she had used the night before from the top of her Gold's Gym bag, and walked to the far end of the room, where she made up a makeshift bed and lay down. She glanced at her watch. It was 11 o'clock. The only other occupants of the lounge, an older man and a woman who was probably his middle-aged daughter, sat talking softly on one of the couches at the opposite end of the room.

Cece's eyes grew heavy in the dimly lit room. She was almost asleep, when her eyelids struggled half-open briefly and took a quick look around the room, before closing again. She knew her subconscious was trying to tell her something. Something was different in the room. But what? Eyes still closed, she could hear the man and his daughter at the other end of the room, still chatting quietly. But now another man sat motionless in the half dark room. She could barely see him in her mind. *Oh God, he's back!* Her eyes jerked open, and she sat up suddenly. *Stupid! You should have rolled over and put your back to him. Now he's looking at you.*

"Bad dream?" he called over to her softly.

"The worst," she said, avoiding his eyes and looking down at the floor. Adrenaline pumped furiously through her system again, and her heart beat as loud as a jackhammer. Her ears started ringing.

Cece, still staring down at the floor, saw a pair of brown dress shoes approaching. They stopped right in front of her. She was too terrified to look up.

"Grace, I see you're still awake," Brad Johnson said. Cece glanced up at him. "Listen, I'm not trying to come on to you or anything, but my room has two twin beds. I thought that maybe you might want to shower and get a good night's sleep. I'll understand if you say no. I just know I didn't rest very well out here last night, and I know you're from out of town and all," he stammered.

"Oh Brad, that would be wonderful," Cece said, quickly jumping up and folding the blanket and placing it on the pillow. She grabbed her purse with the precious disks inside and tried not to make a mad dash for the door.

"Where's your bag?" he asked.

"I'll get it later," she called over her shoulder. "It's in grandma's room."

Brad walked across the hall and punched in four numbers on the door's keypad. Cece practically mowed him down getting through the door.

Collapsing onto the closest bed she said, "Brad, you just saved my life."

"That's a little extreme, don't you think?" he said chuckling.

"I mean, I feel like if I don't get a shower and some decent sleep, I'm just going to die. I'm so exhausted."

"I know what you mean. Anyway, there's still a clean set of towels in the bathroom. Do you want me to get your bag from your grandmother's room?"

"No, but thanks. I'll get it later."

"Well, I'm gonna turn in," he said, sitting down in the chair and untying his shoes.

Cece stood in the shower for a long time, letting the hot water pound her tense muscles. She used some of Brad's Head and Shoulders, and washed her hair twice. Finally she turned off the water and toweled her hair and body dry. She used Brad's comb, careful to remove any of her stray hairs, then finger styled her hair. Cece donned the white shirt, which came to her knees, and picked up her jeans and wig.

She crept quietly back into the bedroom. Brad was snoring softly. Putting her things down on the chair, she tiptoed silently to the window. She ran her hand through her hair. It was a relief to get out of that scratchy wig. But it had probably saved her life. She slipped two fingers through the closed mini-blind and spread the slats so she could look out. She had a full view of the front parking lot, where about a dozen cars were spread out over the area.

Bama was frustrated when he completed his sweep of the hospital. Had he missed her? Had she escaped from the hospital as he checked the different floors and the cafeteria? *Maybe I should have observed the front exit longer.* Had she circled back around and left by way of the emergency room exit? He couldn't watch all of them at once. He glanced down at his watch and saw it was almost one o'clock. He would take up the hunt again tomorrow.

Cece wasn't sure how long she stood at the window lost in thought, before she noticed a man walking across the nearly empty parking lot. He stopped mid-stride, turned, and looked back at the hospital. It was him! Even though she couldn't see him well, she knew. She quickly closed the slats, her heart racing again.

Finally, she slowed her breathing, and her shoulders slumped in relief. He was leaving. She was safe, at least for tonight. Tomorrow she'd decide what to do.

She crept silently to the bed, pulled back the covers, and lay down. She tried to sleep, but all kinds of thoughts kept shooting through her mind.

If he catches me he'll take the disks, then kill me. If I don't have the disks with me, would he kill me before he gets them? Maybe I should stash them someplace safe, but where? Should I rent a safe deposit box? No, that would take a third of my cash or more. I could mail them to Detective Morgan, but then if he catches me, I wouldn't have anything to bargain with.

Suddenly, she threw back the covers. She would hide them in Brad's briefcase. He was a total stranger and no one could link the two of them together. She didn't think the man had recognized her in the lounge since she had her wig on.

Cece stood quietly for a moment to make sure Brad was still asleep, then crept over to the table. Slowly taking several sheets of printer paper, Brad's briefcase and her purse, she walked cautiously back into the bathroom. She turned on the light, then sat down on the bathroom floor, praying his briefcase was unlocked. Cece pushed the buttons, and it clicked open loudly. She froze and held her breath, hoping it hadn't awakened Brad. Cece heard him turn over in bed, but he didn't call out. Finally, he started snoring again. Slowly she raised the lid, then dug the disks out of her purse.

Cece folded a piece of printer paper around the disks to protect them and pulled a pen out of Brad's briefcase to write a note. When she finished it, she folded it and placed it with the disks in the bottom of the case.

Jazz was exhausted when she walked in a little before midnight and threw her purse on the kitchen counter. She noticed the flashing red light on her answering machine and pushed the button. She had three calls, two from girlfriends wanting to get together, and the last one was from Shark. He asked her to call him, no matter how late she got in.

She kicked off her heels, opened the refrigerator and poured the last of the bottle of Pinot Grigio into a water glass, then grabbed the phone and dialed the familiar number.

After three rings a sleepy voice said, "Hello."

"You sound like you were asleep. I probably should have waited to call you in the morning."

Shark sat up in bed. "No, I'm glad you called. I wanted to hear your voice. How was your day?"

"We won't go there. And yours?"

Shark briefly filled her in on his new case. "Campbell called and wanted us to meet her in Savannah. But someone fired off a shot and scared her off before we could talk to her. What are you doing right now?"

"Drinking a glass of wine and peeling my clothes off."

Shark groaned. "So what's hit the floor so far?"

"Suit jacket, blouse and skirt."

"So you're standing in your bra and hose. I know the shoes are already gone. What room are you in?"

"The kitchen. I'm leaning up against the counter."

Shark groaned. "I wish I was there with you."

"Me too. So you're in bed?"

"Yeah, I crashed about an hour ago. When can I see you?"

"I don't know. This case is a bear. Any chance you can run up here?"

"Yeah, sure, I'll just put a triple homicide on hold and run up for a little hanky panky."

"Hanky panky sounds good."

"You're killing me here."

Jazz laughed. "It's only been a week."

"What do you mean only? I want to come home to you every night."

"I know. But even if we lived in the same town, between your job and mine, I'm not sure how much time we would get to spend together."

"So how do we solve this dilemma?"

"I don't know."

"Why don't you quit your job, marry me, stay home and have babies?"

Jazz laughed nervously. "I'm not the staying-at-home type. I love my job, in spite of the long hours and the low-lifes I have to deal with. Listen, I'm wiped out and need to get in the shower."

"I'll let you go then. I'll call you tomorrow night. I love you."

"I love you too. Sweet dreams."

"They're all about you."

Cece was sound asleep when a loud shrill woke her. Brad flipped on a light and quickly picked up the phone. Cece glanced at her watch. It was 3:10.

Brad listened for a minute, then said, "I'll be right there."

"Your dad?" Cece asked.

"Yes," he said, pulling his pants on swiftly. "His heart rate and respirations are falling rapidly."

"Do you want me to come with you?"

"They've called my mother, but it'll take her a little while to get here. Are you sure you wouldn't mind?"

"Not at all. You shouldn't be alone at a time like this," Cece said, throwing back the covers and slipping into her jeans.

"Thanks," he said as they hurried out the door.

Brad was a younger version of his father, Franklin, who lay struggling for each breath. No tubes or IVs marred his handsome appearance, only a urinary catheter hung discreetly on the lower bed rail.

Brad picked up his father's hand and held it lovingly between both of his.

"Dad, I'm here. Mom is on the way. If you can, just try to hold on long enough for Mom to get here. You know how upset she'll be if she doesn't get to give you a kiss before you go. Remember that time you forgot to kiss her, when you rushed out to go to work? And how she called you on your cell phone and made you come back home, and give her a kiss, just in case you had an accident or something on the way to work? And don't you be worrying about Mom. I'll take good care of her, I promise."

Tears streamed down Brad's face as he spoke. Cece reached over and put her arm around his shoulders. She was transported back to another hospital room, where her mother lay dying just the year before. But she had been attached to IVs and wires that monitored her heart rate and respirations. Somehow, without all the equipment intruding, it seemed so much more peaceful.

A short time later, Brad's mother arrived, and Cece excused herself. Turning to her, Brad whispered, "Thanks Grace. Just push four, three, two, one on the key pad to get back into the room."

Brad's mother glanced over at her with a funny look on her face. "Mom, it's not what you think. Her grandmother is a patient here."

Cece crept out of the room, hurried down the hall, and retrieved her bag from the lounge. Crossing the hall, she punched in the numbers on the keypad, and sat down on her bed. She felt sorry for Brad, he seemed like a really nice man. She wished she could do something to comfort him, but didn't know what it would be.

An hour later, Brad returned, his eyes red from crying. "Well, it's over. He's at peace."

"Is there anything I can do?"

"Only pray that God receives him into Heaven and that He comforts my mother. He was a good man."

"I'm sure he was. I'll pray for both you and your mother."

"Thanks for staying with me until Mom came."

"I was glad to do it. Where is your mother now?"

"The neighbor who drove her here took her home. I'm headed over there now."

"Do you want me to drive you? I can take a cab back."

"No, I'm all right. Why don't you go on back to bed and get some sleep?" he said, as he gathered his things.

"Let me help you carry your stuff to the car. That's the least I can do."

"Thanks. That way I'll only have to make one trip."

Fifteen minutes later, under the hazy lamps of the parking lot, Brad loaded his stuff into the trunk. "Well, I guess this is good-bye," he said, standing with his car door open. "I hope your grandmother gets better."

"Thanks. Who knows, maybe we'll run into each other again sometime. Stranger things have happened," Cece said.

Chapter Nine

Dell climbed into Shark's car Monday morning at seven o'clock and handed him a brown lunch sack bulging with blueberry muffins.

"Hey thanks. These smell wonderful and they're still warm. Did Josh bake them?"

"Okay, smart ass, giv'em back. Yes, he baked them while I was getting ready. He doesn't have to go to Charleston today."

"Now I know why you married him."

"You just think you do. I really married him for that sexy ass of his."

"I thought only guys talked like that."

"What, you think women don't check out men's anatomy the same way you guys check out our boobs?"

"I think it's time to end this conversation before you shatter all my images of the female gender, and probably embarrass me as well."

"Chicken! Anyway, I'll see what I can find out today about radiation and cell phones since that's what Dr. Kline had been working on," Dell said.

"I'm going to call Randall Palmer again, Kline's boss," Shark replied. "I can't come up with anyone else but the cell phone manufacturers who'd want to keep his research under wraps."

"Me either. Think Campbell will contact us again?"

Shark glanced at Dell. "I'm not holding my breath. I think she's long gone. Who knows where she could be by now? I seriously doubt she's still in Savannah."

"Do you really think this is all about Kline's research, or could there be another motive, like a jealous husband or something?" Dell asked.

"I don't know. It bears looking into, of course. But, why destroy the computers and try to kill Campbell if it's not about the research? That's the only thing they were both involved with, as far as we know. Maybe you should look into Campbell's background, just to make sure we're not totally off base here. Maybe she was selling trade secrets or something, or having an affair with her boss."

"Okay. I'll see what I can scrounge up."

Shark swore when he saw that traffic had come to a stand-still on the Broad River Bridge, the result of a fender bender. But at least there were already a couple of officers on the scene.

Dell pointed toward the Citgo station on the corner. "Why don't you pull over and I'll run in and grab a cappuccino and get you a cup of coffee."

"Might as well. Hey, pick up a couple of packs of Winstons for me while you're in there."

"Nope. That's where I draw the line. I will not be a party to your addiction."

"Damn it, Dell," Shark said as he parked and climbed out of the car.

Cece woke up a little after nine. At first disoriented, she nonetheless felt more rested than she'd been in days. *Guess that's because I feel safe behind that locked door.* Unfortunately she knew it was only a temporary haven.

Standing in the shower, trying to decide what her next course of action should be, Cece tried to ignore the sounds emanating from her stomach. It quickly became obvious her brain needed food before it was going to function properly.

She dressed in her same old dirty clothes, donned her

wig and picked up her bag. Slowly opening the door, she peered out into the hall. No sign of *him*. Maybe she should give him a name. *What do they call all the bad guys in the movies? The Terminator, that's it.* She shivered. If naming her stalker had been meant to make her feel better, it wasn't working.

Cece boarded the city bus and breakfasted at the same hotel again. After stuffing herself with enough food to feed half the starving in Bosnia, and squirreling away a couple of extra muffins, she settled back in her chair and took a sip of coffee. It was just the way she liked it, strong enough to act like intravenous caffeine. She could never understand people who drank decaf coffee. Decaf was a bit like cutting swearing out of a Tarantino film.

At some point over breakfast, while devouring a bagel and cream cheese, she had decided to go on the offensive. She had been behind the door when they were passing out patience. And after all, now she knew what he looked like. Hilton Head wasn't that big. How hard could it be? And what would she do if she found him? *I'll just call the detective and tell him where to pick him up. Isn't that what the lady detective, V.I. Warshawski, did in all those Sara Paretsky books? Then I'll just retrieve my disks and go on* "Sixty Minutes" *and blow the whistle on all the cell phone manufacturers.*

Cece caught the next bus to Oglethorpe Mall, then walked across the street to the Wal-mart. She grabbed a cart and hit the lingerie department first—clean underwear was a priority. Wandering the aisles leisurely, she added a box of Summer Blond hair color, a pair of sunglasses, and a straw beach hat. She mentally kept a running tally in her mind of her purchases. Wishing she had enough money to buy a pair of jeans and a couple of T-shirts, she headed toward the long checkout line.

With her shopping complete, Cece returned to the hospital and punched the proper numbers into the keypad on the door of the room where she'd been staying. Sticking her head in around the door, she called, "Anybody here?"

Getting no answer, she walked in and carried the box of hair color to the bathroom.

"Mr. Palmer, have you heard about what happened to Dr. Kline?" Shark said.

"Yes, his wife called me. I was shocked. Anthony Kline was a renowned researcher. It's such a loss. Have you discovered who did such a terrible thing?"

"Not yet, but we're working on it. I need you to tell me exactly what Dr. Kline was doing for your company."

Randall Palmer explained the research the committee had hired the doctor to do. "I understand from his wife that all the research was destroyed. Any chance of us recovering some of it?"

"The computers were wiped clean, and we haven't been able to ascertain if there were any backup disks. We're still checking on that."

"Wouldn't his research assistant, Miss Campbell, know?"

"We haven't had an opportunity to interview her yet. We've been unable to locate her."

"She's missing? Mrs. Kline said she came by the house the morning after her husband was killed."

"That's true, but she disappeared right after that."

"But why?"

Because somebody's trying to kill her, too moron. "I really can't get into that right now. Has she contacted you at all?" Shark asked.

"No."

"If you hear from her, please have her call me immediately."

"Certainly."

"I want you to fax me a list of all the members of the committee who hired Dr. Kline."

"I can do that, but why? You can't possibly think anyone on the committee had something to do with Kline's death. We've paid a fortune for that research, and now the study will have to be started all over again."

"Just send it right away."

"I'll have my secretary fax it to you today."

Shark hung up, opened his top right-hand drawer, pulled out the large bottle of Tums he kept there, and popped two into his mouth. He made his way over to the water cooler and filled a small cup. Then he plopped down in the chair in front of Dell's desk and balanced his feet on the edge. "You've been banging on those computer keys for hours. Found anything interesting?"

"Well, I didn't find anything unusual in Campbell's background. But this stuff on cell phones is pretty mind boggling, and I've only read a fraction of what's out there. Did you know that there are over ninety thousand cell phones sold every day? And there are currently over seventy million cell phone users in the United States alone.

Shark whistled. "Maybe we should buy some stock in those babies."

"Yeah, like we can really afford it on our salaries. Anyway, that's not the half of it. I found studies dating clear back to 1982 showing changes in the hippocampus of the brain, due to long term exposure to non-ionizing radiation—whatever that is. A guy by the name of V.S. Belorinski reported that in Russia."

"I didn't even know Russians had cell phones in 1982."

"Well, I don't know if the source of the radiation was a cell phone or not, but radiation is radiation. I've got a list of sixty-two articles published from 1982 to 1999 listing a whole range of side effects attributed to cell phone usage."

"What kind of side effects?"

"Everything from increased incidence of certain types of brain tumors, to effects on the body's immune system. Also memory loss, and decreased ability to concentrate. Now I know what's been scrambling your brain," Dell said.

"Not funny."

"You're right, this stuff isn't funny. It's scary as hell. And get this, in the past few years, Lloyd's of London has refused to insure cell phone manufacturers against the risk of damage to user's health. Said they felt there was too great a risk of litigation, like what the tobacco industry has just gone through. They cited 'mounting concerns about research that suggested long-term effects may be linked to illnesses such as cancer and Alzheimer's disease.' "

"Wow! If that's true, maybe we shouldn't buy any stock after all. So why hasn't some government agency been telling us all this?"

"Wait, let me find it." Dell shuffled through a stack of computer printouts. "Okay, here it is. The FDA doesn't regulate cell phone manufacturers. There's a Cellular Telecommunications Industry Association. Their president, Thomas Maravechi, said that 'while these studies may be scientifically interesting, they do not establish a public health concern, and we will continue to leave scientific interpretation up to the scientists.' "

"No wonder someone wanted to destroy Kline's research. Can you imagine if the public found out about this? Sounds like Campbell may be in deep trouble because of what she knows."

"I agree with you. We're talking about fortunes being lost here."

"So if all this information is available on the internet, why isn't the public already aware of the risks?" Shark asked.

"That's a good question. Most of the information is only available in obscure medical and scientific journals. And if I hadn't been looking for it specifically, I wouldn't have paid any attention to it. I don't think the public has any idea there is even a potential problem."

"Well, somebody found out."

Cece caught the bus to the Hyatt Hotel on River Street and boarded the shuttle to the airport.

Stepping off in front of the terminal and crossing the street to the long-term parking lot, Cece realized her cash was disappearing rapidly. She couldn't afford to pay $10 for the shuttle trip to Hilton Head. And then when she got there, she would need wheels, and she couldn't risk driving her own vehicle.

Cece checked 14 cars before she found a white Ford Expedition with an extra key in a magnetic holder under the bumper.

"Well Mom, I guess I might as well add grand theft auto to my list of crimes. First I steal food, now this. But better alive and in prison, than dead I guess. I only hope the person is gone on an extended trip and I can put this vehicle back before the owner discovers it's gone."

Noting carefully where the car was parked, Cece climbed in and looked around. "Geez Mom, it's huge. I can even lay that back seat down and sleep in here if I need to."

Cece adjusted the seat and started the engine. "Yes, almost a full tank of gas. Wonder where the parking ticket is and how much it'll cost to get it out of here?"

Cece pulled down the visor and searched where she always left her ticket, but it wasn't there. Leaning over in the soft brown leather seat, she popped open the glove box. Not only did she find the ticket, but a Platinum Gold Visa, as well, in the name of Richard Donovan. "Looky here, Mom, I can go shopping and rent a room. What do you think? Dare I use this?"

When there was no answer, Cece said, "Okay. I'll only use it if I don't have enough cash to get out of the parking lot."

Cece drove to the exit, handed the parking ticket to the attendant, and held her breath. "Twenty dollars please."

Relieved, Cece dug in her purse, and handed the attendant two 10s.

"Thanks, and have a nice day," the heavy-set black woman said, pushing the button to raise the bar.

"Time to find the Terminator." But how, that was the big question?

"I'm gonna need a little heavenly intervention here, Mom."

* * *

Bama was pissed. Hungry and bored, he had been parked in the Huddle House lot since eight o'clock, hoping the detectives would lead him to Campbell again. He had been close yesterday. He had sensed it at the hospital. Was she still there? Had she seen him? This job was taking a lot longer than he had anticipated. He should have been back in Ft. Lauderdale by now doing some fishing.

Cece waited for some divine intervention to form a plan, and somehow communicate it telepathically as she crossed the bridge onto Hilton Head. The smell of the marsh at low tide welcomed her home. She noticed the ferryboat to Daufuskie Island off to her right. A familiar sight that always made her feel she was almost home whenever she would return from a trip. It was a sunny day, a light breeze blowing the fronds of the palm trees, and she was glad she had purchased a pair of sunglasses.

Am I making a huge mistake returning to the island? Probably, but doing something instead of just waiting to be picked off seems better somehow. Maybe I should drive straight to the sheriff's office and give them a description of him. Let the authorities do their job. After all, I'm not really a detective like V.I. Warshawski, my favorite heroine.

Cece drove slowly down William Hilton Parkway, cars racing past her in the left-hand lane. The Expedition was much larger and handled differently from her small Honda.

Cece turned left at the Starvin' Marvin convenience store, passed the Huddle House, pulled into the parking lot of the satellite office of the Beaufort County Sheriff's Department, and cut the engine. Should she or shouldn't she? *But what if the Terminator followed the detectives yesterday and that's how he found me? What if he's watching right now?*

Her eyes scanned the small parking lot. Nothing seemed amiss. But suddenly a cold chill marched down her spine and her heart rate almost doubled. "Okay, Mom, what are you trying to tell me? I know, something doesn't feel right."

Cece restarted the engine and made herself pull sedately out of the parking lot. *Maybe I'll just call them and set up a meeting someplace.*

Bama saw the white Expedition pull into the lot next door. The blond had just sat in the car, then after a couple of minutes, left. *Guess she changed her mind about reporting her boyfriend or something.* As he leafed through *The Island Packet*, the local newspaper, an article on page three caught his eye.

Detective Speaks to Zonta Club
on Domestic Abuse

Detective Dell Hassler, a death investigator for the Beaufort County Sheriff's Department, spoke to the Zonta club at a luncheon October 30th at the Marriott Crown Plaza Hotel. The detective stated that one out of every three women would be a victim of physical or emotional abuse at sometime in their life. Whether it is from. . . .

Bama didn't need to read any more of the article. A plan was already forming in his mind. He started the car, pulled onto William Hilton Parkway, and drove to a florist shop he had noticed earlier.

A few minutes later, he walked out with a large arrangement of fresh flowers in a cut glass vase. When he returned to the car, he set the vase on the hood, popped the trunk and removed his bag. He rummaged around until he found what he was looking for. Hardly bigger than a black speck, the bug would let him hear what was going on inside the detective's office, and hopefully lead him to Campbell faster. He stuck it on the ladybug in the floral arrangement—it looked like just another black spot.

Bama drove back down William Hilton Parkway and turned in at the convenience store where he'd noticed a small crowd of Hispanics hanging out, hoping for day work from the local contractors, he assumed.

He found a young man who could speak a little heavily accented English, and offered him $10 to deliver the flowers. The young man quickly pocketed the bill and jumped into the car.

Bama parked under his favorite tree in the Huddle House lot, and pointed to where the flowers were supposed to go. The young man climbed out of the car hesitantly when he saw the sign for the sheriff's department, then slowly shuffled across the lot. He looked back over his shoulder frequently, and Bama was afraid he would run off before making the delivery. Relieved when he entered the building, Bama inserted the tiny microphone into his ear.

Deputy Pickford walked over and held out a large bouquet of flowers to Dell. "These just came for you."

Dell jumped out of her chair and hurried around the desk. "For me? Are you sure?"

"Detective Hassler is the name on the envelope."

"Wow! They're beautiful. Wonder who they're from?"

"Well, why don't you read the card, Ace, and then you'll know," Shark yelled over to her.

Dell pushed things aside on her desk and carefully set the beautiful arrangement next to her telephone. "I still can't believe someone sent me flowers. It's not my birthday."

"Is Josh in the doghouse?" Shark asked.

"No, not at all," Dell replied, her nose in one of the pink roses. "Shark, come over here and look at these beautiful flowers."

Shark reluctantly pushed back his chair and stood up and stretched, then sauntered over to Dell. "Maybe you have a secret admirer. You been holding out on me?" he asked, reaching for the card.

Dell quickly grabbed it and hugged it to her chest.

"Open the card," Shark and Pickford yelled in unison. "And you have to read it out loud," Shark added.

Dell tore open the envelope and pulled out a pale blue rectangle. She shielded it from Shark. Then she smiled, and read it out loud. "Thank you for your wise words yesterday, from a woman who's been there."

"So one of the Zonta ladies sent it," Shark said.

"Yes, wasn't that nice?"

Shark rolled his eyes, then ambled back to his desk, dropped down in his chair, and resumed going over his notes on the Kline murder.

Dell fussed over the flowers for the next few minutes, moving them various places on her desk, before finally settling back down in her chair.

Chapter Ten

Cece hurried to the bank of phones in The Mall at Shelter Cove and pulled some coins out of her purse. Hoping she was doing the right thing, she dialed.

"Beaufort County Sheriff's Department. How can I help you?" a gruff male voice asked.

Cece hesitated, then said, "Detective Morgan, please."

"Morgan here."

"This is Cecilia Campbell."

"Miss Campbell, are you all right? Where are you calling from?" he asked quickly.

"I'm okay, but I need to meet with you. I have some information. Can you be in front of the Banana Republic in the mall in an hour?"

"The one here on the island?"

"Yes, at Shelter Cove."

"Absolutely! And Miss Campbell, please be careful."

Cece hung up and made her way to the food court, where she would have a good view of the store. The smells made her salivate like the old beagle hound her dad used to have. She ordered a Coke, curly fries and a sandwich at the Chick-fil-A counter and sat down at a table to wait.

For the next 45 minutes she observed the shoppers walking to and fro. A few minutes before the rendezvous time she saw a man, a large scar running down the side of his face, and a young redhead stop in front of the entrance to

Banana Republic. They began searching the faces of the women as they sauntered past, comparing them to a paper the lady held in her left hand.

Then she saw him, dressed in the same clothes he had been wearing at the hospital, strolling nonchalantly towards her in the food court. *Oh crap!* She quickly pulled the brim of the straw hat lower. She picked up her sunglasses and put them on, then immediately removed them. She decided wearing sunglasses in the middle of the mall may draw attention. She turned sideways in her seat, her back to him.

Gathering her courage, she glanced over her shoulder at the man who was trying to kill her. She was very uncomfortable not being able to observe him. If he made the least little move in her direction, she was out of there.

He chose a table at the edge of the food court, giving him a good view of the detectives. Then he began to scan the crowd. *He must be following them, not me.*

Should she get up and move, or would that attract his attention? But how long could she sit there nursing a Coke before he noticed her?

By 3:10 the detectives were pacing and glancing nervously at their watches. They looked as if they were ready to pounce on any female that approached the entrance to the store.

A group of shoppers finally plopped down at a table between Cece and the Terminator. Now was her chance. She took a deep breath and casually stood up, keeping her back to him as she made her way to the trash receptacle and threw away her cup, then ambled in the direction of the Victoria's Secret store. She entered and stood browsing where she could see the detectives out of the corner of her eye. *I'm not making contact, so please, just go.* She mentally tried to send the message to them.

Finally, at 3:30, the detectives took one last look around and started strolling toward the exit, frequently looking back over their shoulders.

Just before they reached the door, *he* got up and started in their direction. Cece let several shoppers get between

them before she stepped out into the mall and followed
him.

As soon as she got outside, she saw the detectives getting
into their vehicle. She watched as the Terminator hurried
to a dark colored car, a few rows away, and climbed in
behind the wheel. As he backed out of his parking space,
she couldn't tell what make of car it was, but she did catch
the Enterprise Rent-A-Car license plate. Now she had
someplace to start.

Cece drove to the rental car office on Pope Avenue. She
pasted on her best smile and went inside. *Here goes nothing.*

A tall middle-aged black woman, Nell, according to her
nametag, was behind the counter. No one else was in the
room. "Can I help you?" she asked pleasantly.

"Oh I hope so, Nell. Do you believe in fate? Well, let
me tell you what happened yesterday. I'm recently divorced, my ex-husband beat me, you know. And I prayed
to God to send me a sign that everything would be okay.
Divorce is so depressing. And to my surprise when I was
at the mall today, there *he* was across the food court—my
first love. Terry and I dated our senior year of high school
and then he went off to college. Well, I won't bore you
with all the details, but before I could chase him down, he
was out the door and across the parking lot. Here I am
waving my arms furiously and yelling at him, but he
backed right out and left. I know he would have stopped
if he'd seen me. However, I saw he was driving a dark
colored car, I'm not sure what kind, but it had one of your
plates on the back. He's about six feet with brown hair, a
wonderful haircut, and handsome with his blue eyes and
all. If you ever saw those eyes you'd never forget them—
bedroom eyes. You know what I'm talking about. Anyway,
you've just got to help me. My whole future rests in your
hands. If you can just tell me for sure it was him, and not
some figment of my imagination, I'll search the island till
I find him. Won't you help me, please?"

"Well, that's certainly some story, but I don't think I can do that. Our records are confidential. But I will tell you, a nice looking young man with pretty blue eyes was in here yesterday, if that helps."

"I knew it. I just knew it was him. I don't want you to do something you're not supposed to—I don't want to get you in any trouble. But could you just check and see if it was him?"

Nell hesitated, then said in a low voice, "What did you say his name was?"

"Terry Grainger," Cece quickly replied. It was the first thing that popped into her mind.

Nell flipped through a stack of white rental contracts. After a couple of minutes she turned back to Cece and said, "Well, honey, I hate to disappoint you, but there's no one here by that name. The guy I was talking about with the pretty blue eyes, now his name's not Terry, it's Dave."

"Dave?" Cece asked with a puzzled look on her face.

"Yeah, Dave Garrett. I'm real sorry it's not your man."

"Well, of course. There was a Dave Garrett in our high school. I think he was a year younger than me. Maybe that's why he looked so familiar. From Tulsa, right?"

Nell flipped through the contracts again. "No, this guy was from New York. Sorry."

"Well, you win some and you lose some. Guess I better keep praying. Nell, I can't thank you enough," Cece said, sliding her hand across the counter and picking up Nell's hand in both of hers. "You have a good day now. And if I ever need to rent a car, I'll be sure and use Enterprise."

"Don't you give up on love now, you hear me."

"Oh, I won't."

Cece could hardly control her excitement as she returned to the Expedition. She climbed in and hit the steering wheel with her fist. "Yes, yes, yes! This detecting business isn't so tough after all. But now what? I guess maybe it's time to call Detective Morgan and give him what I've got," she said to the empty passenger seat.

Cece drove halfway around the Sea Pines traffic circle

and barely avoided a collision with a silver Jaguar as she entered William Hilton Parkway, the only major highway on the island. The Jag, with a custom Maryland plate that read "Big Daddy," changed lanes and pulled right in front of her, then abruptly hit his brakes as the stop light turned red. By the time she got stopped, her bumper was about two inches from his. "Tourists," she uttered. "That's all I need. To have an accident in this stolen car."

She pulled into the lot of the next convenience store she came to. Retrieving some coins out of her jeans pocket, Cece walked toward the pay phone. Damn! No phone book. She hurried inside and asked the bored-looking clerk to borrow one to look up the number. She would have thought that she would remember it by now, but she didn't.

Cece asked to speak to Morgan again. When he came on the phone she blurted out, "He followed you to the mall. He was there. I saw him."

Shark motioned for Dell to pick up. "Are you sure it was him?"

"Listen, I know what he looks like. And his name."

"How?"

"Because I was within spitting distance of him twice yesterday. You don't forget what the guy who's trying to kill you looks like, trust me. His name is Dave Garrett and he's driving a dark colored rental car from Enterprise."

Shark was scribbling furiously. "Describe him."

"About six feet, brown hair and blue eyes. He looked pretty ordinary. Unfortunately, he doesn't have 'assassin' tattooed on his forehead."

"How was he dressed?"

"Black jeans and a white Izod shirt."

"We need to get you with a sketch artist. Will you come in?"

"I'll have to think about it. After all, you've led him to me twice now."

"I understand your hesitation under the circumstances, but we really need to get a good sketch so that we can distribute it immediately and get this guy before he finds you."

"Like I said, I'll think about it."

"Miss Campbell, Dr. Kline's computers were destroyed. Do you have any information on the research you guys were working on?"

"I have backup disks of all the data."

"Do you have them with you?"

"No, they're in a safe place."

"We really need that information. It would assist us in our investigation. When can we meet?"

"I'll get back to you on that." Cece quickly hung up.

"Miss Campbell, Miss Campbell!"

"Holy cow!" Dell uttered. "She said she was within spitting distance of him twice, and he didn't recognize her? Lucky gal! And how did she find out his name and that he's driving a rental car from Enterprise?"

"Beats me, but more power to her."

"Do you think she'll agree to meet so we can get a composite from the sketch artist?"

"I hope so. But she seemed upset that he followed us to the mall, so getting her to come in may be difficult. How do you suppose he knew we were going to meet her? We didn't even know until an hour ago." Shark said, his brow wrinkled in deep concentration.

"Were you watching for a tail?"

"No, I wasn't. But I will be from now on. Why don't you go on down to the car rental place and I'll wait here in case she calls back. And watch your back. If you spot anyone that seems to be following you, give a holler and we'll have the closest patrol car assist you. Maybe we can beat him at his own game."

"Okay," Dell said grabbing her purse.

Bama was stunned. *How the hell did she find out the name I'm using and the car I'm driving?*

Bama threw his miniature poker game onto the passenger seat, quickly started the engine, and headed toward the Hilton Head airport. He had only gone a block before traffic had come to a standstill. He heard a siren and his immediate instinct was to flee, but there was no place to go. He watched in the rearview mirror as a Beaufort County Sheriff's Department cruiser attempted to thread its way through the maze of vehicles. He held his breath, sure that they were coming for him. Finally, he exhaled as it crept by and stopped about a half-mile up the road. When he heard another siren, and saw an ambulance in his mirror, he realized there must have been an accident.

Twenty minutes later, he finally pulled into the long-term parking lot at the local airport, grabbed his bag out of the trunk, and made his way to the Avis counter inside the terminal. He whipped another fake driver's license in the name of Mark Halsteader out of his bag, and rented a white Pontiac Grand Am.

After putting his bag in the trunk, he roared out of the lot. As he headed down the road he reviewed the conversation he'd overheard between the detectives. *So I was really close to her two different times.* He racked his brain as he pulled onto William Hilton Parkway and tried to figure out how that could have happened.

I made two passes through the hospital. It had to have been there. But where? Who was I close to twice that she would be able to describe me, even down to my blue eyes?

It took him a while, but then he knew—the dark-haired girl in the critical care waiting room was the only person he spoke to twice who was about the right age. *She must have been wearing a wig. Damn, I was so close. I can't wait to kill her very, very slowly.*

Dell returned from the Enterprise office with a copy of Dave Garrett's rental contract.

"I fed his name into the computer while you were gone to see if he has a sheet, but nothing came up," Shark said.

"I'll see what I can find out about him." Dell plopped down in front of her PC.

"Did you do any good?" Shark asked.

"No tails, and I didn't learn much more than Campbell already told us. He's driving a dark blue Taurus. Did she call back while I was gone?"

"Unfortunately, no."

"I hope you didn't spook her. We really need that sketch."

"I only hope he doesn't find her before we can get it."

Chapter Eleven

Cece had a plan. She stood at the pay phone in front of the Hilton Head Diner and dialed the number from memory.

"Schilling's Boat House."

"Bob, this is Cece Campbell, Dr. Kline's assistant."

"Oh hi, Cece. I was so sorry to hear about Doc and your aunt."

"Thanks, Bob. Ruth said it would be okay for me to take the boat out and just get away from everything for a little while. Would you fill up the gas tank and put it in the water for me, say in about half an hour?"

"Sure, no problem."

Next she dialed Morgan.

"It's me again. Bring your sketch artist and come by boat to the red marker off Dolphin Head at six. I'll be in a white Pursuit with a green bimini top. And don't write this down or tell *anyone* where we're meeting. Not even your partner or the sketch artist until you're on the boat."

"I can do that. Will you have the disks with you?"

"No."

Shark hung up and glanced at his watch. "Well?" Dell asked.

"Yeah, it was her. Come on. We've got some arrangements to make."

Dell quickly grabbed her purse and practically had to run to catch up with him.

As she buckled her seat belt she asked. "What kind of arrangements?"

Shark roared out of the lot, checking his rearview mirror to see if anyone was following them. "We need a boat. Call the office in Beaufort and find out who's on marine patrol. Then contact them and have them meet us at the boat landing at the bridge at five. Also call Cal, the artisté, and tell him not to miss the boat."

"We're meeting by boat? But where?"

"I promised Campbell I wouldn't tell anyone until we're aboard."

"Not even me?"

"Not even you."

"Sounds like Campbell's one sharp lady. She's sure not taking any chances this time."

"Do you blame her?"

"Not in the least. I think paranoia is a healthy state for her at the moment. Is she bringing the disks?"

"No."

"Damn."

Cece stopped at the Harris Teeter grocery and quickly ran inside and threw a few things into her cart. As she stood in the checkout line she kept looking over her shoulder. She felt extremely vulnerable out in the open. If the Terminator only had 666 tattooed to his forehead it would help.

She planned to stay on the boat overnight. There was a small cuddy cabin where she could sleep. It seemed as safe a place as any, and the price was right. Cece didn't think Bob, the guy in the tackle shop, would call Ruth to check if it was okay for her to use the boat. She was usually the one who called to have the boat put in the water anyway, and she had gone out fishing with Tony frequently, so they knew her.

Pleased with her plan, she tried to relax the rigid muscles in her neck. It should be easy to spot any other boats hanging around in the middle of Port Royal Sound, and if Dave Garrett was following the detectives, maybe he'd be caught off guard when they boarded a boat.

Cece parked in the lot at The Boat House, grabbed her groceries and gym bag, and stopped in the tackle shop to pay for four bags of ice.

Loading everything into a two-wheeled cart, she pushed it down the long ramp to the floating dock. The sight of the water was immediately calming to her. It was high tide, water covered the marsh grass that was visible at low tide. Three pelicans hung around the fish-cleaning table hoping for dinner, as the charter boat captain from the *Wave Runner* cleaned his catch of the day.

Cece wheeled the cart to the middle of the floating dock where Tony's boat, *Salt Shaker*, was tied up. She stepped carefully onto the back of the boat, unsnapped the cover and removed it, and breathed a sigh of relief when she saw the keys in the ignition, where Tony usually left them.

After transferring her things aboard, she iced down the food and drinks in the large built-in cooler. Next she picked up the green canvas bimini top off the floor, and had to stretch on her tiptoes to reach high enough to insert both sides into the holders at the same time by herself. Before, Tony had always been there to help. After latching the top down, Cece stood quietly for a moment, her head down and her eyes closed. She said a silent prayer for Tony, then grabbed the keys from the ignition and unlocked the cuddy cabin and threw the cover inside. She gratefully pulled on the black insulated vest Tony always left hanging on a peg in the cabin. The scent of Old Spice on the collar brought tears to her eyes and threatened to spill onto her cheeks. *Get a hold of yourself Campbell. There will be time for tears later. Now you've got to concentrate on staying alive.*

Looking around the cabin, Cece was relieved to see Tony hadn't removed the sleeping bag and small pillow. She knew it would get downright cold once the sun went down.

As she lifted the radio and global positioning satellite antennas, she looked around and was pleased to see the dock was pretty deserted. Next she raised the engine cover and flipped the batteries on.

Cece loved this boat and hated to think of it being sold. She knew Ruth probably wouldn't keep it since she had gone out with them only occasionally and then only if Tony twisted her arm. Ruth didn't seem to enjoy being around the water. Not like Cece, who dreamed of living on a large boat one day and cruising around the world.

Pulling herself back to reality, Cece turned on the bilge blower to remove any gasoline fumes that had accumulated while the boat sat at the dock, then choked it for a full two minutes. When it had been in dry storage for a couple of weeks, all the lines got drained. She turned the key, and the powerful Mercruiser engine roared to life. Reaching down, she flipped off the bilge blower.

"Kevin," Cece called to one of the dockhands, "can you grab my lines?"

"Sure thing," he yelled back, tying off another boat and heading in her direction.

"I couldn't believe it about Doc Kline. What a terrible tragedy. And I read about your aunt and her house being burned down. I'm so sorry," Kevin said as he untied the bowline and threw it aboard. "Do they have any idea who killed them?"

"Not that I know of."

"You ought to buy this boat, you love it so much," he said, walking toward the stern line.

"You're right, but I can't afford it. I'm going to stay out overnight so don't worry if the boat's not here when you come in tomorrow morning."

"Okay, but you be careful out there by yourself," Kevin said, pushing the boat away from the dock with his foot.

"Thanks, Kevin."

Cece pulled slowly away from the dock and stopped momentarily to retrieve the fenders, then threaded her way between the sandbars, a path she knew well. She maintained idle speed through the NO WAKE ZONE of Skull Creek Marina, gazing fondly at all the boats moored there.

Once she cleared the NO WAKE ZONE, she gunned the engine up to 35 miles per hour. The water was smooth as glass, the way she liked it.

Private docks raced by on her right until she cleared the tip of the island. Turning into Port Royal Sound, she encountered a little chop on the water.

It took just a few minutes to cross the sound and anchor off Bay Point at the end of St. Helena Island. The small strip of pristine white beach, only accessible by boat, lay deserted.

Leaving the engine running while she walked up to the bow of the boat, she threw the anchor over. Cece was early, wanting to observe the surroundings before the meet. Once the anchor caught, she looped the line around the cleat and walked back and shut the engine off. She reached down into the cabin and grabbed the binoculars, then pulled a Diet Coke from the cooler, popped the tab, and settled in to wait.

Bama came to attention. So they were going to meet again. Good. But Morgan hadn't said where they were going to rendezvous. Damn! Now he would have to follow them. He would have preferred to be there before Campbell arrived.

Bama hung back until there were several cars between him and the detectives. They headed north, off the island. Just before the second bridge, Bama saw Morgan flip on his left turn signal and shoot through a narrow gap in the stream of traffic. As he shot by, unable to change lanes in time to follow, he saw a sign indicating it was a public boat landing. He could see several trucks and boat trailers in the parking lot.

Bama continued on to The Pantry convenience store just across the bridge, then turned around and approached the boat landing from the opposite direction. As he parked, he saw the detectives walking down the ramp.

Bama pulled his ball cap low on his forehead and casually strolled in that direction. He was shocked to see a

Beaufort County Marine Patrol boat tied up to the floating dock. He watched as Morgan shook hands with a short, balding man who carried a briefcase. Then the detectives and the bald man stepped onto the boat, and the officer who had been aboard headed up the ramp. In a matter of seconds, Morgan steered the boat away from the dock.

Bama let out a string of obscenities. *They must be meeting somewhere by boat. That must be the arrangements Morgan referred to. Or maybe this has to do with a totally unrelated case. Nah, it's Campbell all right. I can feel it in my bones.*

Bama hastily did an about face and practically ran to his vehicle, started the engine, and roared out of the parking lot. *No use waiting around here. Where would she get a boat?*

As he stopped, waiting to be able to cross traffic, his sphincter tightened when he saw a Beaufort County Sheriff's cruiser approaching, turn signal on. *Damn!* He turned his face away as the cruiser pulled in. Heart racing, he watched in his rearview mirror as the cop who had left the boat flagged down the cruiser.

Finally, there was a break in traffic, so he shot across three lanes and turned left, then returned to The Pantry. He parked in front of the pay phone, jumped out of his vehicle, and groaned when he pulled out the gum-encrusted phone book. He had a mild phobia about germs. Telling himself there could be no active germs left in the hardened blobs, he still avoided touching the grungy mess. Gingerly, he flipped through the Yellow Pages to Boat Rentals. Several were listed. He wouldn't know where to start. *Where else would she get a boat? Maybe from a friend? If so, he was screwed.*

And then, for some reason, he flashed back to the night of the murder. His subconscious was trying to tell him something. But the snap of the over-sized American flag flying practically overhead, and the sounds of the heavy traffic, were distracting.

Bama closed his eyes and willed himself to concentrate.

He was back in the doctor's house. He mentally walked from the foyer, through the living room, and back to the office. After destroying the computers, he had surveyed the room. Finally, he had it. There on the shelf above the desk was a picture of the good doc fishing on a small boat. He had noticed because his boat was a much larger and better-equipped version of the same brand. Figuring the man wouldn't leave his boat in the salt water, he quickly flipped the pages to Boat Storage. The dry storage closest to Port Royal Plantation was Schilling's Boat House on Squire Pope Road. Bama glanced at his watch. It was 4:50. He quickly dialed the number.

"Schilling's."

"Hi, a friend of mine, Dr. Kline, said he stored his boat there, and he raved about what a good job you guys do."

"Right, Doc Kline. It was terrible what happened to him."

"Yes, tragic. Tell me, do you have a space for a thirty-six foot boat?"

"This is the tackle shop. You need to talk to the front office. Hold on, and I'll transfer you."

Bama quickly hung up. Well, if Campbell was on Kline's boat, and he'd bet she was, she'd have to come back to the dock eventually. And the chase would be over.

Chapter Twelve

At 5:30, Cece observed the police boat pull up close to the marker and drop anchor. Through the binoculars she could see two men and a woman. She watched them until just before six, then pulled anchor and headed in their direction. Traffic had thinned, and now there was just an occasional fishing boat headed in from the off-shore reefs and a popular fishing place, called The Hole in the Wall. None of them had stopped in the vicinity of the detectives.

Five minutes later Cece pulled alongside their craft, threw her fenders over, and tied off to their boat.

"Miss Campbell, I presume. Permission to come aboard?" Shark asked.

"Sure. There're more seats over here."

Shark climbed aboard, then turned and gave the lady detective and a short man a hand. "I'm Detective Morgan, this is my partner, Dell Hassler, and Cal Miers, the sketch artist. Miss Campbell, we're very glad you're safe. I think we have a lot to talk about."

"Have a seat, and please call me Cece."

"I'd like to have Cal get started before it's completely dark. Maybe we can talk as he works."

"That's fine. But don't worry about the approaching darkness. There are plenty of deck lights."

Cal opened his briefcase and pulled out a sketch pad. "Now, Miss Campbell."

"Please call me Cece."

"Okay, Cece. Now I want you to close your eyes, and pull up the man's face. First up, all I want you to concentrate on is the general shape of his face. Is it more round, or oval?"

Cece was silent for a moment, then said, "More round."

"Good. Now does he look like anyone special? An actor or a famous athlete, perhaps?"

Cece didn't say anything for a minute. "Well the shape of his face is kinda like Bobby Knight's, the basketball coach who used to be at Indiana University. Know who I mean?"

"Of course. That's good. Now what about his hair?"

"It's medium brown, and parted on the left side. Kinda like John Kennedy's was."

"Very good. Now what about the ears. Are they large, small, sit high or low?"

After Cece gave him some basic information, he began drawing. As he worked, she told the detectives everything that had happened since the morning she learned of the doctor's death—except for "borrowing" the Expedition, and where she had hidden the disks.

Shark and Dell just shook their heads in amazement when she repeated the story of how she had learned Dave Garrett's name at the car rental agency. And they were shocked to learn that at one point, she'd been parked right outside their office.

"He's following you, you know. I saw him again at the mall. That's why I didn't make contact."

"Can I interrupt for a moment?" Cal asked. He held up his sketch. Cece gazed at it for a moment, then said, "The nose isn't quite right. Maybe a little broader."

While Cal made some adjustments, Shark said, "When Dell left today to go to Enterprise, I didn't see anyone follow her, and she observed no signs of a tail. Also, I didn't detect anyone following us on the way to the dock today."

"All I know is, both times I was supposed to meet you, he showed up. So you'd better watch your back."

"Speaking of watching your back, if you give us those disks, your life should no longer be in danger," Dell said.

"I disagree. I don't think he'll kill me until he recovers the disks. I see them as my insurance policy. I won't tell you where they are. I will tell you that I've made arrangements that if something happens to me, they'll be personally delivered to you. That's all I'm going to say."

Again Cal offered his pad. "The eyes need to be a little closer together I think."

"Don't you realize whoever has them is also in danger?" Shark asked.

"I don't think so. It's not anyone who can be connected to me in any way."

Finally, Cece felt that the sketch was as good as it was going to get.

"We'll make copies and start checking all the hotels in the morning. Miss Campbell, why don't you follow us back to the boat dock and let us take you into protective custody?" Shark asked.

"No. Like I said, I think he's following you. I feel safer here."

"You're planning on staying on the boat tonight?" Dell asked skeptically.

"Yes."

"I'm not sure that's a good idea," Shark said.

"I've done it lots of times before. I'll be fine."

"What about tomorrow?" Shark asked.

"I don't know yet. Maybe you'll find him tomorrow."

"So do you need anything?" Dell asked, glad that she was going to be safely tucked into her warm bed tonight.

"I'm running short on cash. I'm afraid to write a check or use my credit card. On TV it seems that the bad guy always tracks his victim down that way."

"Well, you probably shouldn't do either one, just to be safe," Shark said, pulling out his wallet. Between the three of them, they came up with $120.

"How am I going to pay you back?" Cece asked. "I could give you a check to hold until all this is over. Would that be okay?"

"If it will make you feel better, that's fine. But be assured I won't cash it. Or we can worry about it later."

"No, let me get my purse out of the cabin. I'll feel better if you take it. That way if something happens, you'll get your money back."

As Cece handed Shark the check, Dell asked, "Do you have a cell phone?"

"Not anymore. It was in the house."

"Where can we leave one for you to pick up in the morning?" Shark inquired.

Cece thought for a moment. "In the tackle shop at Schilling's Boat House."

"What time do they open?"

"At eight."

"We'll leave one for you there first thing. What else?" Shark asked.

Should I tell them about the car? I wonder if they can fix grand theft auto?

"Just your prayers," Cece muttered softly.

"You've got them," Dell said. "Thanks for meeting with us. This sketch should help a lot. Try not to worry. We'll find him. And if you change your mind and want to go into protective custody, just give us a call."

They stepped aboard the police boat. But before Shark started the engine he called over, "I don't feel good about leaving you out here alone. Where do you plan to anchor for the night?"

"My game plan was to stay in the May River, but it's too dark for me to head over there now. I'll probably just go back over and anchor off Bay Point."

"Why don't I come back and stay with you after I drop them off, or better yet, leave Dell with you now?"

"No, that's not necessary, but thanks for the offer. Frankly, I don't want your police boat anywhere near me. It would attract too much attention. One boat at anchor is a common sight around here, two boats tied up to each other is another matter."

"Do you have a weapon?" Dell yelled over.

"No, and I don't want one. I'd probably shoot myself in the foot. I have trouble not cutting myself with a filet knife."

Bama pulled into Schilling's parking lot a little after five. He was surprised to find so many cars. Then he noticed the restaurant, The Boat House Grill.

He ambled down the ramp to the floating dock and tried to act like a tourist, going from boat to boat. Four small boats were tied off to cleats. There was a large empty space that would hold a couple more boats. *Good! She shouldn't have any trouble finding a space to tie up when she returns.*

Bama paced back and forth along the deserted dock, gazing in one direction, then the other. He watched as a couple of dolphins frolicked close to a sandbar. Deciding he didn't want to be standing on the dock if she came back, afraid she would recognize him and take off again, he strolled back up the ramp.

Inside the restaurant, he asked for a table by a window so he would have a good view of the floating dock. He ordered a Jack and Coke, then studied the menu. When the waitress brought his drink, he ordered the salmon special.

As he quickly drained his drink, and motioned for the gal to bring him another, he watched a couple of large ferryboats tie up at the next dock up. *Maybe I should go back to the boat landing and see if she returns on the police boat.* He thought about her actions so far. He had to give her credit. She was either very lucky, or smarter than he had anticipated. *No, my gut tells me she'll show up here. And my gut is usually right.*

By the dim anchor light, Cece propped her tired legs up on the seat and ate a bologna sandwich with provolone cheese—Tony's favorite. She hadn't even realized that as she bustled about the busy grocery store, she was automatically picking up the same things she always did when shopping for one of their fishing trips. Even down to the chocolate chip cookies. Tears slid silently down her cheeks. She sipped a Diet Dr. Pepper, again Tony's favorite, and wished she had brought a six-pack of beer instead.

Suddenly, a dam opened up, and Cece began to sob uncontrollably. Being on the boat alone, without Tony busily changing the tackle on their lines, or pulling up anchor and instructing her to move the boat to a more advantageous spot, made her face the harsh reality of his death. She had been so busy trying to stay alive, that she really hadn't had time to think about Aunt Sophie or Tony very much.

Beginning to shiver, Cece stepped down into the cabin, pulled the sleeping bag out of its tote and tossed it up on deck. She returned topside, opened a storage compartment to get a tissue, and saw Tony's Marlboro lights and his Nascar lighter. She had to smile. Ruth wouldn't let Tony smoke at home, and he seemed to do fine kicking his habit until he had all the fishing lines in the water. Then he always reached for a cigarette. Once, when Ruth had finally agreed to accompany them, she'd found his hidden stash. Tony had tried to convince Ruth that they were Cece's, but she hadn't been fooled. Cece grabbed the cigarettes. She'd never been a smoker, but she thought that maybe if she had just one, it would bring Tony back. Just for a minute or two.

Cece blew her nose, settled back down on the seat, and wrapped the sleeping bag around her. She pulled a cigarette out of the pack, and lit up. After a couple of puffs a wave of dizziness washed over her. But the smell reminded her of Tony.

How patient he had been with her in the beginning. She'd hardly been able to get through a day without crying. Tony had initially thought that she was afraid of him, until finally, fearful that she was about to lose her job, she had told him about her fiancé.

From that day on, Tony had treated her like the daughter he'd never had. And when he found out she used to go fishing with her father, a special bond had been formed. He had taught her how to fish for cobia, Spanish mackerel, and shark. For the past three years, every spring Tony had been determined that this was the year they were going to catch their first marlin. But they never had, and now Tony never would.

Cece glanced down at her watch, and was surprised to find it was almost 11 o'clock. She stared up at the sky, filled with a half moon and occasional stars. It was the first time in days she wasn't looking over her shoulder, fearful that at any minute she was going to be killed. She wondered where she would go and what she would do when all this was over, and how long it would take the detectives to find their man now that they knew what he looked like. Relaxed by the motion of the boat, she began to yawn. But before turning in, she checked the anchor line to make sure it was secure, as Tony had taught her.

She climbed down into the cabin and stretched out on the V berth, stuck the filet knife under her pillow, and covered herself with the sleeping bag. The rocking motion of the boat and sound of the waves quickly put her to sleep.

Bama sat at the Boat House Grill, nursing several drinks and smoking an entire pack of cigarettes until just before midnight. Finally, deciding Campbell wasn't going to show up, he disgustedly threw several large bills on the table.

He returned to his boat, *The Oasis,* took a quick shower and fell into his bunk. Just before falling asleep he mentally ticked off all the things he needed to do tomorrow. He would have to change his appearance. Brown contacts and a mustache should do the trick. He'd also move his boat to the other marina, Palmetto Bay, first thing in the morning, in case the cops came looking for him, now that they knew what he looked liked. Then he'd return to Savannah and track down the guy Campbell had spent the night with at the hospital. That shouldn't be too tough. Then he would head out in his boat and circle the island and see if he could find Kline's boat.

* * *

Cece was in a deep sleep when something suddenly made her sit up. The noise of a boat, a big boat, sounded as if it was practically on top of her. Her heart racing, and fearing that maybe she was about to be rammed, she grabbed the filet knife, as if that would do her any good, and stuck her head out of the cabin.

Off to the right, in the dim moonlight, she could see a tugboat pushing a huge barge laden with what looked like timber. She exhaled with relief. *He must be headed for Daufuskie Island.* The captain of the tugboat tooted his horn, to let her know he had seen her.

Cece checked her depth gauge and anchor line before returning to bed. She slept fitfully after that, and at dawn climbed out of the cabin, the sleeping bag wrapped around her, and pulled a soda out of the cooler. She needed caffeine. *God, what I wouldn't give for a cappuccino right now.* As she sipped her soda, she heard the blowing noise of several dolphins swimming close to the boat.

Cece knew she had to decide what her next move should be. She couldn't pick up the cell phone until eight, when the tackle shop opened. Once she did that, she would head back to Savannah and return the car, praying it hadn't yet been discovered missing. But then what?

Cece thought of Brad Johnson. She hoped he was so busy with the funeral arrangements for his father that he hadn't opened his briefcase and found her letter and the disks yet. She wondered if the funeral would be today or tomorrow. And what about Aunt Sophie and Tony's funerals? When would they be? She knew it wouldn't be safe for her to attend either one. So as the sun began to break through the clouds and the sky turned a pinkish orange, she said her good-byes. She told each of them, as if they were sitting next to her, how much she had loved them and how they had impacted her life.

A little after eight, Cece glided the boat expertly up to the dock and tied it off to the cleat. She squirted soap into the bucket and filled it with water from the hose on the dock. She scrubbed the boat down from bow to stern, lowered the antennas, raised the engine cover, and flipped the batteries to Off. Next she removed the bimini top, folded it and placed it on the cooler. Finally she reached down into the cabin, pulled out the boat cover, and snapped it into place.

At the top of the boat ramp, she turned and took one last look at the boat, then wrote on the chalkboard for it to be returned to storage. Cece's eyes filled with tears, as she made her way toward the tackle shop. She knew it was the last ride she would ever take on the *Salt Shaker*.

She looked around carefully, before walking into the tackle shop. "Good morning, Bob," she called to the familiar face behind the counter.

"Hey, Cece. A deputy just dropped off this package for you. Is everything okay?"

"Yes, thanks," she said, putting on a smile and taking the sack from him.

"I still can't believe it about Doc. Do they have any idea who did it?"

"I really don't know," she said walking toward the door. "They're still investigating."

Once in the Expedition, she pulled out the small cell phone and note from Detective Morgan with his and his partner's mobile numbers. He'd also given her the name of a detective on the Savannah Police Force, Tim Michaels, and his number. Morgan's only request was that she keep in contact with him at least once a day.

Cece searched all over the phone, but she couldn't find anything with the phone number for the unit. Oh well, the only person she would have given the number to was her dad, and it was probably best if he didn't know it, or he'd be calling her every few hours to check on her. She slipped the phone and note into her purse and headed for the Savannah Airport.

Cece had difficulty keeping her eyes on the road, frequently checking the rearview mirror to see if she was about to be stopped by a cop. She had visions of being pulled over and handcuffed, thrown into the back of a squad car and arrested for grand theft auto. Cece was relieved to pull into the airport 45 minutes later. She drove to Section B and tried to park the car as close to where she had found it as she could. It was two rows back and over to the right a little from its original location. She only hoped the owner would be too tired to notice.

Cece used a T-shirt from her gym bag to wipe her prints away, then left it just as she'd found it. She prayed the owner hadn't returned yet.

She grabbed her purse and bag and walked to the terminal. Immediately, she bought a newspaper and a cappuccino, and sat down in the lobby. What she longed for was a long shower to wash all the salt and grime away and some fresh clothes. Pushing those thoughts away, she turned to the page with the obituaries and read about Brad's father. The funeral was tomorrow.

Cece read the entire paper, as much to kill time as anything. She was glad she had, when she discovered a small blurb about Tony's funeral tomorrow, as well. She wished she could be there for Ruth, especially since they had no children, but knew the risk was too great. She felt Tony would understand.

Now what? Cece knew her father would be frantic. She needed to find a way to e-mail him again or send a FAX. She knew that if she called him on the cell phone he would argue with her about coming home, or insist on flying down to help her. At least with an e-mail, she didn't have to worry about fussing with him.

Cece found a bank of pay phones and pulled out the directory. She turned to the yellow pages and looked for cyber-cafes. There was no listing. *Why did I think Savannah would have something so techno?* Then she looked under FAX. There were several businesses listed that offered the service. *But wait, wouldn't the library have computers? They did on Hilton Head. She could e-mail her father from there.* Cece flipped through the book until she found the address for the Chatham County Library.

She threw the newspaper and her empty cup into a trash receptacle, and looking over her shoulder frequently to make sure she wasn't being followed, descended to the baggage claim area and boarded the courtesy van for the Hyatt Hotel once again. From there, she could catch a city bus to Bull Street where the library was located. After she completed that task, she had no idea where she would go or what she would do.

Chapter Thirteen

The following morning the sun had barely peeked out from behind the clouds when Bama pulled anchor and guided his boat expertly out of the slip and into Broad Creek. As soon as he was out of sight of the marina, he threw his anchor over again between two of the multitude of private floating docks that lined the entire waterway. Then he leaned over the stern and peeled off the black letters, changing the name on the back of the boat to *The Runabout.*

His first task completed, he stepped down into the cabin and pulled out his Dopp kit. Bama removed a white plastic rectangular case and a bottle of saline, then inserted non-prescription brown contacts. Next he placed small pads into the top of his cheeks and pasted on a brown mustache. He pulled an old fishing hat off the peg and pulled it down low on his forehead, and carefully perused his reflection in the mirror. He hardly recognized the face that stared back at him. It always surprised him how little one had to do to alter his appearance. The plumper cheeks alone made a dramatic difference.

Bama was satisfied that even Campbell wouldn't be able to recognize him, so he pulled anchor and continued the short distance down to Palmetto Bay Marina. He tied off to a cleat in front of the fuel dock, then sauntered up to the Harbourmaster's office. The flavor of this marina was totally different than the one he had just left. There was a glaring absence of luxury yachts that had been the norm at Shelter Cove. He noted much smaller craft, and even a couple of old houseboats. But what struck him most was the abundance of sailboats.

Bama wrenched open the door to the office and approached the white-haired gentleman behind the counter. "I'd like to tie up for a few days. I live over on Wilmington Island and thought I might try my hand at shrimping. We don't have a shrimp baiting season in Georgia like you do."

"We get lots of guys coming over from Georgia during the six weeks of the baiting season. How long do you think you'll be staying with us?" the elderly man asked.

"Don't know for sure. Guess it depends on how well I do. How much do you charge per night?" he asked.

"Eighteen dollars, or one-twenty for a week."

"Why don't I go ahead and pay for three nights."

"Sounds fine to me. They've been doing pretty well. Most guys been filling their coolers about every night."

"That's what I wanna hear," Bama said, peeling off two twenties.

"You'll be in slip J32. It's on the end."

Bama moved his boat to the appointed slip, changed clothes, and called a cab. He returned to Shelter Cove, retrieved his car from the parking lot, and headed toward Savannah.

Traffic was heavy as he threaded his way down Highway 278, then turned left onto a beautiful stretch of road lined with old churches and huge live oaks dripping with Spanish moss that formed a canopy over the road. Would he find Campbell back at the hospital? Now that he knew what her disguise was, it should be a lot easier to spot her.

Once he reached the hospital, he strode briskly to the bank of elevators that would take him to the critical care waiting room. Bama held his breath as he entered the room, but there was no sign of Campbell, or the guy she had spent the night with. Disappointed, he ambled down the hall to the nurse's station.

"Can I help you?" an attractive black unit clerk asked. Her blue plastic nametag read Tanya Simpson.

Bama pasted on his sincere smile. "I sure hope so. Sunday night a man left a brief case in the waiting room down there. I don't know his name, but he was sleeping in a room right across the hall. I think he has a relative who's a patient here." Bama described the young man.

Tanya flipped through a loose-leaf notebook and said, "That was probably Brad Johnson. His father died that night."

Bama attempted to put on an appropriate face. "I'm sorry to hear that. Would you happen to have his address so I can return his briefcase?"

"No, I'm sorry I don't. But let's try the phone book."

She flipped to the J's and ran her long red polished nail down the page. "Here it is, Bradley Johnson, 2230 Norwood Place. That's a subdivision on the south side. Here," she said grabbing a piece of paper. "I'll write down the address for you."

A couple of minutes later, he slipped the paper into his shirt pocket. "Well, thanks for all your help. I know he'll be glad to get his briefcase back and I'll be sure and tell him how helpful you were, Tanya."

Bama tipped his hat, and tried not to chuckle as he practically skipped down the hall. *Like taking candy from a baby.*

Bama made a quick sweep through the cafeteria looking for Campbell, then returned to his car. He followed the directions on his city map to Johnson's house. Ten minutes later he pulled in the drive behind a late model midnight-blue Ford Mustang. He retrieved a fake private investigator's license from his bag and slipped it into his pocket.

Bama approached the one-story brick ranch and rang the bell. Shortly, the man who had invited Campbell to share his room answered the door. "Are you Brad Johnson?" Bama asked with a smile on his face.

"Yes. Can I help you?"

Bama quickly flashed his PI license. "Jeff Blakely, private investigator. I need to speak with you for a minute."

Surprised, Brad hesitantly motioned for him to enter. "What's this about?" he asked standing stiffly in the foyer.

"This is about a lady named Cecilia Campbell."

"There must be some mistake. I don't know anyone by that name."

"That's interesting. You shared your room at the hospital with her the other night."

Taken aback, Brad said, "The lady who shared my room was Grace Parker. And how do you know about that?"

"I told you, I'm a PI. Can we sit down? I won't take much of your time, but I have a story I need to share with you."

Warily, Brad closed the door and shuffled into the living room.

Bama sat down on the brown leather sofa, and Brad almost fell into a matching chair. "Cecilia Campbell, aka Grace Parker, escaped from a mental hospital in Charlotte, North Carolina, and her family has hired me to find her. She's a paranoid schizophrenic. When she doesn't take her medication, she thinks people are trying to kill her. She frequently carries around a couple of blank computer disks that she says contains information about a conspiracy. Something to do with radiation from cell phones causing brain tumors."

Wide-eyed, Brad said, "Wow, that's pretty bizarre."

"I know what you mean. Did she give you any disks or anything when she stayed with you the other night?"

"No. She said her grandmother was a patient there, like my dad. She seemed so normal. But I didn't really spend much time with her that night because my dad died a few hours later."

"I'm terribly sorry. So she didn't tell you anything or give you something to hold for her?"

"No, nothing."

"Well, since you befriended her, she may try to contact you again. If she does, please call me right away at this number," he said, passing a business card over to Brad. "If she happens to show up, please try to stall her until I can get here. She's attempted suicide twice, so you could possibly save her life."

"Certainly. I'll call you right away if I hear from her, but I doubt I will," Brad said, convinced beyond a shadow of a doubt that what he had just heard was true.

Bama stood up. "Thank you for taking time to talk with me. Again, I'm sorry about your father. I won't keep you any longer."

Bama could hardly keep the smile off his face as he backed out of the drive and pointed his car in the direction of Hilton Head. *God, people are so gullible. I think I could have told him she was really an alien and he would have believed me. I guess it's time to return to my listening post and see if the Keystone Kops will lead me to Campbell.*

Chapter Fourteen

Late Tuesday afternoon, Shark and Dell met up at the office. Both had struck out. Dave Garrett hadn't been registered at any of the hotels, and no one had recognized his picture. They had covered villa rental places and RV resorts as well.

"So where the hell is this guy?" Shark asked, throwing his pen disgustedly down on the desk.

"Beats me," Dell answered, her hands busy massaging her tired feet.

The phone shrilled loudly on Shark's desk. He picked it up on the second ring and listened for a minute, then hung up and turned to Dell. "They found his rental car at the airport."

"So do you think he flew the coop?"

Shark picked up his pen, tapping it nervously on the desk as he considered the possibility for a moment. "I don't think so. Not with Campbell still on the loose. What do you think?"

"I agree. He may have just switched vehicles. I'll call the other car rental places, then let's run by the airport and flash his picture around on our way home."

Deputy Sayles sauntered in and handed Dell a stack of computer printouts. "Thanks, Sayles," she said as she began to leaf through them. "Well, we're back to square one. He's using a fake ID. Dave Garrett died in New York four days after he was born."

"Well, at least we have a good sketch of him."

"Has Campbell checked in with you today?" Dell asked.

"No, not yet."

"Think she's still out on the boat?"

"Don't know, but that wouldn't be a bad place to hide."

"Have you read any of these printouts on the effects of radiation from cell phones? I can't believe, with all this information available, that the public hasn't become aware of the dangers. Me, I'm going to get one of those headphone things just to be safe."

"Don't you think it's kind of ironic that the cell phone manufacturers are the ones funding the research and collecting all of the data? You'd think some regulatory agency would be doing that."

"That makes too much sense," Dell said, stacking the pile of documents on her already cluttered desk. "So how are we going to find our guy?"

"Frankly, I have no idea. If he's not in a hotel, villa or RV, where could he be?"

"Maybe he's staying in one of the hotels up by I-95 in Hardeville or Ridgeland."

"I'll send some guys up to check it out this evening."

"Well let's get started to the airport. I'm about ready to call it a day. Maybe I can still get home in time to actually cook dinner for my husband."

"How is Josh?"

"Good. Have you spoken to Jazz lately?"

"Yeah. I called her last night. She's busy on a robbery/ kidnapping case. The trial started today. Sounds like she's going to be tied up for a while. The feds are involved, which she says is a royal pain in the ass."

"You know, she had a few dates with some FBI guy in the Charleston office before I introduced you two. You better hurry up and marry her before she discovers all your faults and looks for greener pastures."

"Thanks, Dell. You really know how to make a guy feel

good. She's the one that doesn't want to rush into anything so soon after her divorce. Me, I'm ready. Hopefully I'll see her next weekend. We're supposed to be in a fishing tournament in Charleston."

"You better hope we've got our guy in custody by then, or there's not a chance in hell you'll be in that tournament."

Shark's cell phone rang. "Maybe it's Campbell," he said, pulling it quickly out of his shirt pocket. He listened for a minute and gave Dell a thumbs up. "Where are you?" he asked. "So okay, forget I asked. Just tell me if you're still on the boat." Shark rolled his eyes as he listened. "Okay, okay. No more questions. Won't you reconsider going into protective custody?" He listened momentarily, then said, "No, we haven't caught him yet. He's using a fake ID. The real Dave Garrett died when he was four-days-old. We checked all the hotels and villas on the island, and no one recognized him. We've located his rental car at the airport and we're headed over there now to see if anyone can ID him. So we haven't given up. I'm also sending some guys up to I-95 to see if he's staying up there somewhere. Check in with me again tomorrow about this same time. Be extremely careful, and call if you change your mind about protective custody."

"So she wouldn't tell you where she is?" Dell asked.

"No, she wouldn't even say whether she was still on the boat or not."

"That is one stubborn lady."

Shark tapped his pen on the desk and stared into space for a moment, then turned to Dell. "Maybe we should think about setting up a false meet somewhere and see if he follows us."

"That's an interesting idea. What have you got in mind?"

Bama smiled and started his car as soon as he heard that Campbell may still be on the boat. There shouldn't be that many boats anchored around the island tonight, especially ones captained by a woman. Not only that, but he knew she was in a white Pursuit with a green bimini top. He was sure glad he had noticed that picture in the doc's office.

Bama made a quick stop at the BiLo Grocery and picked up some cold cuts and chips. Then he proceeded a couple of doors down to the liquor store and bought a liter of Jack Daniels. Once he had acquired the necessities for an evening cruise, he returned to the marina. As he made a couple of sandwiches he fantasized about all the delicious things he would do to Campbell when he found her.

Cece peeled $39 off her meager roll of bills for a room in a seedy motel in downtown Savannah. Behind the locked door, she collapsed onto the full-sized bed and tried not to think about all the germs she knew must be on the floral spread. It was better not to look too closely. She should have turned the spread back before collapsing. But she was too tired to move, and tried to focus on relaxing the tense muscles in her neck and shoulders. It wasn't long, however, before the smell of food from the Burger King bag she'd thrown on the tiny table drew her off the bed.

As she inhaled the Whopper and french fries, a large brown cockroach suddenly appeared on the corner of the table. It just stared at her for a moment, its antennae moving slowly back and forth. When she had first moved south, she'd freaked out every time she had seen one. One evening in Aunt Sophie's kitchen, a huge roach had scooted across the tile floor in her direction and she had grabbed a can of roach killer out from under the kitchen sink. Standing halfway across the room, she'd sprayed enough in its direction to drown a rat. To her horror, the roach had flown directly at her and had landed on her blouse. Hysterical, in her haste to strip, she had ripped two buttons off her shirt. She was shocked the buggers could fly!

Her aunt, hearing Cece's screams, had run into the room, demanding to know what the crisis was, only to find Cece stomping all over her new silk blouse, finally grinding the damn roach practically to a powder. After Sophie had quit laughing, she'd politely informed her niece that in the south they had a more genteel name for them—palmetto bugs.

After finishing the last morsel of her dinner, she searched every nook and cranny in an attempt to discover if she'd be sharing the room with any other obvious critters. Cece felt creepier by the minute, and contemplated returning to the antiseptic-smelling hospital, but she desperately needed a shower and a good night's sleep.

Cece mustered her courage and strode into the tiny cubicle of a bathroom, fearful of the condition in which she would find it. She pulled back the pink vinyl shower curtain and peered into the rust stained tub. There was no way she was going to sit down in that yucky-looking tub to take the long bath she had envisioned. The hospital was sounding more attractive by the minute.

Cece returned to the bedroom and stripped, except for a pair of white socks, and then made her way back to the bathroom, carrying her tennis shoes. She washed her face and brushed her teeth, then put her dirty underwear and bra in the sink to soak.

Next, adjusting the water temperature of the shower, she stepped into the tub, socks and all. The hot water revived her, as it played over her tired body and washed the salt residue away. She washed her hair, then let out a deep sigh as she stood, hands braced on the front of the shower, letting the water play over her stiff neck. She really did feel safe for the moment, but realized it was a temporary respite. She knew she had to make some decisions, and her life depended on making the right ones.

After toweling off, she removed the wet socks, donned her tennis shoes, and dropped the socks into the sink to soak with her other things. By the time she'd put on the long white shirt, rinsed out her undies and hung them over the towel bar to dry, she had come up with a plan. She wasn't convinced the police were going to be able to find the man who had shot Tony and was trying to kill her. Cece knew she'd been damned lucky, but felt her luck was bound to run out eventually. She decided to contact Brad

Johnson and pick up her disks. Then she would get copies made of them and send the originals to Detective Morgan. The duplicates she would give to a newspaper reporter. Maybe Brad knew someone she could contact at the *Savannah Morning News*. Once the information hit the media and the public became aware of the results of all the studies, maybe there would be no reason left to kill her.

Meanwhile, she'd move to a different part of the country, even change her name if necessary, and start over again. Cece was getting tired of starting over. How many times was she going to have to pull up roots and move someplace where she knew no one and didn't have a job?

She had hoped, when she moved south after Mark's death, that she could get settled and start a career. Cece was tired of always having to make new friends, find a beautician who didn't hack her hair to death, and a dentist she didn't despise. And she had thought her career was finally on track, working as Tony's research assistant. A couple of her college friends she had kept in touch with were already married, and on the fast track at work. One was even a vice president at a bank. As for her, she had no husband, no place to live, no career, and someone was trying to kill her.

Cece returned to the bedroom, picked up the glass ashtray off the table and placed it on the floor directly under the doorknob. Then she rummaged in her purse until she found five quarters, which she stacked on the doorknob. That way, if anyone tried to enter her room, the quarters would fall into the ashtray when the handle was turned, and it would wake her up. She had learned that little trick one year from her college roommate when they'd been on spring break in Miami.

Pleased that she knew what her plans were for the following day, she pulled back the bedspread and tried to ignore the dingy gray sheets, and the pillows that looked as flat as pancakes. She rummaged around in her gym bag and removed the flashlight and little tube of nerve spray, wishing she had more substantial weapons. Damn, she should have thought to bring the filet knife from the boat. She placed her meager weapons next to her on the bed, then collapsed into the lumpy mattress and turned out the light.

"Mom," Cece whispered. "I feel so alone. I have no one I can trust and I don't know what to do. Please help me. Why did you have to die? I desperately need you. I'm so sorry about Aunt Sophie. I know I'm the reason she's dead. It's not fair after she opened her home to me. But life isn't fair is it? Please help me." Cece began to sob.

By the time Bama was ready to pull out of the marina, it was almost five o'clock. Since the entire area was a NO WAKE ZONE, he slowly threaded his way to the mouth of Broad Creek. Huge houses stood, elbow to elbow, with an occasional older single-level home, which originally had probably been a summer home before the island was developed. Most of the newer places had floor to ceiling windows facing the water so they could admire their private docks and large fishing boats. Beautiful flowerbeds and professionally manicured lawns laced with faux-cobblestone walks extended down to the water's edge. Many of the yards sported gazebos, or screened-in porches right on the dock. If he could only get this job finished, and maybe do just a couple more, he might be able to afford something similar one of these days.

He finally reached the mouth of the river and gunned his engine up to around 40 mph, then turned left in the direction of Harbour Town, which was at the south end of the island. It took only a few minutes to pass the lighthouse, at which point he had to slow down dramatically because of the shallow depth and sandbars. Finally making it around the tip of the peninsula and into deeper water, he revved her up again. As he skimmed over the surface of the choppy water, he polished off the sandwiches and a couple of beers. There were few boats on the water, which made his search a lot easier.

It took him over three hours to completely circle the island, search the May River and the largest of the surrounding creeks, but he didn't find her. He knew he would eventually, and then he would extract sweet revenge for all the trouble she'd put him through. It wasn't just a job anymore, now it was personal.

Chapter Fifteen

When Cece awoke Wednesday morning, she was initially disoriented. But peering around the room, it didn't take her long to recognize her dismal surroundings. It looked worse in the daylight. There was even a big crack in the ceiling right over her bed. But she'd gotten some much-needed rest. She glanced over at the doorknob, and saw the quarters were still in place. As deeply as she had slept, the Terminator could have waltzed right in and carted her off, and she wasn't sure she would even have awakened.

Cece yawned and stretched her cramped muscles, then sat up on the side of the bed and slipped her feet into her sneakers and tramped into the bathroom. After washing her face and brushing her teeth, she dressed in the same old pair of jeans, but at least she had clean underwear, even if the elastic was still a little damp.

Desperately needing caffeine, Cece grabbed her room key and purse and headed next door to the Burger King.

Once she'd savored her breakfast sandwich and accompanying tater tots, she leaned back in the booth and leisurely sipped the strong black stuff that was passing for coffee. She knew she should have gotten take out and gone directly back to the room, but the damn place was so grungy and depressing. At least here she could look out the window and see the sun and sky.

She grabbed a newspaper off the next table when Mel, a supervisor at Midas Muffler according to his nametag, hiked up his brown polyester pants and headed for the door. As she leafed through the pages and came across the obituary page, she remembered that both Brad's father's and Tony's funerals were today. When she'd made her plans last night, she had forgotten. There was no way she was going to bother Brad today, so suddenly she had a whole day to kill.

Cece returned to the dreary room, and at 10 o'clock, the appointed time for Tony's funeral to start, she switched off the television and sat quietly on the side of the bed, head bowed. She'd driven by the church Ruth attended occasionally, but had never been inside. She wondered what the sanctuary looked like. She hoped Ruth had picked out a beautiful casket, and had had the decency to have it closed. Cece didn't think Tony would have liked people staring at him. Were there lots of flowers? How many people were in attendance? Was Ruth holding up reasonably well? And what about Sophie? What was happening with her body, or what had been left of it? Had they contacted Cece's father, since he was the only other relative? Just what her father needed, another burial to take care of. And she also thought of Brad Johnson. Too much death, and too many funerals.

Suddenly there was a knock on the door. Cece jumped off the bed, and began frantically pulling things out of her gym bag, searching for her nerve spray she had put away a few minutes earlier. She heard a key in the lock. She thought she was going to pass out from lack of air, and stood frozen to the spot as she watched the door handle turn slowly. She realized she was helpless. She could not move.

As the door opened a crack, Cece heard someone call out, "Maid service," and then a road-weary, bleached-blond stuck her head in the door. Cece finally took a breath.

"Lord girl, you look like you seen a ghost. Sorry, I didn't mean to scare you. I didn't hear anything so I thought you'd already cleared out."

Cece grabbed her bag. "I was just getting ready to leave now."

"Well, technically you got another half-hour before you got to be out or pay for another day. You want me to come back in a few minutes?"

"No, it's okay, really."

Not sure where she was going, or how she was going to spend the day, Cece hit the sidewalk and just started walking. She passed the bus station and kept on strolling down Oglethorpe Street. She wandered around the old district, noticing many of the attractive homes that had been restored and were presently being used for offices. And she loved all the little memorial parks scattered throughout the city. She tried to guess which one Tom Hanks had sat in when he'd filmed part of *Forrest Gump*. Cece knew she needed to get off the street, and find someplace that would shelter her from onlookers. As she passed the old Lucas Theater, which had been closed for years, she didn't pay much attention. She strolled on by, and was halfway down the block, but suddenly turned and looked back at the old building.

Cece caught the next bus to the south side of town. When she stepped off, she was practically in front of Southside Cinemas. She strode over to the ticket booth, but it wasn't open yet—not for another half-hour.

Looking around, she spotted a convenience store about a block away. Cece dashed between the parked cars stopped for the red light, then entered the Circle K and bought a couple of packages of cheese crackers, a Snickers candy bar, and two Diet Cokes. She wasn't about to pay the outrageous prices they charged at the theater. She jammed her snacks into her gym bag.

Cece took her time ambling down the block, frequently looking over her shoulder to see if she was being followed. She was anxious for the theater to open, so she could get off the street.

As she studied the different movies that were currently playing, she realized she must really have been working too much. She hadn't heard of most of them. Then she spotted one with Clint Eastwood and Tommy Lee Jones. Their movies were usually at least entertaining.

When the ticket booth opened she bought a ticket for *Space Cowboys*. Bypassing the snack bar, she went directly in and sat down in the aisle seat in the back row of the totally empty theater. That way she could see everyone who came in.

Only three older couples entered before the movie started, so Cece hunched down in her seat and began to watch in earnest. To her surprise, she found herself actually laughing at times, and forgetting about all her problems for a little while.

Detectives Morgan and Hassler sat in the back row of St. Andrews Methodist Church trying to appear inconspicuous. Dell had even put on a skirt for the occasion, which was about as rare as snow in the Low Country. Dr. Kline's open casket was positioned in the front of the church, just below the pulpit. The large sanctuary was only about a third-full, not surprising since he had lived on the island for only three years. His body was to be returned to New Jersey for final burial.

Ruth Kline, supported by her sister and brother-in-law, sat in the front row, her face hidden by a black veil.

Several arrangements of fall flowers, including every color of mum known to man, were in evidence. A blanket of red roses and white baby's breath covered the lower section of the casket. One floral arrangement was so large it dwarfed all the others and almost looked out of place. Shark couldn't fathom how much it must have cost.

"Jeez, I've never even seen some of those exotic looking flowers before. Wonder who it's from?" Shark said softly to Dell.

"I know what you mean. I bet it's from all the cell phone manufacturers who hired Dr. Kline to do the study."

"Guess that means none of them are showing up for the service."

"That'd be my assumption."

"I feel sorry for the widow. At least when Laura died I knew it was coming and had the chance to say good-bye," Shark whispered.

"Well, at least the good doctor left her financially secure. It's not like she has to worry about running out and getting a job," Dell replied.

"Trust me, money can't replace your mate."

"Yeah, but I bet it helps ease the loss."

The organist began to play softly and as the service started, Shark was transported back to Laura's funeral, what little he remembered of it. She had fought so gallantly against the malignant melanoma that had ravaged her body. But by the end, she had looked like a Holocaust victim, bald from the chemotherapy and skeletal; not like the lively woman she had been just a few months previously.

He was still angry with God. He couldn't imagine an omniscient presence that could create the cosmos, only to direct the lives of men with such petulance and caprice. The reason for deadly disease and natural disasters escaped him. And he couldn't comprehend why bad things happened to good people. In his job he saw that every day. He had had to learn to compartmentalize his feelings, in order to keep his sanity.

Shark was shaken out of his reverie as the service ended and people began to file past the casket to express their final condolences to the widow. He and Dell searched the faces of the mourners as they moved by slowly, but unfortunately they didn't find the one face they were looking for.

Frustrated, they returned to their car and headed back to the office where they reported their lack of success to the sheriff.

Shark hung his sport coat over the back of his chair, sat down at his desk, and picked up a report Deputy Pickford had left for him. He and another deputy had checked all the hotels up by I-95, but no one had recognized the sketch.

Shark turned to Dell. "Let's talk some more about setting

a trap for our guy. If Campbell is correct, and he's following us, then maybe we can use that to our advantage."

"What do you have in mind?" she asked, filing a broken nail on her left index finger.

"I'm not sure yet. Just go with me here for a minute. What if we sent some plainclothes guys in somewhere, maybe a restaurant or someplace kinda off the beaten path, then we raced out of here like we were going to meet Campbell. If he really is watching and follows, we could apprehend him. What do you think?"

"Can't hurt I guess. It's better than sitting here with our heads up our ass."

"So you got any idea where we could set this up?"

"Let me think for a minute. It should be somewhere where there's not a lot of other people around, but enough that he won't be suspicious. Someplace where he would stick out like a sore thumb. Wait, I've got it! A laundromat!"

"Laundromat?"

"Yeah, that way we arrest any guy who shows up without a basket of laundry and a bottle of Clorox."

"You're kidding, right?"

"No, I'm not. We could have a couple of undercovers inside folding laundry, and a couple of guys sitting in their cars, as if they were waiting on their wives. Have an unmarked car follow us there, and we see if he shows."

"You know, that's not bad. It's also a logical place a woman might pick out for a meet. Think we could get it set up by this afternoon? Maybe we could use the one over in Triangle Square."

"I think you'd better run it by Sheriff Grant before you get too excited. See if he has the manpower available."

"Maybe if you batted those long eyelashes at him, and showed him your legs since you have on a skirt today, he'd find enough people."

"And maybe I could sue your ass for sexual harassment and get a partner who's not a total wuss. Come on, we'll both go ask him," Dell said rising from her chair.

* * *

By three o'clock, all the arrangements were in place. Two female deputies dressed in plain clothes stood in the Shipyard Coin Laundry on New Orleans Road folding clothes, their weapons hidden under some towels. Deputies Sayles and Roberts were in unmarked cars in the parking lot.

At 3:15, Shark and Dell rushed out the door of the office, ran to the car, and sped away. Deputy Sanchez, in an unmarked Ford Mustang parked in the lumberyard on Matthews Drive, watched them fly by a couple of minutes later. He let two cars pass before he pulled in behind them. He was afraid that if he let too many vehicles get between them, he wouldn't make the stop light.

Once they both turned onto William Hilton Parkway, he let them get a little ahead of him in the left lane, and he swung into the right lane. They had decided to use the laundromat on the south end of the island, since the one at Triangle Square was just a few blocks from the office, and wouldn't allow them enough time to see if someone was following them.

By the time they reached mid-island, Sanchez didn't think anyone was tailing the detectives, but it was hard to tell for sure with so many cars darting in and out behind Shark and Dell. The speed limit was 45 mph, but traffic seemed to be moving along at about 55. Boy, he could have given out a slew of tickets. He liked creeping up on a speeder in his Mustang, the person totally unaware that a cop was behind them, until he hit the blue light and siren. He had actually clocked one guy flying down the road doing 70 at 6:30 one morning.

Shark turned on his left turn signal as soon as he passed Shipyard Plantation, then pulled into the turn lane for New Orleans Road. Anticipating his move, Sanchez had entered the left lane just prior to the plantation. Three cars separated him from the detectives.

When the signal turned green, he followed them past Reilly's liquor store, and when they turned into the Ship-

yard Coin Laundry, he sped on by and watched in his rearview mirror to see if any other cars pulled in behind them.
None did, so he made a left into the dental office parking
lot and turned around, then drove back and pulled in next
to Sayles. He glanced over at the deputy and indicated there
had been no tail. Eyes glued to his rearview mirror, he
could see Shark and Dell pacing inside, as if they were
waiting for someone.

Twenty minutes had passed when a silver Saturn, with
an Avis-Rent-A-Car tag, pulled into the lot. The sole oc-
cupant, a young man, fumbled around on the floor of the
passenger seat, then exited the vehicle and ambled slowly
toward the front door. Deputies Sayles and Sanchez were
instantly alert, both drawing their weapons and keeping
them out of view as their eyes were glued to their rearview
mirrors. Why would a guy be walking into a laundromat
with no laundry?

Shark and Dell, seated in hard plastic chairs by this time,
were surprised to see the young man, dressed in camouflage
pants and a black T-shirt, walk in, look around, and then
turn around and walk back out. Instantly Morgan and Hassler were on their feet, racing out the door.

"Halt! Police!" Shark yelled, as the man approached his
car door.

As the young man turned, he was shocked to see two
deputies, guns pointed at him, come racing around the back
of his vehicle. He immediately raised his hands in the air.
"What's going on?" the man asked, as the man and woman
from the laundry, guns drawn also, joined the deputies.

"Just take it easy," Shark said as he approached him
slowly. "We just need to ask you a couple of questions. Do
you have some ID?"

Trembling, the young man said, "Yes, in my wallet. It's
in my car, on the seat. What's this all about?"

"Why did you come in the laundry, then turn right
around and leave?" Dell asked.

"Because it didn't have any of those big washers for

oversized loads. I got a couple of sleeping bags in the trunk. I need to wash them."

Dell glanced over at Shark. He moved to the passenger side of the car. "Okay, I'd like you to slowly reach in the car and get your wallet."

"Yes, sir."

Tentatively, as if he was convinced a bullet was going to enter his back at any moment, he opened the car door and reached over and grabbed his wallet. Dell reached for it, and once he handed it over, he put his hands back in the air. She opened the wallet and removed his driver's license. She read out loud, "Jason Oliver, birthdate October 10, 1975, from Augusta, Georgia."

"What are you doing down here, Jason?" Shark asked.

"Working construction out at Sun City."

"And where are you staying?" Dell asked.

"I'm camping out at Stoney Crest Plantation right outside of Bluffton."

"Okay Jason, you can put your hands down. Why are you driving a rental car?" Shark asked.

"Because my truck got hit and it's in the shop."

"Jason, I just need you to do one more thing. Just open your trunk and show me those sleeping bags," Shark said.

"Can you stop pointing those guns at me?" he asked nervously.

Shark motioned for the two deputies to lower their weapons. He and Dell did likewise. Jason slowly lowered his hands and walked to the back of the vehicle and opened the trunk. Inside were two sleeping bags, just as he'd described. "Okay, Jason, everything's fine. You can leave now. You happened to wander into an undercover operation. Sorry for the inconvenience," Shark said.

"Inconvenience? You call having guns rammed in your face an inconvenience?" he said as he opened the car door and climbed in. "You guys are really nuts!" he yelled out the window as he roared away.

* * *

As the parade of vehicles headed back to the office, Bama chuckled and stuck his hand into the almost-empty bag of pizza-flavored Doritos. He was hunched down behind the steering wheel in the Colony Building parking lot, practically across the street from the laundromat. So they'd thought they were going to trap him this afternoon. Fat chance! Thank goodness he could hear what was going on inside the squad room. He hoped the flowers he had sent didn't wilt for a while. This was working even better than he had anticipated.

Bama had considered already being in the laundromat doing his clothes when they set up their little sting. He knew it would be fun to watch their scheme fizzle. But he had been afraid he wouldn't be able to keep from laughing when he saw the disappointment on their faces. He'd contemplated going fishing for a few hours, but he just couldn't pass up the opportunity to watch the detectives make fools of themselves. And they'd certainly done that. What a show they had put on with that kid. He was surprised the poor guy hadn't wet his pants when he saw all those guns pointed at him.

Bama brushed the crumbs off his hands onto his jeans and then started the engine. It was time to get back to his listening post under his favorite tree in the Huddle House parking lot. He glanced down at his watch. It was getting close to the time that Campbell usually checked in. Maybe he'd get a hint where she was hiding.

Cece sat through four different movies until her butt felt like the dentist had injected it with Novocain, and her stomach demanded something more than cheese crackers and a candy bar.

She stretched her stiff muscles as she left the theater and hurried to the bus stop. Darkness had descended and she felt uncomfortable standing there alone. Cece stood back away from the curb, fearful the Terminator, or someone just as evil, would pull up and try to force her into his car.

She was relieved when she saw the bus come roaring down the street, until the diesel fumes almost choked her.

Ten minutes later she exited the bus at the Oglethorpe Mall, then crossed the street and walked about a block to Shoney's Restaurant.

She ordered the soup and salad bar since that was pretty easy on her wallet. She was into her second bowl of corn chowder when the toddler in the next booth peered over the back of the seat and looked at her. The little girl had red hair, held out of her eyes by a Winnie the Pooh barrette, and a smile that would someday make her father have to beat off the boys with a baseball bat. Her dark-brown eyes sparkled with mischief.

"Well, hello." Cece said softly. "Did you finish your dinner already?"

"Bye, bye," she replied, waving her pudgy little hand and smiling.

"So you're ready to go bye, bye?"

"Kaeleigh, sit down," she heard a man say from the next booth.

"Kaeleigh. What a pretty name."

Suddenly, the little girl's arms flew up in the air and she squealed as she disappeared from sight. "I told you to sit down!" a gruff male voice bellowed.

Cece lowered her spoon, suddenly transported back to those long talks she and Mark had had about having children. She had wanted three; Mark, at least five. He loved kids, having come from a large family of four brothers and two sisters. Twins ran in his family, and he used to tease her about how big she would get if she ever got pregnant with a pair, but that he would love her anyway. They had often speculated about what their children would look like. He had been blond, with piercing blue eyes. Since he had died, she had tried not to think about what might have been. Why did so many people she loved have to die? Mark, her mother, Tony, Aunt Sophie. It was as if everyone she grew to love disappeared. There was only her father left.

Fighting back tears, and pushing those memories back

into another place for later, she tried to get her emotions under control. She couldn't afford to let her guard down, not even for a minute. Her eyes swept the room, but no one seemed to be paying her undue attention.

Cece caught the last bus of the night to the west side of town, to St. Joseph's Hospital. She had a plan.

She walked briskly from the bus stop, and approached the multistoried structure, looking over her shoulder frequently. She tugged on the main doors, but they were locked. Cece felt a moment of panic, then made her way around to the emergency room entrance and was relieved to find the doors unlocked.

As soon as she stepped inside she saw a nurse dressed in pink scrubs, hurrying down the hall with a bag of intravenous solution, and asked for directions to the surgical suite.

Finally locating the elevator, she punched the button for the fourth floor.

Double doors with NO ADMITTANCE in large red letters announced the entrance to the surgical area. The hallway was deserted. Cece peered through the glass, took a deep breath, then stood in front of the doors and waited for them to open. Nothing happened. She searched for a handle, but there was none. Next she tried pushing on them, but they wouldn't budge. She stepped back perplexed. *Maybe they lock them at night.* As her eyes scanned the doors again, she noticed a gray rectangular pad on the right hand wall. When she pushed on it, the doors magically opened up. *Yes!*

When no one appeared after a few seconds, Cece crept into the hallway, her head moving back and forth as she cautiously made her way past the nurse's station. If someone walked out of one of the operating rooms, she wasn't sure what she was going to say, but no one confronted her.

All of the operating rooms appeared deserted. Cece hadn't gone very far before she saw a door with a sign said NURSE'S LOUNGE. She pushed the door open a fraction, just enough to hear if anyone was talking inside. After about 30 seconds of silence, she slowly stuck her head in. It was empty. She darted into the room and looked around. The wall to her right held lockers, some with padlocks. A door, with SHOWER ROOM stenciled in black, was in the back corner. There was a three-shelf stainless steel cart with green surgical scrubs, hats, masks, and plastic things to slip over your shoes in a variety of sizes. Off to the left were a couch and a couple of chairs.

Cece strode purposefully over to the cart and rummaged through the paraphernalia and grabbed one of each. Then she entered the shower room. She quickly stripped, took a two-minute shower, then emerged a few minutes later in her new uniform. The green scrubs were a little large, but comfortable, and the hat made her look totally different. She made her way to the couch. If she slept with her back to the door, and someone entered, they might think she was resting after having spent the night assisting someone in surgery. After all, it was a big hospital, and surely people didn't know everyone. At least it was safer than spending another night in a critical care waiting room, even if it was a different hospital. Since *he* had found her at a hospital before, he might be checking the other hospitals in the area. Tomorrow she would have to find someplace else to spend the night.

Cece lay down on the couch, turned her back to the door, and used her gym bag for a pillow. The room was chilly. She longed for a blanket, but didn't see any lying around. She closed her eyes and tried to sleep. The intercom seemed to page someone every few seconds. Cece always had trouble falling asleep if she was cold. She wrapped her arms around her body in an attempt to get warm. But the chill just wouldn't go away. Reluctantly, she hauled herself back over to the cart. Cece dug to the bottom of the pile of scrubs until she found an extra-large top. Returning to the couch, she gratefully draped it over her arms and curled into a fetal position. Finally, after blocking out the noise and cold, she drifted into a fitful sleep, her dreams filled with visions of a man in a long black hooded coat reaching out for her.

Chapter Sixteen

Thursday morning Shark was yawning when Dell slid into the passenger seat next to him.

"Late night? Did you run up to Charleston and see Jazz?" she asked, buckling her seat belt.

"Nah. She's still tied up on that kidnapping case. I went shrimping with my neighbor, Gary, last night."

"Do any good?"

"We got almost a cooler full."

"So where's mine?"

"I didn't see you out there throwing a cast net or pinching off the heads. But I plan on going again tonight if you want to tag along."

"Yuck. You know how I love shrimp, but I don't think I could stand pinching off their heads while they're still alive. How about if I loan you Josh instead?"

"How is he with a net?"

"Not good, but he could drive your boat while you do the casting."

"I guess that'll work. You know, I don't get it," Shark said as he headed over the Broad River Bridge. "The guy only follows us when we're in fact meeting Campbell. It's almost as if he knows ahead of time. I have a hunch I want to check out as soon as we get to the office."

"What kind of hunch?"

"Remember those flowers you got a few days ago? What

if our guy sent the arrangement and put a bug in them? He would know every move we're about to make."

Dell thought about that for a moment. "I think you've been reading too many espionage novels. You're just mad because we didn't catch him yesterday after tying up all those officers most of the afternoon. Frankly, I still think it was a good plan."

"Not good enough apparently."

"Anyway, I thought of something last night. We checked everywhere for our guy except the marinas. Maybe he's staying on a boat."

Shark didn't say anything for a moment. Then he looked over at her and said, "Damn! I should have thought of that."

"You mean I'm not allowed to have a brilliant idea once in a while?" Dell asked grinning at him.

"Just as long as it doesn't happen too often. You don't want to ruin my reputation."

"Well, there are only a couple of places that allow live-a-boards on Hilton Head. Broad Creek Marina used to have just a few, I think. But most of them tie up at Shelter Cove or Palmetto Bay."

Shark looked at her and rolled his eyes. "What, you think I didn't know that? As soon as we get to the office, and I check out your flowers, I'll run by the marinas."

"Good, because I want to work some more on that list of CEOs that Randall Palmer faxed us. I'm checking the airlines to see if any of them were in the vicinity when the doc got shot. Seems to me like they still have the best motive."

"I know what you mean. Actually, that's about the only motive that makes sense. Especially since the computers were destroyed, and he's after Campbell too. I can see them hiring someone to do the Kline hit, but not spoiling their manicures by doing the deed itself."

"Well, we don't have any other leads to pursue at the moment."

A few minutes later they walked into the office and Shark made a bee line for Dell's desk. He slowly removed each flower and inspected it closely, then dropped the mutilated bloom into the wastebasket by Dell's desk.

"Are you satisfied?" Dell asked as he dropped the last lily into the trashcan.

"No. I was so sure."

He stood with his hands on his hips, a crease in his brow. Suddenly he picked up the lady bug that was lying on the desk blotter and slowly began to tear it apart. First he removed the eyes and inspected them closely. Then he began to rip at the body.

"Aha!" he said, holding up a small black dot. "Look at this. All the other dots are painted on."

"I'll be damned," Dell whispered.

"Let's go check the car."

They hurried out to the parking lot and each knelt down on opposite sides and began to run their hands under the bumpers. "Got it!" Dell said as she pulled the transmitter out from the left front wheel well.

"Now maybe we've leveled the playing field a little," Shark said as he crushed it under his heel.

Shark had no luck at Broad Creek Marina. But when he showed the sketch to the dockmaster at Shelter Cove, the guy started nodding his head.

"Yeah, he was tied up here for a little over a week. But he's gone now."

"Do you know what kind of boat he was in?" Shark asked, pulling his notebook out of his pocket.

The man typed some information into the ancient-looking computer on the counter. "Looks like it was a forty-five foot Grady White, named *The Oasis*."

"When did he pull out?"

"Couple of days ago, I think."

"What name was he using?"

The man glanced down at the screen. "Dave Garrett."

"Do you know where he was from?"

"Nope. Don't recollect that he ever said."

"Were there any distinguishing features on his boat?" Shark asked.

"Don't know. Never saw it. I just recorded the info he gave me into the computer."

Disappointed, Shark handed the man one of his cards. "If he happens to show up again please call me right away."

"Sure enough. Why you looking for him anyway? This got something to do with that doctor that got shot?"

"Yes, as a matter of fact, it does. That's why it's so important for you to contact me immediately if he shows up again."

Shark threaded his way through the heavy traffic to Palmetto Bay Marina and pulled up in front of the dockmaster's office.

He flashed his badge to the elderly man and said. "I'm looking for a guy by the name of Dave Garrett. He's in a big Grady White named *The Oasis*." Shark pulled the sketch out of his pocket. "Recognize him?"

The man studied the photo briefly, then shook his head. "Afraid I can't help you. Haven't seen him."

"Have you had anyone tie up the last couple of days?" Shark asked.

"At least a dozen boats. Lots of guys over here right now for shrimping season."

"Can I look at your logbook there?" Shark asked, pointing over to the desk behind the counter.

"Sure," he said, reaching over and grabbing it.

Shark ran his finger down the entries for the last few days. "I'd like to take a look at these boats. Can you tell me which berths they're in?"

"I'll write 'em down for you."

Shark searched the dock, but found no trace of *The Oasis*, Dave Garrett, or a 45-foot Grady. He flashed the sketch to a couple of men working on their boats, but no one seemed to recognize the man. He was turning to leave when he spotted a Pursuit 3400 Express Fisherman, his dream boat, moored in one of the berths on the dockmaster's list. He couldn't help himself. He had to have a closer look.

Shark approached the beauty with a sense of awe and called to see if anyone was about. There was no answer. Tempted to step aboard, he nonetheless made himself remain on the dock. The detective walked the length of the beauty and admired the largest of Pursuit's sportfishing boats. Shark knew it had a 350-gallon gas tank, and all the bells and whistles any fisherman could dream of. He actually had a picture of one on his bulletin board at home. Shark didn't need to step aboard to know where all the coolers and tackle boxes were located. He also knew the cabin would sleep four and had a nice galley and head. The envious detective chuckled when he noticed the black letters: *The Runabout. That's exactly what I'd like to do, run about on that boat.*

Discouraged that he hadn't found his man, but delighted that he'd gotten a look at his dream boat, Shark lazily made his way back to the car. The sun was out, and it looked as if it would be a perfect day on the water, not much wind. He hoped the weather would hold for his shrimping expedition that night. It wasn't nearly as much fun when the wind kicked up and the waves tried to bounce you off the front of the boat as you threw the net. Especially with an inexperienced captain like Josh.

Shark made a quick stop at Ronnie's Bakery on the way back to the office and picked up some apple fritters, Dell's favorite. They smelled so good that he inhaled two in the short time it took to drive to the office.

Dell was just crossing the squad room, coffee in hand, when he dropped the sweet-smelling bag on her desk, then plopped down in his chair.

Dell squealed with delight, grabbed the bag and tore it open and stuck her nose inside. The smell of apples filled the air. "How did you know I was having a sugar fit? But there's only two, didn't you get any for you?"

"I guess if you're having a fit, I'll just have to let you have both of them, being the gentleman that I am."

"Bull. You already ate some didn't you? So how many did you eat?"

"I plead the fifth. Anyway, getting down to business, our guy was staying on a boat called *The Oasis* at Shelter Cove Marina, but he pulled out a couple of days ago."

"What kind of boat?"

"A forty-five foot Grady White."

"Do you think if we give the Coast Guard the name and type of boat they could find him?"

"Possibly. If he hasn't reached his destination yet we may have a chance."

"How far could he get in a couple of days?"

"It takes about eight hours to get from here to Mrytle Beach up the intracoastal waterway by boat. He could have gone quite a ways in two days."

"Well, it's the only lead we've got at this point," Dell said.

"I agree. It can't hurt. I better fill in Sheriff Grant."

Once that was done, Shark contacted the Coast Guard station on Tybee Island to get the wheels in motion.

The soft voices jerked Cece awake. She glanced down at her watch. 6:00 A.M. She kept her back turned, feigning sleep until the two women had closed their locker doors and moved on. As soon as they were gone, Cece grabbed her bag, crept to the door and peered out into the hall. It was teeming with activity. She straightened the cap on her head, grabbed a surgeon's mask off the cart, and tied it into place. Mustering her courage, she strode purposefully into the hallway. Cece hoped the lack of a hospital ID hanging from her neck would go unnoticed as she exited the surgical suite.

Cece forced herself to take her time. At the elevators she pushed the down arrow and fidgeted until the elevator door slid open. She rushed inside, stabbing at the L button. Once on the ground floor, she located a restroom and quickly locked herself in a stall. She took a couple of deep breaths and her heart rate began to return to normal.

Cece peeled off the surgical scrubs and left them hanging

on the hook inside the stall. She wrinkled her nose in disgust as she pulled her grungy clothes back on.

After washing her face and brushing her teeth, she ran a brush through her tangled hair. She couldn't help but smile back at the image in the mirror. *Well girl, you pulled it off.* She'd managed to stay alive one more night, although she had no idea where she was going to spend the next one. All she was certain of was that it wouldn't be in another hospital.

Cece followed the signs to the hospital cafeteria where she bought a blueberry muffin and a large coffee to go. It was time to take matters into her own hands again. She was getting tired of wasting time while the police failed to perform. Morgan had told her, when she checked in yesterday afternoon, about the trap that had failed to capture their quarry.

She didn't want to bother Brad Johnson at the office, especially on his first day back after his father's funeral. She had decided to just show up at his house when he got off work. She had looked up his address in the phone book and had discovered his house wasn't too far away from the hospital. But what was she going to do with the hours that stretched out ahead of her?

Cece caught a bus downtown to the Hyatt Hotel. She ambled through the spectacular atrium filled with lush plants, fountains, and comfortable-looking chairs, then exited one level down onto River Street.

She knew the multitude of shops that lined the riverfront wouldn't be open yet. But she remembered there were benches where you could sit and watch the large container ships make their way down the narrow channel to the Georgia Ports Authority. Cece had taken a trolley tour of Savannah when she first moved to Hilton Head and had been amazed to learn that Savannah had the 10th largest container port in the United States. She liked to try and figure out what country the large vessels were from by the flags they flew. She and Tony had often seen the ships when they fished for Spanish mackerel in the Savannah River Channel.

Cece lowered her bag onto the bench and sat down as a small tugboat appeared in her peripheral vision. It was leading a large ship up the treacherous narrow channel. A friend who had lived on Hilton Head for a decade had told her about the time one of these monsters had struck the old bridge several years ago. For months, all traffic had to go clear around the back way to get into the city. Since then, they had dredged out the channel and added a higher bridge.

Dark clouds hung low over the water and there was no doubt in Cece's mind that it would start raining soon. Wind whipped off the water and had a chill to it. A little over an hour later, Cece felt the first raindrop. Needing another hit of caffeine and shelter, Cece hurried back up the street to the hotel. She entered through a different door and found herself in the conference center. She passed the Magnolia Room, and the Tulip Room. Just outside the door of the Azalea Room, she ran into a small knot of people lined up in front of two silver coffee urns and a table laden with bagels, a variety of Danish and muffins, and a scrumptious pile of fresh fruit. Cece casually checked out the middle-aged mixed crowd of men and women. Almost all had plastic nametags around their necks, with some kind of strange logo that Cece didn't recognize. But not *all*. Dare she?

She hesitated for only a second, then tucked her bag down in a corner behind a towering Ficus tree and stepped into the food line. Once she had filled her plate, and served herself a cup of Colombian Special Blend, she carried her unexpected brunch to the farthest sofa and ate greedily.

After she finished, she returned to River Street. The rain had stopped and the sun peeked out behind a cloud. Cece knew that soon one of her favorite places, Savannah Sweets, would be opening up. She never failed to stop there when she was in Savannah to pick up a box of pralines. She remembered how they made them right on sight, and even gave away free samples from the huge tub in which they stirred the sweet confection. Cece had tried to make them at home in the microwave from a recipe she had found in the newspaper. They turned out okay, but nothing like the originals.

Mid-morning, Cece caught a bus to the library and e-mailed her dad again. She read three newspapers and several magazines, glancing frequently at her watch. Finally, boredom drove her to the bus stop and the #10 to Oglethorpe Mall. She did five laps around the large interior, working out all the kinks she had acquired from her night in the nurse's lounge. She had done way too much sitting the last few days. In the past she had tried to work out at the gym at least a couple of times a week, and when she couldn't, she took long walks on the beach or pedaled her bike through the plantation's many trails. Ruth was the one who had gotten her started going to the gym; she had raved about one of the trainers there, and even given Cece a complimentary pass for a couple of visits. Before long, Cece had signed up for a full membership.

She wondered how Ruth was doing. Tony had said Ruth didn't like Hilton Head much, that she missed New York. She had always seemed more of a big city person, into the arts and theater—the exact opposite of Tony, who loved the beach, fishing, and boating. Ruth had complained a lot when they first moved to the island, but recently had seemed to settle in. She had taken up quilting, and of course, working out at the gym. Cece wondered if Ruth would make a move right away. She knew she should have no trouble selling the beautiful oceanfront home, at a sizable profit no doubt.

As Cece walked, she tried to plan ahead for what she should do after making the information on the disks public. Would it be safe to immediately go back home and visit her father in Indiana? Or should she wait for a week or 10 days to allow time for the story to be picked up by large newspapers like the *Wall Street Journal* and *USA Today*? Would "Sixty Minutes" or "Dateline" want an interview?

Maybe she would be talking to Barbara Walters on "20/20" one of these days.

Cece tried to think where she could hang out for a little while with her limited resources. She had about $90 left from the money she had gotten from the detectives that night out on the boat. That wouldn't pay for lodging and food for very long, more like a couple of days. Where could she stay that wouldn't cost her anything?

Cece wracked her brain as she dodged in and out of the busy shoppers. She could afford a Greyhound bus somewhere if it was fairly close. There was a large lake and cabins for rent upstate at Santee Cooper. She doubted all of the cabins would be rented this time of year. Maybe she could stay in one of them. But breaking and entering didn't sound too appealing.

What about a deserted youth camp or something? There were dozens of them up in North Carolina. Maybe the bunkhouses wouldn't have locks on the doors. No, she needed something closer. She had an acquaintance whose husband drove the large ferry boat back and forth to Daufuskie Island, just off the tip of Hilton Head. Maybe he knew the manager of one of the two large developments there who would be willing to comp her a room. *Yeah, in your dreams maybe. Or I could stay on one of the large deserted yachts at the marina in Shelter Cove if I can find one that isn't locked up tight.*

Cece suddenly stopped mid-stride, and the elderly man who was practically on her heels ran into her. "Sorry," he mumbled, then hurried on his way.

Aunt Sophie used to check an empty house in the plantation once a month for a friend that she occasionally played golf with. The lady's mother had owned the house, but she had died a couple of years ago. And her friend only made it down to Hilton Head a few weeks a year. But how would she get in? She didn't have the key. Then Cece remembered the time Aunt Sophie had gotten tied up at a doctor's appointment and a service man was scheduled to check the air conditioning at the house. She had telephoned

Cece and asked her to meet him, and informed her that
there was a key hidden in a bag of grass seed in the garage.
But should she risk going back to Hilton Head? And the
house was only about a half-mile from Tony's place. But
then again, she should no longer be a target once the media
picked up the story. She could take a courtesy van from
the Savannah airport to the Westin Resort, which was in
the plantation, and only a short walk from the house. Yes,
she would hole up there.

Pleased that she had a plan, Cece walked to the bank of
pay phones, dug some coins out of her purse, and dialed
Brad Johnson's house. She let it ring until the machine
clicked on, then hung up without leaving a message. She'd
give him another hour, then try again. She paced in front
of the entrance to Ruby Tuesday's, before finally succumb-
ing to the aroma drifting out. She ordered a house salad
and treated herself to a piece of key lime pie. She would
need all her strength for her meeting with Brad. At least
that's what she told herself.

Chapter Seventeen

A little after 8:00 P.M., Cece hurried up the driveway of the low ranch-style house in the Norwood Place subdivision. Only a sliver of moon cast a faint glow on the smooth concrete and Cece stumbled on the top step up to the porch. Several lights were on in the house, so she had no trouble finding the doorbell.

She hesitated only briefly, then punched the button. A few seconds later the porch light snapped on and almost blinded her.

Brad Johnson, in rumpled gray sweats, took a step back when he saw her. "Grace, what are you doing here?" A half-eaten slice of pizza dripped cheese in his left hand.

"I need to talk to you for a minute. May I come in?"

Brad's hesitation puzzled her. "Well, I'm kinda busy. What do you want?"

"Please, I won't take up much of your time. But it's really important."

"Well, if you insist."

Cece edged by him into the foyer while Brad closed the door behind him. When he turned, he seemed to have relaxed a little.

"I was just eating dinner. Would you like a piece of pizza?"

"No thanks. But you go ahead. We can talk while you eat."

Brad headed toward the kitchen, and Cece followed him silently. They sat down at the round kitchen table. "How about a beer?" Brad asked.

Cece noticed his half-empty bottle of Budweiser on the table. "Sure, that would be great."

Brad pulled another bottle from the refrigerator, grabbed a towel and twisted off the top, before handing it to her. When he sat back down he closed the pizza box.

"It's really okay for you to go ahead and eat. Pizza's not nearly as good once it gets cold."

"That's okay. I'm not hungry anymore. What did you want to talk about?"

"First of all, I'm sorry to bother you right after your father's funeral. Secondly, my name isn't Grace Parker."

Cece had expected surprise, maybe even shock. Certainly confusion. She couldn't understand Brad's calm question. "So what *is* your name?"

"Cecilia Campbell. I need to tell you a story. You may already know part of it."

"Why's that?"

"Did you read about the murder last Friday night over on Hilton Head?"

"I don't think so. When I wasn't at work, I was at the hospital with Dad. Who was murdered, and what does that have to do with you?"

"I worked for the man who was killed. His name was Dr. Anthony Kline, and I was his research assistant. The man who shot him is also trying to kill me."

Brad leaned back in his chair and crossed his arms, his eyes looking everywhere but at her. His silence was unnerving, but Cece stumbled on.

She told him about the torching of the house she had been living in on the same night. "I was hiding from the murderer at the hospital the night we met. That's why I used a phony name."

"Grace, or Cece, or whatever your name is, don't you think you've seen a few too many movies?"

"It's all true, I swear to you. Actually, you saved my life."

"How do you figure that?"

"Remember the night you asked if I wanted to share your room?"

"Yeah, so?"

"He was there! The murderer had shot at me that afternoon in front of McDonald's where I was to meet a couple of detectives, and he followed me back to the hospital. A few hours later, he showed up in the waiting room asking everyone if they knew a Cecilia Campbell. He didn't recognize me because I had on that hideous Cher wig. He came back a couple of hours later and was sitting right there when you walked out and called me Grace."

"This is just too outrageous to believe. Are you sure you're not on drugs or something?"

"I can prove it to you." Cece pulled out Detective Morgan's business card and turned it over to where his home number was written. "Hand me the phone, and I'll let the detective tell you it's all true."

Brad reached for the cordless phone on the kitchen counter.

Cece let it ring several times, and then the answering machine picked up. She hung up without leaving a message.

"Not home? How convenient."

"Listen, I know another way to prove it to you. I hid some computer disks in your briefcase that night. They have all the information on them from our research. Didn't you find them?"

"No. I was so busy with the funeral I didn't even open my briefcase."

"But what about today at the office?"

"I was out doing an appraisal on a warehouse most of the day."

"Is your briefcase at the office?"

"No, it's been in my trunk since that night at the hospital."

"So why don't you go get it, and I'll prove to you that what I've said is true."

As Brad walked slowly to his car, he tried to figure out how he could get a hold of Jeff Blakely, the private investigator who had shown up at his door, without tipping off Cece. And could he keep her there long enough until he arrived? Blakely had been right—she was nuts and needed to be back in the loony bin.

Grabbing his briefcase, confident that there would be no disks inside, he wondered what fantastic story she would spin to explain their absence.

Brad moved the pizza box over to the counter and set the briefcase on the table. He glanced at Cece, then flipped the latches. The folded letter with his name on the outside was tucked down under his files. He stared at it for a moment, then, as if it would burn him, he picked it up with his fingertips and flipped it open.

Dear Brad,

My name isn't Grace Parker, it's Cecilia Campbell. I'm sorry for the ruse, but it's necessary. I have placed some computer disks in your briefcase. I ask that you hold them for me until I contact you. My life is in danger because of them. Please, I need your help. The story is too involved to get into now, and I don't want to put your life in danger. I ask only, that in the event you read of my death in the newspaper, that you deliver these personally to Detective Morgan of the Beaufort County Sheriff's Office on Hilton Head Island.

I took one of your business cards and I'll contact you to retrieve the disks as soon as possible. I'm sorry to involve you, especially at a time like this, but I have nowhere else to turn. Thank you in advance for your help.
Grace/Cecilia

Brad refolded the letter and stared at the floppy disks. "So what's on these that's worth killing someone for?" he asked, holding them up to the light as if he could discern what was on them.

"We were studying the effects of radiation emitted from cell phones. We had scientists from all over the United States and Europe feeding us their data."

"What did the studies reveal?" Brad asked skeptically.

"That there is an increased incidence in brain tumors, headaches, loss of concentration, and that the radiation also affects the body's immune system."

Brad laid the disks on the table. *Just what Jeff Blakely said she'd say. I have to figure out how to get him over here so he can take her back to the hospital.*

"So what do you plan to do now?" Brad asked.

"I'm going to make copies of them and send one set to Detective Morgan, and I want to give the other set to a newspaper. Once the information becomes public, I think my life will no longer be in danger. I was hoping you might know a reporter I can turn them over to."

And Brad immediately knew how he could get Blakely here to pick her up. "As a matter of fact, I do know someone. Why don't I call him and see if he can come over?"

"I need time to copy the disks. Maybe you could call him and I could meet him at the newspaper office tomorrow."

"Why don't you just meet him here tomorrow, say about noon? I'll come home for lunch.

That way I can introduce the two of you, and then you can go on down to the newspaper office together."

"That would be great if you're sure you don't mind."

"Not at all."

Cece dropped the disks into her handbag and stood up. "I'd better go. I've taken up enough of your time."

"Uh . . . where are you staying?" Brad asked.

"That's not important. It's really better if you don't know. I'll get these copied in the morning and then meet you here at noon."

Brad was relieved to close the door behind her. He leaned back on it and took a couple of deep breaths. If Jeff

Blakely hadn't told him about her, he would almost have believed her story. She had sounded so convincing. But he had read that paranoid schizophrenics really believed their hallucinations were real.

Brad raced into the kitchen and pulled out the kitchen drawer where he had thrown Blakely's card. He dug around among the notepads, pencils and pizza coupons until he found it. He stood looking at it, and knew he should pick up the phone and call him immediately. But there was something about Grace's bizarre tale that made him hesitate. Could she possibly have been telling the truth?

Chapter Eighteen

Bama sat on the deck, feet propped up on the side, having a conversation with his best friend, Jack Daniels. The sound of the waves lapping against his boat was making it hard to stay awake. The sky was almost black, just a random star peeking out from behind the clouds. A sudden ringing broke the silence. His legs dropped to the deck, and he reached down in the cabin and grabbed his cell phone off the counter.

"Yeah?"

"Is this Jeff Blakely?"

Bama's heart rate picked up, and he was instantly alert. He recognized Brad Johnson's voice. "Hey Brad, what's up?"

"She was here, tonight. She was here!"

"Slow down. Tell me what happened."

"She just showed up on my doorstep about eight, said people were trying to kill her, just like you said she would. Then she claimed she had hidden some computer disks in my briefcase that night at the hospital. Sure enough, when I looked, there they were."

"You mean you've had the disks all along? Where is she now?"

"I don't know, but she's coming back tomorrow at noon. She wants me to introduce her to a reporter from the newspaper, so she can give him a copy of the disks she took with her. She thinks people will stop trying to kill her then. Can you come and pick her up tomorrow? I don't need to wonder every time my doorbell rings if it's some loony."

"Is a frog's ass watertight? You bet I'll be there." For the first time in a week, Bama smiled.

"She told me that crazy story about radiation causing brain tumors and stuff.

"I told you she was nuts."

"But you know what's really scary? At times she seemed so normal."

"I know what you mean. And she does do pretty well when she takes her medication regularly. Did she tell you where's she staying? Or give you a phone number to contact her or anything?" Bama asked.

"No. She said it would be safer if I didn't know," Brad said, chuckling.

"I'll come by about eleven-thirty, in case she shows up early."

"That'll work out fine. I have to do an appraisal at nine, but I should be done by then. When she comes, how about I introduce you as the reporter?"

"Sounds like a plan to me."

Bama smiled as he sat back down and picked up his drink. It wouldn't be long now. He pulled a fat Cuban cigar from his shirt pocket. He sniffed it, savoring the almost cherry aroma, then clipped off the end, and lit up. As he worked on his drink and relished his cigar, he began to plan all the delicious things he would do to Campbell for the ton of trouble she'd caused him.

After leaving Brad's house, Cece returned to the Hyatt Hotel. She wandered around the rooms in the conference center, where several meetings had just broken up. In the Magnolia Room, she noticed two workmen setting up a table with a white skirt around the base and four chairs on a raised platform. It looked to be in preparation for a panel discussion the following day. After they left, Cece made her way down the center aisle and stepped up onto the carpeted stage. She pulled out the chairs and threw her bag underneath the table, knelt down and crawled under, then scooted the chairs back up into place.

She lay down on her back and stretched out. With the carpeting, the floor didn't feel half bad. She had her bed for the night. It almost reminded her of the tiny treehouse her father had built for her one summer in the old maple. It was the summer she was 11, and two of her cousins had moved in with them. Their cousins' father had been in the Navy, and their mother was deemed "unfit" by the courts. At first it had seemed like it would be fun having someone just a year older than she was to do things with. But by the time she and her sister had each shared their rooms for several months, Cece had been ready to run away from home. Sensing she needed some space, her dad had thrown up some boards in the old tree and told her that it was her place. She had reveled in the solitude that she so desperately needed.

A short time later, just as Cece was about to doze off, the lights went out in the room, and she heard someone lock the door. Good, she was secure for the night. Now no one could get in. But then again, she also couldn't get out. Could she make it until morning without needing a bathroom? Suddenly, the infinite darkness seemed to descend like a funeral robe. What had seemed like a cozy little shelter now felt as confining as a casket. If only they had left the lights on. What if there was a fire and she couldn't get out? Visions of Aunt Sophie being consumed in her bed by raging flames danced before her eyes. Cece's heart began to do flip-flops, and it wasn't long before she felt she was trying to breathe against a heavy weight on her chest. Soon her fingertips and lips felt numb, and she recognized the signs of a panic attack. She hadn't had one in years. Cece frantically reached for her gym bag. Crouched over so as not to hit her head on the table, she rummaged around in the bag and pulled out her small flashlight. She fumbled with the switch, then pushed it forward. Nothing. Tears began to slide down Cece's checks. Trying to quell her rising panic, she banged the light on the floor, and a feeble beam lit up her small space. A sob caught in her throat. She pushed back the chairs, crawled out from under the table, and tried to get herself under control. The room was pitch black except for a tiny sliver of light at the back under the door.

Cece wasn't sure how long she sat huddled on the floor before she began to calm down. She kept telling herself that after she turned over the disks tomorrow she would be able to get her life back and quit running. Weariness finally overcame her and she scurried back under the table and rearranged the chairs. Cece eventually fell asleep, the flashlight clutched tightly in her hand as if it were her sole lifeline.

Early the next morning, Cece heard someone throw open the doors to the conference room. Suddenly the room was ablaze in light and the melodious strains of "Georgia On My Mind" filled the room. Something squeaked. It sounded as if the individual who was whistling was rolling a piece of equipment in her direction. Cece froze. Next she heard the warbler approaching the stage. He was almost upon her. She held her breath. There was a small thud on the top of the table, just above her. Then the song began to fade.

A couple of minutes later everything was quiet. Cece looked at her watch and made herself wait a full five minutes before she pushed the chairs back and peered around the edge of the table. The room was empty, except for an overhead projector in the aisle. Quickly she gathered up her bag and crawled out. She smiled when she saw a pitcher of ice water and several glasses on a silver tray in the center of the table. Cece replaced the chairs, and sprinted down the aisle to the door. Cautiously, she peered out into the hall. She sighed with relief when she saw several members of the hotel staff setting up a continental breakfast.

Cece draped the strap of her bag over her shoulder, hurried out the door, and sedately made her way down the hall. After a long pit stop in a restroom that was larger than

most small residences, she returned to the conference center
and availed herself of the generous spread.

After breakfast, Cece sauntered to the front desk and
asked for a piece of paper and a pen. Then she approached
the bank of pay phones over by the cocktail lounge. She
leafed through the Yellow Pages and wrote down three
names of computer businesses on the south side close to
Brad Johnson's house that should be able to copy her files.

Outside, the air felt heavy, and dark clouds moved rapidly overhead. She hoped the bus would arrive before the
rain started. She didn't have an umbrella or a change of
dry clothes, although what she was wearing sure needed a
good washing.

Cece had no trouble getting two copies of the disks made
at the first business on her list. The originals she addressed
to Detective Morgan, and dropped the envelope into a mail-
box she passed on the street. She would give the reporter
from the newspaper a copy, and still have a copy for herself. Now, she just had to kill an hour and a half until it
was time to go to Brad's.

Bama arrived precisely at 11:30, with his cheek pads,
colored contact lenses, and hat pulled low on his forehead.
He was convinced Campbell wouldn't recognize him.

"Now, when she comes in I'll introduce you as the newspaper reporter," Brad said, setting a coffee mug down in
front of his visitor.

"Good. Then I'll ask her to accompany me to the newspaper office."

"Then what will you do?" Brad asked, adding a packet
of sweetener to his coffee.

"Once I have her in the car, I'll just drive her back to
the mental hospital in Charlotte."

"Won't her family want to see her first?" Brad asked,
his forehead wrinkled in confusion.

"I already talked to them after you called last night.
They'll meet us there."

*   *   *

Cece noted the white Grand Am parked in Brad's driveway behind his Mustang. *Good, the reporter must already be here.*

She barely had her finger off the bell before Brad was opening the door.

"Hi! Come on in the kitchen, Jeff's already here. We're just having a cup of coffee. Can I pour you one?"

"That would be great."

Cece followed Brad down the hall. The man seated at the table wore jeans and a red windbreaker, a black Atlanta Braves ball cap pulled low on his forehead, his head bowed over the white mug that sat in front of him. "Grace, ah, I mean Cecilia, this is Jeff Blakely. What do you take in your coffee?"

"A little sugar and milk, if you have it. Mr. Blakely, it's nice to meet you." Cece approached the kitchen table. She noticed that Blakely wouldn't meet her eyes, just stared down at the table, and played with his mustache. There was something about him that seemed vaguely familiar, but she couldn't put her finger on it. She pulled out a wooden chair and sat down opposite him.

"I don't know if Brad has told you why I need to speak to you," she said, reaching into her purse and pulling out the floppy disks. She laid them on the table in front of her. "I worked for Dr. Anthony Kline, the doctor who was killed over on Hilton Head a week ago."

"I think we should go to the newspaper office, where we can talk privately," the man said, reaching up and massaging his right ear lobe.

And then it hit her. *Oh my God! It's him!* Her heart pounded so loudly in her ears she thought she might faint. She swallowed the bile that rose in her throat. She hadn't recognized him at first with the mustache, but it was definitely her stalker. She had to get away, but wasn't sure her legs would support her.

Trying not to show the panic that threatened to engulf her, she stood and glanced at Brad, who was just returning the gallon of milk to the refrigerator. "Excuse me, but could I use your bathroom?"

"Sure. I'll show you where it is," he said, slamming the refrigerator door.

"I don't think so." Bama sprinted out of his chair and grabbed her wrist.

"Brad, it's him, the man who's been trying to kill me. Help me!" she pleaded, trying to twist her arm away.

"Now, Cecilia, don't get upset. I'm here to take you back to the hospital," Bama said, moving between her and Johnson.

"Please, Brad, you have to believe me. He killed Tony and he's going to kill me!" she screamed, beating at her captor with her free hand and aiming useless kicks to his shin.

Bama cursed and wrenched her arm up behind her back, then pulled her to him with his free hand.

"Cecilia, calm down. He's a private investigator that your family hired to find you and return you to the hospital so you can get back on your medication. You should go with him quietly." Brad spoke as if she were a quarrelsome child.

"No, please listen to me. I don't know what he's told you, but he *is* the killer. Help me," she pleaded.

Bama pulled Cece toward the front door. She tried to dig in her heels. "He's right. Once you're back on your medication these delusions will stop. Now be a good girl, and come with me."

Cece struggled as he forced her toward the front door. "Brad, call Detective Morgan. He'll tell you what I'm saying is true!"

"Johnson, help me hold her while I give her a shot. It's a mild tranquilizer," Bama said, trying to reach into his windbreaker pocket with one hand while he held Cece with the other.

Brad hesitated, then moved to take Cece's arm.

"Brad, no. You've got to listen to me before it's too late.

He's going to *kill* me, and it'll be your fault!" Cece screamed. And then she began to cry.

Bama pulled the cap off the syringe with his teeth, then plunged the hypodermic into Cece's arm, injecting the straw-colored liquid. She continued to struggle, but the men were too strong. There was no fighting the effects of the drug. Before long her arms felt as if they weighed 50 pounds apiece, and her legs had begun to shake.

"Help me get her out to the car," Bama said to Brad, as Cece sagged against him.

With one man on each side, they dragged her to the Grand Am. By the time they had deposited her in the passenger seat, Cece was completely unconscious.

"Thanks for your help, man," Bama said walking quickly around the car.

"Are you sure she'll be okay?" Brad asked, concern apparent in his voice for the first time.

"She'll be fine. She'll just sleep for a couple of hours, that's all." Bama hit the automatic door lock as soon as he'd slid behind the wheel. Ignoring the seat belt, he started the engine and backed down the drive.

Brad stood watching until they had pulled out of the subdivision. He knew he had done the right thing, that she needed help, but he had a bad feeling. There had been something almost vicious about Blakely's handling of Cece. Then he glanced down at his watch and realized that, if he didn't hustle, he would be late for his next appointment. He locked the front door and sprinted to his car—Cecilia Campbell, alias Grace Parker, fading from his mind.

Chapter Nineteen

Cece was thirsty, but when she tried to lick her lips her mouth wouldn't open. She flinched at the roar of thunder and the crackle of lightning striking close by. Slowly, she became aware of the pounding rain.

Cece tried to open her eyelids, but the effort seemed too great. She was so sleepy. Her shoulder hurt, but she didn't have the strength to change positions. A rocking motion, which reminded her of a cradle, encouraged her to drift back off to sleep, but something in her subconscious kept demanding that she wake up.

Ever so slowly, she became increasingly aware of her discomfort; her cramping legs and aching arms screamed for relief. If she could just get something to drink. Gradually, as if she were pulling layers of gauze away from a wound, she became more alert and heard the sound of waves crashing against something. Another minute or so passed before she realized she was on a boat. But how did she get there?

Cece felt her eyelids must surely be weighed down by boulders. Finally, mustering a Herculean effort, she managed to force them open briefly, but a laser beam of bright light sliced through her brain. Her forehead wrinkled, and she closed her eyes instinctively. Maybe she'd just go back to sleep.

"I know you're awake. I saw you open your eyes."

The voice seemed to come from far away, almost like the person was speaking from the end of a long tunnel. She knew that voice from somewhere. But where? Cece tried to remember, but her brain was full of cobwebs.

Then she flashed back to the critical care waiting room, and *he* was there talking to her. Her eyes flew open.

He sat on a cushion, elbows propped on a small table, his chin resting on his hands. A huge black gun with a long silver silencer lay in front of him. He wore a smug expression, his mouth turned up in a smile.

"It's about time you woke up."

Afraid to say anything, Cece just glanced around the small room and realized she was in the cabin of a boat. She noted a small galley on her left and at first thought there was someone else in the tiny room, but it was just a black wetsuit hanging on a peg next to the cabin door. To her right was the opening to the head.

Cece tried to move, but realized her hands and feet were bound, her hands behind her back. She strained at the restraints, but they wouldn't budge. Cece tried to say something, but her mouth was covered with tape.

Then it all came flooding back. The realization that it was *him* in Brad's kitchen. She knew she was going to die now; it was just a matter of how and when.

Forcing her eyes open again, she glanced over at him. He'd removed the mustache and ball cap, and looked just like the kind of clean-cut guy she'd have been interested in if she had met him in a bar.

She tried to hide her terror, but was sure he could smell it from across the room. Maybe if she could just get him talking. Cece recalled the magazine article she had read several months ago that said the longer a kidnapper kept his victim alive, the harder it was to kill them.

Cece attempted to talk, but all that came out was a mumble.

Bama picked up the gun and moved toward her. "What did you say?" he asked, then laughed.

"Water," Cece attempted to say again.

"Wawa?" he mimicked. "What's the matter? That shot make your mouth feel like a desert?" He just stared at her for a moment. "Sure, why not?

He leaned over to the mini refrigerator, and took out a bottle of water. He shoved the gun against her temple. "You make a sound when I take that tape off and you'll be dead before it ever leaves your mouth. Understand?"

Cece nodded.

Bama ripped the tape off her mouth. It was difficult not to cry out, but she forced down her scream and just looked up at him. He put the bottle of water between his legs and awkwardly unscrewed the cap slowly with his left hand, his right still holding the gun. He lifted it to her lips. Cece sat up as best she could, her back against the side of the boat. She drank greedily, water dribbling down her chin and onto her T-shirt.

A few seconds later, he took the bottle away. "More, please," she whispered. He tipped the bottle up again and she took another long pull on the water.

Bama backed away, the gun now pointed at her heart, and set the bottle down in the galley. He just stared at her for a moment, then lay the gun down on the counter within easy reach, grabbed the roll of duct tape, made a quick incision in it with a knife from the drawer, picked up the gun, and walked back over to her.

"Please, I won't utter a sound if you'll just leave it off. I promise," Cece whispered. "It makes me feel like I'm going to be sick."

"Sorry, I don't believe you," he said, as he approached.

"Wait, can I ask you just one thing?" she whispered.

"What's that?"

"Why? Is this all because of our research?"

Bama paused. "I guess you might as well know what you're dying for." And then he told her.

Cece was stunned. Grasping for anything, to play for time, she said, "Look, can't we work something out here? Why don't you just let me go and I'll disappear. No one will ever hear from me again. Your employer will think you killed me and threw me overboard. Please, I beg you, just let me go. I won't tell *anyone* what you've told me."

"Sorry, a deal's a deal, and I probably shouldn't have told you who hired me. And you've been a royal pain in the ass. I'm going to enjoy myself a little before I take you out," Bama said as he slapped the tape back on her mouth.

He reached over and turned on a portable marine radio. "As soon as this storm let's up we'll be heading out. Don't want to hang around here too long, in case old Brad starts having second thoughts."

Cece wondered if they were docked in Savannah, Hilton Head, or maybe one of the surrounding islands. She prayed the storm would last for days, but she heard the announcer on the radio say it would be moving out in a couple of hours.

"Damn! I was hoping to get underway soon." He set the gun on the counter in the galley and pulled on a pair of welder's gloves, the kind he often used for removing fish hooks. "I guess we might as well entertain ourselves until then, eh?"

Cece closed her eyes against the horror of his smile and scrambled into the far corner of the bunk. Hot bile rose in her throat, and steel bands of fear cut off her breath. Whimpering, she curled herself into a ball. At his approaching footsteps, she dared a glance and swallowed hard against the overwhelming urge to vomit.

Bama stood next to the bunk, glaring down at her. "Normally, I'd say it's a shame to waste a pretty little body like yours on shark bait, but you've been a real pain in the ass, you know? All the trouble you caused me, I'm gonna enjoy providing those babies with a little incentive." His voice dropped to a whisper. "They say a shark can smell a drop of blood in the water from a mile away."

In one swift motion Bama grabbed a handful of her hair, jerked her head up, and landed a left jab squarely in the center of her face.

Beneath the tape Cece felt her lip split, and blood spurted from her nose. The pain was numbing. She gagged, struggling for air when the next blow descended. And the next. As he continued to pummel her, she tried to clear her mind of her surroundings, to block the pain and control her breathing, as she had learned in her attempts at meditation after Mark died. She focused on the sound of the roaring thunder and beating rain . . .

Another thunderstorm. She'd been a child. She and her father had been fishing one night in a pond on the farm where they rented a house. They had had a wonderful time and caught several catfish when it suddenly started to rain. Her father had handed her a stringer of catfish and told her to go back to the house. Cece had hesitated, afraid of the fish, until he assured her they were dead.

She had set out across the pasture, the stringer held stiffly as far away from her body as she could get it. A few minutes later, a couple of the fish began to flop. Cece screamed, dropped the stringer of fish, and started running—which caught the attention of Samson, the farmer's prize bull.

By the time she reached the house she was crying hysterically. Her mother met her at the back door. Cece flung herself into her mother's arms, and it was a few minutes before she could calm down enough to tell her what had happened. When her father came in an hour later, he was in a mess of trouble with her mother, and Cece was in trouble with him for dropping the fish.

Suddenly she was jerked back to reality as she felt the cold, hard barrel of the gun pressed against her temple. Cece ignored the threats of her captor and forced herself to escape again into another memory. This time, when she was a little older, she and her dad had been fishing in a private pond. She remembered they had had only seven night crawlers, and didn't expect to catch much of anything with so little bait. Instead, they'd gotten into a school of bluegills and as soon as she would throw her line in the water, a fish would grab it and take off running. They ended up catching 33 fish and three large turtles. She remembered her dad, trying to remove their shells with a hammer and a crowbar, as they scurried all over the driveway. She could see the chunks of meat, moving as if they were still alive, in the frying pan. At first she had refused to taste the golden-colored delicacy, but after much cajoling by her father, she had managed to gather her courage and take a bite. Surprised by the sweet taste, if she hadn't known better she would have sworn she was eating chicken.

Finally, Bama drew off his gloves, pleased with his work and sure that he had beaten any resistance out of her. She had stopped trying to dodge his blows a while ago. It was almost as if she wasn't there anymore. Her eyes were open, but she rarely blinked, just stared off into space, almost as if she were catatonic. He knew he had broken her spirit completely, which had been his goal all along. But, as a safety measure, he checked to make sure her hands were still securely bound behind her back. Then he removed the knives, and anything else she could use as a weapon, from the galley and took them with him to the flybridge. The storm had stopped. It was time to get underway.

Chapter Twenty

Shark and Dell moved about as if they were in a stupor. A pall hung over the squad room. They'd been called out earlier to the home of one of their fellow officers, Roger White, who worked in the burglary division. His wife had died two years earlier in an auto accident. Today, his six-year-old son had shot his four-year-old sister while the babysitter sat eating popcorn, glued to the Jerry Springer show. Sara had died before the paramedics could get her to the hospital.

"I still can't believe he would keep a gun in the house with small kids around, unless it was under lock and key," Dell said, shaking her head.

"It's not like he just left it lying around out in the open. It was in a shoebox on the top shelf of his closet."

"Well, I'm sorry, but that's not good enough. The kid knew where to find it."

"Roger said he had forgotten it was even there. It was his wife's gun. He'd bought it for her since she was a nurse and didn't get off work till around midnight. And he didn't know it was loaded," Shark replied.

"Do you believe the kid's story that they were playing house?"

"You mean the part about him playing the dad, so that's why he got the gun down?" Shark asked.

"Yeah."

"Yes, I do. Can't you just see him wanting to play a cop, like his father? This whole senseless tragedy may not have happened if he hadn't fallen off that stool and discharged the weapon." Shark said, staring off into space.

"Just think, that kid is going to have to live the rest of his life knowing he shot his sister. How do you handle something like that?"

"I don't know," Shark said, shaking his head.

"I feel so sorry for Roger. First he loses his wife, and now his daughter." Dell fought back tears.

"It was hard for me losing Laura. It must be even worse with a child, especially so soon after his wife's death."

"If it was up to me, I'd throw that damn babysitter's ass in jail," Dell said, anger now flashing in her eyes.

"I know what you mean."

"I'm whipped. I think we should just go home and finish the rest of the paperwork tomorrow. What do you say?"

"I agree."

"Good. I don't think I can even think anymore today. By the way, did Campbell check in with you earlier?"

"Crap, no she hasn't. Let me try to call her."

"She usually checks in by four. Hell, it's almost seven. Think something has happened to her?" Dell asked, trying to put the papers on her desk in some semblance of order.

"God, I hope not. We don't need another tragic case to deal with today," Shark said, punching the keypad of his phone.

"Well, I still think all those muckity-muck CEOs are behind it. But for the life of me I can't come up with a good suspect out of the list. I've spent hours researching all of them and not a single one has anything more serious than a traffic violation. Even though they may not be the shooter, I'll still bet you ten bucks they hired him."

Shark let Cece's phone ring ten times. There was no answer. "I don't like this. She's always checked in on time. I wish she'd let us take her into protective custody."

"There's nothing you can do about it. She's an adult. She can make her own decisions. Come on, we'll try her again in the car in a few minutes. I want to throw some chicken on the grill when I get home. Josh's been in Charleston all day and should get home about eight-thirty. Want to come over for dinner?"

"No thanks, I don't think I'd be very good company. I need to see Jazz after a day like this. I'm going to call and see if she can meet me for dinner on this side of Charleston."

"How's her case going?"

"She was hoping it would go to the jury today. Damn, I wish Campbell would call. I'm worried about her."

"Sitting around here taxing your brain isn't going to help. Come on, let's hit the road." Dell said, grabbing her purse.

There wasn't much conversation on the way home, each lost in their own thoughts about their depressing day. Shark couldn't get Campbell off his mind. He had a bad feeling. She had never failed to check in.

Shark dropped Dell off and headed on to Charleston. He had called Jazz on their drive home, and she had agreed to meet him at the little Mexican place they went to frequently.

Dell was in the backyard taking the chicken off the grill when Josh appeared at the back door. He walked over and gave her a peck on the cheek. "Hey, babe, that smells wonderful."

Dell set the platter down, turned to him and buried her face in his chest as she began to cry.

"What's the matter? Are you okay?"

"I need a hug."

Josh put his strong arms around her and began to rub her back. "Bad day?" He'd only seen her like this a few times since they had been married—and it always had something to do with a case she was working on.

"Want to talk about it?"

"No, just hold me."

"As long as you want," he whispered in her ear.

After a couple of minutes, Dell dried her eyes and looked

up at him. "Thanks. I needed that. I don't know what I would do if you weren't in my life."

"Well, I'm not going anywhere," he said as he leaned down and kissed her tenderly.

Cece had no idea how long she lay in the dark before she realized she was alone. It had stopped raining, and the boat was moving. Her face was crusted with dried blood, and the coppery taste of it lingered in her mouth. She hurt all over and was afraid to move. She attempted to take a deep breath, but cut it short when a shooting pain pierced her side. She felt exhausted, physically and emotionally. She knew she should do something before he returned and killed her, or worse yet, tied her to an anchor and threw her overboard. But she didn't think she had the will to even move. Cece knew she was going to die. It was just a matter of how.

Finally, calling on an inner strength to survive, she wriggled around until she could sit on the side of the bunk. The pain was so severe that she would have cried out if not for the tape that stilled her screams. Nausea washed over her, and she swallowed repeatedly. Finally, her stomach settled down.

Cece sat there for a moment in the dark, overcome with dizziness. When the cabin stopped swirling she forced herself to stand, her legs shaking so badly they would hardly support her. The tape around her ankles seemed to have loosened up a little during the beating. Cece took another shallow breath and tried to clear her head. She needed to free her hands. Thankful for her years of gymnastics and her tall lithe frame, she slowly worked her bound wrists down the back of her legs, then sat down on the bunk and worked her hands under her feet so her hands were now in front of her. Cece ripped the tape off her mouth, then used her tongue to find the end of the duct tape on her wrists. Finally, she managed to work the end loose with her teeth, then unwound the tape from around her hands and then her feet.

Thinking a little more clearly, she tried to push past the pain and what she had just gone through. Now she had to try and survive. She contemplated her options. *Maybe I should try and find something to kill or disable him, then take control of the boat. Fat chance, he's bigger and armed. What else? Wait to be killed, or jump overboard? I have no chance on the boat, and very little in the water. But what choice do I really have? Water, I'll need drinking water.* She had made a decision. Whether it was the right one or not, only time would tell.

Cece grabbed the pillow from the bed and stripped off the case. She groped her way in the darkness over to the refrigerator, then reached inside and put anything that felt like it contained liquid into the pillowcase. She popped the tab on one can and washed the taste of blood from her mouth with the ginger ale, then poured some into her palm and attempted to cleanse her face of the dried blood as best she could, before she drained the rest. She opened the cabinets above the refrigerator and moved her hands cautiously over the contents. There were mostly heavy cans, which wouldn't work. She needed something lightweight. Something appeared to have a twist off lid. Cece threw it into the bag, then fumbled across another small container with a pull top opening on the lid. Since it was light, she added it as well. She knew people could survive without food for a long time, so she needed to take more liquids than anything. And she couldn't take too much, or it would be so heavy it would cause her to sink. She tied the end of the pillowcase into a knot.

Cece wished she knew how much time she had before the boat would stop moving and he would return to the cabin for her. There had to be lifejackets and a throw cushion somewhere on the boat, but where? They could be up top on the deck for all she knew, and she didn't feel she could take the risk of searching around in the dark for them. Also, she was afraid of stumbling into something and making a loud enough noise that would bring him down into the cabin. It was time to go.

As Cece stepped back, she tripped over her tennis shoes that he had removed when he bound her ankles, and almost fell. Did she need them? No, but she could use the shoelaces. Quickly she removed them, and tried to distribute the weight in the pillowcase more evenly. Then she tied a shoestring around each end, leaving just enough room to slip her arms through and hoist the bag onto her shoulders like a backpack. It weighed a lot more than she anticipated. Would it be too heavy? Would it cause her to sink? If so, she would deal with it once she was in the water. Trying not to think about what lay ahead of her, Cece knew that she had to go now, before the realization of what she was about to do set in.

Hand over hand, she inched her way in the dark toward the cabin door. Suddenly she felt something rubbery and stepped back quickly. Then she remembered seeing a wetsuit hanging on a peg when she'd come to earlier. Hypothermia would be an even bigger problem than dehydration. She hadn't even thought of that. Cece quickly stripped off her backpack and pulled the wetsuit on over her clothes. It was a little big, but better than nothing. She repositioned her backpack.

Cece fumbled for the latch and depressed it ever so slowly. She sighed with relief when it didn't make any noise. If the cockpit was right outside the door she would be able to see some light, and she knew if that was the case, she would be dead. Cece inched the door open just a fraction and peered out. She could hardly see anything in the darkness. She pushed it a little further and stuck her head out. She looked up, and saw a hardtop. Relieved that at least there was one more level, she crept out a little further. *The cockpit must be topside.* The roar from the outboards was loud and would hopefully mask any noise she made. *I'll have to be careful to get out of the way of the props when I slip over the side.*

Cece crept silently all the way out onto the deck. The marine radio above her was repeating the weather forecast as she inched her way over to the port side of the boat—

and stumbled into something. She froze. *Did he hear? Is he on his way down here?*

Finally, she couldn't hold her breath any longer and opened her mouth and sucked in precious oxygen. Cautiously she reached out and traced the outline of the object she had stumbled into. It was a small plastic cooler. She raised the lid and felt inside, hoping to find a lifejacket. It was empty. But, she had her flotation device!

Cece quickly removed the pillowcase from her back and dropped it silently into the cooler and closed the lid. She worked her fingers along the edge of the boat and felt a docking line about two-thirds of the way down. Untying it and securing one end to the cooler handle, she bound the other end around her wrist. She didn't want to risk the current taking the cooler away from her when she entered the water. Cece dropped the ice chest into the water and let half the line out, then quickly worked her body over the side. She was hardly in the water before the rope around her wrist wrenched her away from the boat. Waves washed over her head. Saltwater stung her eyes and the cuts on her face and mouth.

She was on her own now. Mingled with the relief of being off the boat were fear, pain, apprehension, hope and hopelessness. Her feelings, all bundled up in a ball of confusion, devoured her as a black hole gobbles up light. Cece felt so vulnerable. No more second chances.

Chapter Twenty-one

Brad Johnson returned to his office late in the afternoon. He had to complete an appraisal for a residential property he had looked at the day before his father died, since the closing was scheduled for 10 o'clock the next day. Brad threw his briefcase on the desk, walked down the hall, and poured out the last of the dregs in the coffeepot. He tasted it, grimaced, then dumped it into the sink and made a new pot.

He pulled his tie off as he returned to his desk. He turned on his computer, pulled up the Uniform Appraisal Report Form, and began sketching in a drawing of the property. Brad knew it would take at least three hours to complete the job.

It was a little after 10 when Brad pulled into his driveway. He hauled his weary body through the front door, set his briefcase on the floor, and threw his car keys onto the credenza in the foyer. Famished, since he hadn't eaten all day except for a couple of granola bars and a package of salt and vinegar potato chips, he headed straight for the kitchen to see what he could find. He flipped on the overhead light, and stopped dead in his tracks. Campbell's purse and computer disks lay on the table, and her gym bag was next to the chair. Damn! He had forgotten all about her in his haste to catch up at the office. Now he would have to call Jeff Blakely again and ask where he should send her stuff. What a hassle.

Brad opened the refrigerator door, reached for a bottle of Heineken and twisted off the cap. He took a long pull on the refreshing liquid. The door standing wide open, he perused his slim pickings and finally took out a package of bologna, a slice of cheese, and the mayo. He opened a drawer and removed the Honey Wheat bread, or what was left of it, which turned out to be one slice and two heels. Brad grabbed the two ends, then disgustedly threw them in the trashcan when he saw the rows of penicillin growing on them. He cursed, then opened the cabinet and took out a package of saltine crackers.

An hour later, while Brad was letting the hot water of the shower wash the tension out of his tired body, the muffled ringing of Cece's cell phone in her purse went unanswered.

Shark continued to dial Campbell's phone every hour on the hour until midnight, when he fell into a fitful sleep, the cordless phone still clutched in his hand.

Bama cut the engine when he reached the area on his chart marked the Snapper Banks. That seemed like an appropriate area to have his way with Campbell and then toss her overboard.

He walked down the stairs to the main deck and reached for the 50-pound anchor and chain that he'd set aside earlier. Should he shoot her first, then tie the anchor to her body and throw her overboard? Or maybe he should just attach the anchor, cut her a little to attract the sharks, and throw her over. He decided he would have a bigger mess to clean up if he shot her. Anyway, she deserved a slow death, after all the hassle she'd caused. But first he would have a little fun.

Bama raised the lid on one of the storage bins and removed the blood encrusted Billy club that he used to knock out fish before he brought them aboard. Opening the door to the cuddy cabin, he flipped on the light. "Time for a little fun and then a swim, Sleeping Beauty."

His mouth formed a silent O and his unbelieving eyes surveyed the room. The bunk was empty. Not sure how she had managed it, but convinced she must be hiding in the head, he wrenched open the door. It was empty. He was furious! Trying to quell his anger and rising panic, his eyes swept the small space again. Then he saw the duct tape lying on the counter in the galley. "Oh God," he whispered.

Bama raced for the cabin door, his hand on the latch, when he noticed the empty peg where his wetsuit should be. "She jumped overboard!" he screamed, then stopped dead in his tracks. *Or maybe that's what she wants me to think. Maybe she's hiding up top and plans to club me over the head or something. But where could she hide? Would she fit in the built-in cooler?*

Bama grabbed the gun out of his waistband and a flashlight from the cabin. He slowly opened the door and made a quick reconnaissance of the deck. Creeping silently, he made his way to the large cooler. Bama stood there for a moment, listening for even the slightest sound, then laid the flashlight down on the seat. Gun in hand, he jerked the cooler open.

The only thing inside was his shrimp net.

Bama turned off his light and collapsed onto the seat. *Think! The water temperature is about sixty-five degrees, and even with a wetsuit she probably can't last in the water more than a few hours without a flotation device. Do I go back and search for her? Or should I head on to Lauderdale, and get out of the area? With the tides, who knows where she'll drift? And she'd be hard to spot in the water in that black wetsuit. But, if by some far-flung chance a boat picks her up, I'm really screwed. And what if Johnson didn't buy my story and called the cops after we left?*

Bama replayed the scene in Brad's kitchen in his mind. Johnson had seemed convinced, but who could say for sure. Then a cold chill crept up his spine. Her purse and gym bag. He'd left them in the kitchen.

Bama cursed, sat down on the seat, and raised his legs to prop them on the small cooler he used for a footrest. But his legs dropped back to the deck with a thud. *Oh no! She has a flotation device. What else can possibly go wrong on this job?*

Bama returned to the bridge, a bottle of Jack Daniels in hand, and studied his map. He tried to calculate where Campbell would drift. He wished he were more familiar with the tides in the area. And he would have to factor in the wind. After studying the chart and making some calculations, Bama decided to backtrack and search for a few hours. If he didn't find her by daylight, he'd head for home. And, he reminded himself, he would need to change the name on the side of his boat at daybreak, just as a precaution.

Bama started the engine, winched up the anchor, and punched the coordinates into his GPS. He sipped straight from the bottle of Jack and tried to figure out what he should do if he didn't find her. He would need to get rid of the boat, which made him almost nauseated to think about. But hey, he could get another boat. Maybe he should take her on over to the Bahamas and sell her there. Then he could fly on down to the Turks and Caicos, withdraw some money from his account, and head on over to St. John's to do a little diving. Bama knew one thing for sure, he definitely needed to get out of the States for awhile, and he never should have told Campbell who had hired him.

The water was cold, much colder than she'd expected, but it seemed to dull some of the pain. Cece reeled in the line still tied to her wrist, hand over hand, until the cooler was by her side. She wound the excess rope around her arm and flung her upper body onto the lid, resting on her stomach. The brisk wind made the night air colder than the water, so she slipped back down into the blackness. She had to conserve body heat as best she could; thank goodness for the wetsuit. Without it she knew she wouldn't last long. Her mind flashed back to the Coast Guard auxiliary boating course she'd taken several years ago. She recalled the HELP position; pulling your knees up to your chest and keeping your limbs as close as possible to your body to conserve body heat. Cece grabbed the handle on the side of the cooler, then pulled her knees to her chest, and floated as best she could. She prayed the swift current would take her far from the boat.

As the wind whipped the waves over her, Cece felt as if the sea would crush her; rob her of her body heat and living breath. *I will die here, and no one will ever know what happened to me.*

What would he do when he discovered she was gone? Retrace his path and look for her? Or would he decide the elements or sharks would take care of his problem and leave the area? She hoped he'd just go on back to wherever he came from. If he started searching for her and saw the cooler, she would have to cut herself free. And she knew that without it, her chances of survival were next to nothing. But she would have loved to see his face when he discovered she was gone. The thought made her smile.

Cece was glad the clouds covered the thin slice of moon. Darkness was her ally at the moment. She wondered where she was. How long ago had they left the marina? But then, which marina had they left from? She wondered if she was close to the Savannah ship channel. If so, maybe a cargo ship would pick her up. *Yeah, sure, in your dreams.*

At the moment she had to concentrate on keeping the salt water out of her mouth as the current pulled her along. Cece couldn't help but worry about sharks. She knew they were night feeders. At least if any came close she wouldn't be able to see the fins in the darkness. Tony had told her that sharks usually bumped their prey before striking. If it didn't fight back, then they went in for the kill.

Bama slowly retraced his path. He ran diagonally, about a half-smile wide, playing his spotlight across the water.

He knew the tides would be changing soon and hoped they would wash her back in his direction.

The longer he searched in the cold wind, the more enraged he became.

Cece knew her body was beginning to shut down; she was shivering, which she recognized as a sign of hypothermia. When she stopped shivering, Cece knew it would be even more dangerous. She had no idea how long she had been in the water. It seemed like an eternity between seconds. The sea had stopped spitting at her, and the waves had lost their curly heads. *It must be slack tide.* Cece feared that it would shift and send her back in the direction she'd just come from. She needed to get as far away as possible from where she had gone into the water, especially if he tried to search for her. Cece could just envision daylight appearing and herself floating just off the bow of his boat. If he found her, she knew it would be all over for sure.

Maybe if she drank a little water it would wake her up. Cece lifted the lid of the cooler, rummaged in the pillowcase, and pulled out the first can she came to. Not knowing if it was a soda, beer, or juice, she felt around and pulled the tab and lifted it to her lips. The bitter liquid washed the salty taste out of her mouth, but she knew that the alcohol content in the beer was not good for her present condition. She took one more sip then put it back in the cooler. What she wouldn't give for a hot cup of coffee, or better yet, a cappuccino.

Cece thought of her father. Whenever she ventured back to Indiana to see him, he would always make fun of her for driving down the hill to the convenience store to buy a cup of cappuccino, when he had a perfectly good pot of coffee already made. She regretted she hadn't made that trip back home in over six months. But it had been hard to walk in that house ever since her mother had died. Everywhere she looked, she would see the swag of flowers her mother had arranged over the couch, or the pictures she'd grouped just so on the wall. A family picture sat on the end table, taken just six months before the cancer ravaged her mother's body and she had wasted away to nothing. Cece missed her mother a lot.

Her father had remarried six months later to a lady who had once been their neighbor for several years, and had hoped they would have at least 10 or 15 happy years together. But unfortunately, his new bride had died suddenly just three months later.

Cece's head snapped up. She thought she saw a light. She didn't hear a boat, so it must be several miles away. Was it a cargo ship or *him*?

Her body tensed as she watched the light move slowly right and left across the water. The current was taking her in that direction. *Damn! He must be searching for me. If he spots the cooler, I'm dead, and no one will know why Tony, Aunt Sophie and I died.*

She thought of her father again. How could he possibly handle another death after losing two wives in less than a year?

"Mom, if there really are guardian angels, I could use one about now," she said, her eyes raised to the darkened sky.

Cece watched the light continue to sweep across the water, the tide carrying her closer by the minute. Something brushed against the side of her face. Quickly she batted it away, then felt something against her upper body. Tentatively she reached out her hand and realized she was in the middle of a tiny island of floating reeds. She had frequently seen patches of them drifting by when she was in the boat with Tony. *Think! Can you use them in any way?*

Cece flipped the hinged white lid of the cooler over so that the dark bottom was now the top. She had forgotten about the pillowcase and barely managed to grab it before it sank. Cece quickly pulled out two tall thin bottles of what she assumed was water and slipped them into the top of her wetsuit, then dumped out the rest of the contents. She knew if she wasn't picked up within a day or two at the most, it wouldn't matter anyway. Grabbing handfuls of reeds, Cece lay them on the cooler. Reaching out again, she felt something hard. Quickly she grabbed it and worked her hand over the surface. It was a small board that had become trapped in the debris. She laid it on top of the reeds on the cooler.

Cece looked over her shoulder. The boat was getting closer.

Should she detach herself from the cooler, since that would be easier to spot than a person in the water? But she knew she wouldn't last long bobbing in the sea without it. No, she had to keep it.

Could she put her head inside and pull it down so it was just above the surface? But if he shot at it he could strike her.

Maybe she should let the remaining line out and try to duck under water a short distance from the cooler. The reeds would help obscure her if she could stay in the middle of the bed. How wide a patch was it? She knew if he was up high on the flybridge shining the light down into the water, it would be easy to spot her.

The boat was definitely searching, working a grid pattern from left to right. She could hear the motor now. Cece guessed it was about a half-mile away. She would let him complete two more sweeps and then she'd have to decide her course of action.

And then it was time. Cece stuck her head underwater and surfaced inside the chamber of the cooler. She grabbed both handles and pulled it down until it touched the top of her head, then pulled harder and lowered it even further until her face was in the water up to her mouth. Cece was surprised how hard it was to keep it pulled down. It wanted to float. She only hoped it would fool him long enough for the current to take her past him.

Her senses had never seemed so sharp. Was it time for her to die? She closed her eyes and grimaced, then forced herself to breathe when she realized she was holding her breath. It sounded as if the boat was right next to her.

*   *   *

Bama continued to sip from the almost-empty bottle of Jack Daniels as he played the light back and forth across the water. He was cold, tired, and more than a little drunk. He had searched for five hours, and it would be dawn soon. If he didn't find her by then, he'd head out. Bama knew he should have left the area by now. He figured he was wasting his time anyway. She was probably already dead from hypothermia. Hopefully, the sharks would take care of her body.

Suddenly he saw something. He picked up his gun and steadied his light on it. It was just a bunch of flotsam. Reeds, beer cans, an old board, and even a can of nuts. But what was that in the middle?

He drove the boat closer. Hell! It was just part of an old cooler. It must have been in the water for a while with all those reeds caught up with it. He lay his gun back down and maneuvered the boat to the left, around the large patch of flotsam, and resumed moving his light back and forth across the water.

Cece waited until she could no longer hear the boat motor before she raised the cooler, flipped it over on its side, and felt around for the piece of board. But she couldn't find it. She turned the cooler upright and pulled her upper body onto the lid. Mentally and physically exhausted, she looked back over her shoulder and could see the boat moving slowly away. But how long before he'd give up, turn around, and head back in her direction?

The adrenaline rush that had fueled her body was beginning to dissipate. She ached all over from holding her muscles so tense inside the cooler while waiting for a shot to ring out.

Her eyes were heavy, and she had to fight to stay awake. But she couldn't allow herself the luxury of sleep in case he turned around. She raised her eyes to the sky. "Mom, I don't know if you or some of your cohorts had anything to do with that patch of reeds, but thank you if you did."

The moaning wind picked up and began to cool Cece's

body rapidly. She forced herself off the cooler and back down into the terminal darkness of the sea.

Even though the sun was up, Bama could hardly keep his eyes open. It had been over 24 hours since he'd slept. The elements, and the bottle of Jack, had slowed him down to the point where he could hardly function. And the warm sun was only adding to the problem.

He pulled out his stick-on letters and changed the name on the side of the boat to *Fishing Fool*. Finally, unable to fight his drowsiness any longer, he checked his map and saw he was just off the coast of Sapelo Island. At least he was out of the area. Maybe he would anchor and catch a quick nap. When he got up it wouldn't take long to get to Brunswick, where he could fill up with gas, top off his spare tank, and eat a little something. Then he probably wouldn't have to stop again for fuel until Daytona. He just needed to sleep for an hour or so and then he would be fine.

Chapter Twenty-two

Brad Johnson searched his empty pantry for something to have for breakfast. He stumbled across a pack of Peaches and Cream Instant Oatmeal that had fallen behind the cans of corn and green beans. The package was hard as a rock, so he whacked it on the counter a couple of times trying to break up the contents a little, then stuck a mug of water into the microwave to heat. When he ripped open the envelope, a chunk of congealed mass fell into the cereal bowl. *I've got to stop at the grocery after work.*

As the microwave shut off he thought he heard something. He turned and could barely hear a muffled ring. Brad looked at his phone on the wall, but it was silent. Then he realized the noise was coming from the purse on the table.

Brad quickly unzipped the brown bag and pulled out a small cell phone. He punched the button and said, "Hello."

Shark was shocked when a male voice answered Campbell's phone. "Who's this?" he asked.

"Brad Johnson. And you are . . . ?"

"Detective William Morgan. Can I speak to Cecilia Campbell?"

Brad paused. *Oh crap, there really is a Detective Morgan just like she said.* "She's not here."

"Then where is she?"

"Probably back at the hospital in Charlotte by now."

Shark sat up straighter. "Is she injured? What happened? And why do you have her cell phone?"

"It's kind of a long story, and I was just about to leave for work."

"Wait! Don't hang up! Her life could be in danger. I need to know what happened."

Brad sighed. "The private detective her family hired to find her and take her back to the mental hospital picked her up here yesterday. That's really all I know. She left her purse and gym bag, and that's why I have her phone."

"Slow down. What you're saying doesn't make any sense. I need you to start at the beginning. How do you know Miss Campbell?" Shark asked, concern apparent in his voice.

Brad pulled out a chair and sat down at the table. He gave a brief synopsis of his encounters with Campbell.

When he finished, Shark, barely able to suppress his rage, shouted, "You fool. You turned her over to the murderer!"

"What murderer?" Brad asked, his voice barely more than a whisper.

Shark quickly relayed the events of the previous week.

Cold washed over Brad's body, as Shark talked. "Oh my God! Then she was telling the truth."

"Yes, Mr. Johnson, everything she told you was true. And if the guy has had her since noon yesterday, she's probably dead by now."

"Please, tell me, what can I do to help?"

"Give me your address and stay put. My partner and I will be there shortly to see if you recognize a sketch of the man we think may have her."

Brad clicked the phone off and sat motionless for a long time, his heart beating as fast as a runaway freight train. He closed his eyes, and could see her face. He tried to blot out the picture of her lying dead, her throat slashed or her body riddled with bullets. Even though he knew he hadn't wielded the knife or gun, he felt responsible. If only he had believed her.

Brad picked the dishtowel up off the table and wiped the sweat from his brow. Then he grabbed the phone, called his office and told his boss he was ill and wasn't going to make it in. He arranged for an associate to deliver the appraisal he'd completed the night before.

Brad felt bile crowding his tonsils, and he barely made it to the kitchen sink.

Dell answered her phone on the third ring.

"He's got her. I'll pick you up in ten minutes."

"What happened?" she asked, as she began pulling on a pair of navy slacks.

"I'll fill you in on the way to Savannah." The phone clicked in her ear.

Shark's car hadn't come to a complete stop in front of Dell's, before she was racing down the drive.

"How long's he had her?" she asked, slamming the door and reaching for her seat belt.

"Since noon yesterday."

"Then you might as well slow down. She's already dead."

"Damn!" Shark yelled, pounding the palm of his hand against the steering wheel.

"It's not your fault. You offered her protective custody, and she refused. Tell me what happened."

Finally blackness turned to gray. A small palette of muted colors began to appear. *I survived the night!* Cece had been brought up to believe she could do anything and be anything. She desperately wanted to believe it.

There was a great emptiness in her stomach, a cramping need for food. She dreamed of a big breakfast, like she always ordered at the Cracker Barrel on Sunday mornings.

The Big Man's Breakfast; two eggs, country ham, fluffy hot buttered biscuits, milk gravy, and grits. She could almost taste it. In an attempt to fool her body, she drew out a bottle of water and took a big drink.

Suddenly a fin slashed the surface close by. Cece tensed and propelled her body onto the top of the cooler. She pulled her legs out of the water, bent her knees and pushed her feet as high as she could get them. Cece pulled her hands to her chest. A svelte blue form cruised underneath her. The large shark swam around her three times. Desperation shook her. She wanted to cry, but forced herself to hold back and choke it down. Cece bit on her lower lip and wept within. *Please God.* It seemed as if an hour passed between every second. Finally, the shark darted off to seek other prey. Silent tears streamed down her face.

Clouds sat motionless in the sky and the sun beat down and warmed her cold, tired body. Finally she allowed herself the luxury of closing her eyes.

Brad Johnson could hardly make his legs work when he heard the doorbell. Slowly, as if he were marching to his own funeral, he made his way to the door.

"I'm Morgan and this is Detective Hassler."

Brad didn't trust himself to speak, just motioned for the detectives to enter.

Once they were seated in the living room he said, "I'm so sorry. I should have called and checked out her story before I contacted the private investigator. I can't believe I was so stupid."

Shark didn't say anything, just pulled the sketch out of his coat pocket and handed it to Brad. "Is this the man?"

Brad studied it carefully. "That's him, but he had a mustache. And his eyes were brown, not blue like it says here."

"Eye color is easily altered with contact lenses," Dell said brusquely.

"What kind of car was he driving?" Shark asked.

"A white Grand Am."

"Plate number?"

"Sorry, I don't know."

Shark pulled out his cell phone and punched in the number for the office.

"Sayles, take the sketch of the guy we've been circulating and draw a mustache on it. Change eye color to brown. Make some copies and check all the marinas. He's driving a white Grand Am. He's got Campbell."

"Now, Johnson, let's go over your story in detail."

An hour later Dell asked, "So where are her things?"

"In the kitchen. I'll show you."

Dell picked up the purse and found the floppy disks beneath it. She dumped the contents of the bag onto the table and went through them rapidly. Shark dove into the gym bag and began searching the contents. When they finished, Dell picked up the disks and turned to Brad. "Do you have a computer here?"

"My laptop is in the bedroom, first door on the right."

Dell retrieved the computer and set it down on the kitchen table. It wasn't long before she glanced over at Shark. "Bingo."

"So why take her and not the disks? It doesn't make any sense."

"Maybe he thought she had them on her," Dell replied.

"You would think he'd take her purse and bag in case they were in them if he was only after her for the information. Are we missing something here?"

"I don't know. I agree, it doesn't seem to fit."

"Come on, let's get back to the office," Shark said, throwing Cece's stuff back into the bag. "As for you, Johnson, don't leave town. We may need you for a lineup when we catch the guy. Write down your office and home numbers for me."

After they left, Brad sat down at the kitchen table, tears streaming down his face.

Shark backed quickly down the driveway. "Everything

has made sense until now. I still think we're missing something."

"But what?" Dell asked, staring off into space. "Let's think about this for a minute. Kline is murdered and his computers destroyed. His assistant's house is burned down seemingly in an attempt to silence her and destroy any backup disks she may have. Logical assumption is that their research is the motive for the deeds. We know it could be devastating to the cell phone manufacturers if the information became public."

"Then why take Campbell and leave the disks? It makes more sense to take the disks and let Campbell go."

"Except she knows what's on them and she can also identify him."

"But so can Brad Johnson. Why not kill him too?" Shark asked.

"Maybe he figured Johnson bought his story. Expected him to be distracted with what he had just gone through, burying his father and all. Let's forget about the research for a minute. Let's just say we have a man murdered in his own house and an attempt made to murder his assistant. What could the possible motives be?"

"Money is the first thing that comes to mind. Kline had a large insurance policy. Plus the oceanfront house is worth a small fortune. But then why try to kill Campbell?" he asked.

"Maybe Cece and Tony were having an affair and the wife found out," Dell said.

"It's certainly worth looking into, but what if Campbell was the target all along, and Kline was killed to muddy up the waters?"

Dell didn't say anything for a moment. "I don't think we can rule anything out at this point."

Shark was silent as he pulled onto the Talmadge Bridge. "So do you really think Campbell is dead?"

"Don't you?"

"Unfortunately, yes. There would be no reason for him

to keep her alive. I guess we have to just concentrate on finding this monster."

"At least now we know for sure what he looks like and what kind of car he's driving. That should help."

Sheriff Grant met them as they entered the office. "We've located the Grand Am at Palmetto Bay Marina, and the dockmaster recognized the altered sketch. I've sent a tow truck to take the car to Beaufort so the team can get on it."

Shark and Dell turned and headed back out.

They arrived at the marina just as the tow truck was pulling out of the lot. Deputy Sayles hurried over to them. "The dockmaster said the guy pulled out sometime last night."

"What slip was he in?" Shark asked.

"I don't know the slip number, but it was down on the end. Big sucker named *The Runabout*."

"Crap! I saw that boat the other day. It's a Pursuit 3400 Express Fisherman. I have a picture of one on my bulletin board at home. That's why I noticed it."

"Are there any live-aboards close to that slip?" Dell asked.

"According to the dockmaster, a few, but I haven't gotten down there yet."

"Okay, Sayles, good job. We'll take it from here," Shark said, patting him on the back.

"You sure you don't want me to stay and help?" he asked eagerly.

"Thanks anyway, but we've got it."

As they walked down the dock Dell said, "I thought the boat's name was *The Oasis* and it was a Grady White. No wonder the Coast Guard hasn't found it."

"The dockmaster at Shelter Cove probably never even saw the boat. He probably just wrote down the information the guy gave him. And it's easy to change the name with stick-on letters."

Shark pulled out his cell phone. "I'll call the sheriff, have him contact the Coast Guard and give them the right information. And ask them to stop any boat like that no matter what name it has on the side."

When they reached the empty slip, Shark stared at the rippling water. If only he'd known . . .

They split up and started boarding vessels, searching for anyone who could give them some information.

On the fourth one, a small houseboat that had seen better days, Shark found a man scrubbing the deck with a long-handled brush. "I'm Detective Morgan, Beaufort County Sheriff's office. The Pursuit at the end of the dock, happen to know what time it pulled out last night?"

The white-haired gentleman leaned on the handle of his brush. "I think it was around eight or nine, after the storm was over. I was down in the cabin since the lightning was so bad. But I heard the engines start up. I was surprised, him pulling out at night and all, especially with the weather."

"Did you ever see anyone else on his boat?"

"Nope, just him. And he wasn't around a whole lot."

"Well, thanks."

"Why you looking for him? He smuggling drugs or something on that fancy boat?"

"I'm sorry. It's a police matter, and I really can't discuss it."

"Sorry, just curious."

An hour later, Shark found Dell sitting on a bench at the top of the dock scribbling in her notebook. "Get anything?" he asked, as he dropped down beside her.

"Yeah. A guy saw him carry a young woman to his boat yesterday afternoon. He told Patterson that she had drunk too much, fallen and hurt her ankle. The old man said she didn't say anything, seemed to be asleep."

"She was probably still out from the hypo he gave her at Johnson's. The boat pulled out about eight or nine, after the storm was over."

"He probably killed her and dropped her overboard. We may never find her body,"

"Damn it, Dell! This shouldn't have happened."

"Beating yourself up isn't going to help. Let's just get this SOB."

Chapter Twenty-three

Bob Needham, the watchstander at the Coast Guard station on Tybee Island, glanced at his watch. Only 12 more hours before his 48-hour shift would be over. Things had been slow. It always was this time of year. There was invariably a lot more going on in the summer—all the inexperienced, crazy tourists out tooling around in boats, getting themselves into jams.

The phone shrilled and he picked it up after the first ring.

"This is the 911 dispatcher requesting Coast Guard assistance for the Beaufort County Sheriff's Department."

Needham grabbed a pen. "Description of vessel."

"Pursuit 3400 Express Fisherman, *The Runabout*. But may be showing a different name. Request you stop all boats of this make. Murder suspect and kidnap victim aboard. Suspect is armed and dangerous."

"Name of the suspect and description please."

"He's using the name Jeff Blakely, and the sheriff's department will fax you a copy of the sketch."

"And the victim?"

"Cecilia Campbell, white female, mid-twenties."

As soon as Needham hung up, he sounded the alert, which would send the crew to the COMMS room. Then he contacted the officer of the day, Charles Wellington.

Wellington immediately notified OP Center at Coast Guard Group Charleston that his watch commander had received a request from the Beaufort County Sheriff's Department for Coast Guard assistance. Wellington gave them a description of the boat, informed them that a possible kidnap victim was aboard, and the sheriff's department requested they stop the vessel and board the boat.

Needham hurried to the COMMS room and briefed the crew. Then he unlocked the door where the firearms were stored, and they drew their weapons. First they donned flak vests. The LED belt came next, which held a 9mm Beretta, expandable baton, handcuffs, holster for a radio, and a tube of OC pepper spray. Next they drew out the boarding kit. Once the boarding team had their gear, they moved quickly down the ramp to the boat, a 24-foot Boston Whaler.

They hastily loaded up and stepped onto the boat. A total of five minutes had transpired since the call had come in.

The duty cocksain, the individual responsible for driving the boat, the safety of the crew, and the accomplishment of the mission, sliced quickly through the jetties then hung a left and cut through Calibogue Sound toward Braddock's Point off the tip of Hilton Head.

The boarding officer and his team began to study their maps and factor in the tide schedules and the wind speed from the previous night.

Wellington contacted the Grady by radio as they moved on past the tip of Hilton Head and headed out to sea. "Suspect may have traveled out of your range. He left Palmetto Bay Marina at nine last night. I contacted Jacksonville station to look for him in their waters as well. Charleston will cover north, so head on south. Department of Natural Resources will also be assisting in the search."

Shark was pacing back and forth in front of Sheriff Grant's desk. "If he left at nine last night he may be out of the Tybee station's region by now. They only extend down to Jacksonville."

"Look, I know you're frustrated that you're not out there in your own boat looking for him yourself," the sheriff replied, "but don't you think the Coast Guard will notify their other stations? He may be heading north for all you know."

"No way," Shark said shaking his head emphatically. "Not with that kind of a boat. That's a serious fisherman's vessel. He'll want someplace warm, where he can fish year round. Trust me, he's headed south for sure. Can't you twist someone's arm at the state police and get a helicopter in the air?"

"I tried that, but they're tied up at the moment chasing some escaped prisoners up in Columbia. As soon as they free one up, they'll give us a call. I also contacted the Georgia State Police since our suspect may have traveled far enough south to be out of our state jurisdiction. They're going to see if they can free up a chopper to search from Savannah to Brunswick. I understand DNR is assisting the Coast Guard in the search. That's the best we can do for now."

"What about contacting the Air Station in Beaufort? They have lots of choppers."

"The Angel One chopper has assisted in search and rescue operations occasionally when we have people in the water, but we can't ask them to assist in a criminal case. You know that. Face it, Campbell is already dead. That boat can only go so far without gasoline, and we've alerted all the authorities along the coast to be on the lookout for it. There's nothing more we can do right now, but wait."

Shark stormed out of Sheriff Grant's office. No one dared speak to him as he marched down the hall.

"Any luck with a state police chopper?" Dell asked, as Shark walked in the door and kicked the trashcan, then grimaced.

"Hell no! They're all out chasing a bunch of drunk drivers who escaped from the pen up in Columbia. Grant's trying to get a Georgia chopper to search south of Savannah."

"Well, does kicking the wastebasket help? I feel just as bad about Campbell as you do, but there's nothing more we can do. We just have to let the Coast Guard and DNR do their jobs."

"I know, but I can't just sit here on my dead ass and do nothing if there's any chance she could be alive." Shark grabbed his coffee cup off the desk and turned around and stalked out.

"Great, that's all he needs, more caffeine." Dell shook her head.

Cece could see fried chicken, mashed potatoes and gravy, all just outside her grasp. She kept reaching for them, but the closer she got, the further away the food moved. She could almost taste the warm buttery potatoes on her tongue. Then a wave crashed over her, and she awoke to reality.

The sun felt good as she lay on top of the cooler. She'd finally stopped shivering, but the incessant gnawing and cramps in her stomach would not go away. She reached inside the wetsuit and drew out a bottle of water. It was about two-thirds empty. Draining the last of it, she tossed the empty plastic container away. Cece watched it slowly drift toward eternity. She had only one unopened bottle left.

Cece wondered how many ships and planes would pass her today, unaware of her struggle to survive. She wasn't sure she could last another night in the water. Was this her last day to live? All she had accomplished in life seemed pointless as she gazed out across the liquid desert and watched sunlight dance off the water.

Cece tried to shift her thoughts to the things that she wanted to do if she were saved. *I'll definitely spend more time with Dad, and I'll let my friends know that I appreciate them and love them.* Next she dreamed of a husband, children, and a home. And hot fudge sundaes. *Stop it! You are not there. You are here, in hell. Don't give yourself false hope. Think of survival!*

But the desire to dream lingered. It was a way to pass the time. The ideas and plans were not only an escape; they gave her a purpose to hang on.

Cece wondered about God. Was there really a Heaven paved with golden streets where her mother and grandparents awaited her? Would she see a tunnel with a glowing light when the time came? Did it hurt to die? Did she really believe in Him?

Cece believed in the universe, nature, and other miraculous things. But a super human being who created all this? She didn't know the workings of that way. Sure she'd gone to church some as a child, but she hadn't been inside one for years now, except for a couple of her friends' weddings. She had occasionally envied the few people she knew who found peace in their religion. They seemed so sure of everything. She had sensed something in them that she lacked, but had never really thought a lot about it. Then there were those who tried on faith the way she tried on shoes. Cece only hoped that, if there was a God, he would be forgiving, and include her in his divine plan.

White fluffy clouds moved slowly across the sky. One looked like the front of a jetliner, another like a huge stuffed mushroom. *Girl, you're beginning to describe everything in terms of food. Get off it!*

Eventually she succumbed to drowsiness again. Visions of being picked up by a ship and transported to a Caribbean island, where she could lie on the warm sand and drink margaritas, danced before her closed eyelids.

Chapter Twenty-four

Bama wasn't sure how long he'd slept, but he knew it wasn't long enough judging from the way his body felt. He longed to roll over and catch a few more zzzs. As he stretched, he lifted his wrist to peer at his watch. Suddenly his feet hit the floor and he sat bolt upright. "Holy crap!" He had slept a little over four hours.

Quickly he slid his feet into his Nikes and headed topside. Grabbing a beer out of the cooler, he hurriedly climbed the stairs to the flybridge. Bama took a long pull and emptied half the can of Bud, then started the engines and winched up the anchor. The sky was filled with rapidly moving cumulous clouds, and the wind was about 10 mph out of the southwest. The sun felt good on his bare arms, and he guessed the temperature was in the mid-60s.

Bama was ravenous, but didn't want to waste time in the galley fixing something. He was only about an hour or less from Brunswick, where he planned to fuel up. He'd get something to eat there, while they were topping off his tanks.

Fifteen minutes after getting underway, Bama noticed a helicopter in the distance to his left. He eased the throttle forward and picked up his speed a little. He watched as the chopper edged closer.

Pulling the bill of his ball cap down further on his face, he slipped on his denim jacket and slid the .38 in his waistband to the small of his back. His pulse began to pick up. It wasn't long before he could read Georgia State Police on the side of the chopper. He smiled and waved, and was relieved when it headed on south. Bama drained the rest of his beer, crushed the can in his hand, and threw it overboard. He put the engine in neutral, made his way down one flight to the lower deck, removed the gun he had used to shoot the doc, and slipped it overboard. He hated to part with the weapon. It had served him well.

Shark was pacing when the phone shrilled on his desk.

"This is the Georgia State Police dispatcher. Our chopper spotted a Pursuit 3400 just off Sapelo Island. However, the name of the boat was the *Fishing Fool*, not *The Runabout*."

"Instruct your pilot to keep the boat in sight, but from a distance, until the Coast Guard can check it out."

"Will do."

"Did they find it?" Dell asked, as Shark punched in the numbers for the Tybee Coast Guard station.

"Maybe. It's the right make, but different name." Shark relayed the information to the watch stander on Tybee.

"But our guy should be a lot farther south by now, wouldn't you think?" Dell asked.

"Who knows. Maybe he had engine trouble or something. Damn, I wish I was out there."

"Well you're not, so let's go get some lunch."

The cocksain on board the Grady White received a call from the officer of the day regarding the boat they might be looking for and the approximate location.

"We're about fifteen miles away. Contact the Jacksonville station, in case he gets to their waters before we can rendezvous with him," the boarding officer instructed.

The cocksain goosed the throttle wide-open and headed due south.

Bama didn't like the fact that, even though the chopper remained a good distance in front of him and to his left, it never really flew on out of sight. Maybe he should try to go on to Jacksonville to fuel up and get out of the jurisdiction of the Georgia Police. But if the wind and surf picked up anymore he wasn't sure he'd make it that far, without running out of gas. No, he would go ahead and stop at Brunswick. If he hung around the dock for a few minutes, maybe the chopper would lose interest in him. And if not, he could just leave the boat, take a cab into town, and rent a car.

Thirty minutes later, Bama expertly slid his boat up to the dock at the Islands Marina, on the north side of Brunswick. He tied off to the cleats and instructed the dockhand to top off his gas tanks. "Any place close around here to get a sandwich?" he asked.

"The Dockside Grill is just up the ramp, on your right."

"Thanks."

Bama's eyes searched the ramp for any unusual activity, but he saw none.

He sat down at an outside table and ordered a cheeseburger platter to go. Bama was halfway through his second cigarette when he almost choked. Two Brunswick City policemen strolled over to a table, sat down and scanned the menu.

A buxom waitress sauntered over, called them by name, and set two glasses of iced tea down on the table in front of them and rattled off the specials of the day. When the two men began to flirt with her, Bama relaxed a little.

Looking at his watch, and becoming increasingly impatient to be on his way, Bama stubbed out his cigarette and was about to rise and head back down to the dock, when his waitress appeared with a bag in her hand. "Here you are. Hope you enjoy." She handed him the bill. "Just settle up with the cashier over there."

"Sure. Thanks." He threw a couple of dollars on the table and strode nonchalantly over to the cashier.

As he walked slowly down the ramp, he searched for the chopper or any signs of suspicious activity, but there was no sign of it and everything appeared normal on the dock. Bama quickly paid for his gas and climbed aboard.

"I'll get your lines," the dockhand said as Bama started the engines.

"That would be great. Thanks." Bama slowly guided the boat away from the dock, his eyes searching the sky again for any sign of the chopper. All he saw was blue sky. He relaxed a little and grabbed a couple of french fries and stuffed them into his mouth. *Damn, I should have asked for some salt.*

Bama made himself adhere to idle speed through the long NO WAKE ZONE. He was anxious to get out of town so he could open her up and get out of Georgia waters.

He bit into the juicy burger. *Mm, that's good!* He flipped on the marine radio and listened to the weather and tide report. They were predicting a 75 percent chance of storms again tonight, but he should be far away by then.

Finally he saw the RESUME SAFE SPEED sign and opened her up. He was finishing off the last few fries when he heard a boat approaching rapidly. Bama glanced over his left shoulder, and a chill ran down his spine. It was the Coast Guard.

Damn! Should I try to outrun them, or would that make me appear guilty? He had a full tank of gas, but he couldn't outrun the chopper, which had suddenly reappeared out of nowhere. *If they try to board, should I let them? Could Campbell still be alive? There's no evidence to tie me to Kline's murder, since I got rid of the gun, but they might charge me with kidnapping Campbell. However, it would be my word against Brad Johnson's, and I disguised my appearance when I met with him. And there's no body. Wait, her tennis shoes are down in the cabin. But hey, they could be anyone's. Maybe it's just a routine stop, to check and see if I have all my safety equipment. I've been stopped before for that. Or maybe they aren't even going to stop me. They could just be en route to someplace.*

Bama turned his head and saw the blue flashing lights. *Damn!*

He slid the gun out of his waistband, opened a storage compartment, and slid it under several maps, then started decreasing his speed. His mind raced, as he tried to think of anything incriminating in the cabin besides the shoes. His false documents were well hidden, so he didn't think they would be a problem.

The Grady White slowly made its way alongside Bama's boat. The cocksain contacted the watch stander with the vessel number, location, and description. Back at Tybee, the officer of the day wrote everything in his log. He would contact the boat every three minutes to check on the status.

McCauley, the boarding officer, waved over at Bama. He would be in charge of the conduct of the boarding. His name would go on all the reports.

Bama forced himself to smile, lifted his hand, and waved back. The Coast Guard boat threw its fenders over the side and pulled up about six feet from the *Fishing Fool*. Bama cut his engines and made his way down to the deck.

The boarding officer yelled over. "Captain, have you been boarded by the Coast Guard before?"

"They've come alongside to check my safety equipment, but I've never been boarded," Bama called back.

"Where are you out of today, Captain?"

"I've spent the last couple of days just fishing the local waters."

"Captain, how many persons are on board?"

"Just me."

"Captain, without reaching for or touching, do you have any weapons on board?"

"A couple of filet knives and a pistol in my map compartment on the flybridge."

"Okay, Captain, we're aware of that now. We're going to come on board and conduct a search."

Bama threw his fenders overboard, and the Grady White slowly came along side. The cocksain radioed to the watch stander that they were preparing to board.

"Why am I being boarded?" Bama yelled over.

"A vessel of the same make and model as yours has been

involved in a crime. Permission to come aboard?" the boarding officer asked.

"Granted," Bama called back, as if he had any choice.

McCauley, and two additional officers, made their way over to the deck.

"What kind of a crime?" Bama asked.

"Possible kidnapping. You say you're the only person aboard?"

"Yes sir."

"And what is your name?"

"Al Jeffers."

"Okay, Mr. Jeffers, we're going to search your vessel now." He nodded his head to his officers. One headed for the cabin, the other for the flybridge. "Captain, I need to search you to make sure you have no weapons. Would you remove your jacket please?"

Bama stripped off his jacket and held his arms in the air. The boarding officer patted him down. "Thank you, Captain. You can put your jacket back on now."

McCauley began to search the storage compartments on deck. He raised the cooler and livewell lids. There was no bait in the livewell and the compartment was bone dry. "How's the fishing been? Catch anything?" he asked.

"Mostly sharks. Nothing of any significance."

"What kind of bait you been using?"

"Mostly Menhaden," Bama answered. As soon as the words were out of his mouth he realized the significance of what he'd said. Trying to change the subject quickly he asked. "So who was kidnapped?"

"I'm sorry, but I'm not at liberty to discuss an ongoing investigation," McCauley said, as he opened the rod storage compartments and searched thoroughly.

On board the Grady White, the cocksain received a call from the officer of the day checking on their status.

The officer from the flybridge returned with a .38 Smith and Wesson in a Ziploc baggie. He handed it to McCauley, along with a small slip of yellow paper. The boarding officer looked at it, then smiled.

"What did you say your name was?" he asked.

"Al Jeffers."

"Then why do you have a credit card receipt from Palmetto Bay Marina on Hilton Head in the name of Jeff Blakely?"

Before Bama could answer, the officer who had been searching the cabin stepped up onto the deck, his gun drawn. "I found this, sir," he said, handing a green canvas bag to the boarding officer. "There are three sets of driver's licenses and credit cards. Also, some surveillance equipment. They were stored in a false compartment in the head. His gun remained trained on Bama. "I also found a pair of ladies' tennis shoes."

Bama tensed his body and looked around for a way to escape. "Don't even think about it," McCauley said, reaching for his handcuffs. He jerked Bama's arms roughly behind his back. Once he had them secure he asked, "Where is she?"

"Who? Those shoes are my girlfriend's."

"And the three sets of ID?"

"Well, I don't think I should discuss those until I talk to a lawyer."

They transferred Bama to the Coast Guard boat, and the cocksain radioed to the watch stander to have the Beaufort County Marine Patrol boat meet them at Braddock's Point, on the tip of Hilton Head.

They attached a towline to the bow of the Pursuit and headed back toward the island.

Chapter Twenty-five

Shark was halfway across the squad room, empty coffee cup in hand, when his phone rang. He sprinted back to his desk and listened for a moment, then gave Dell a thumbs up. "What about Campbell?" he asked.

His eyes closed momentarily. "I'll contact the Marine Patrol. Thanks."

"They got him?" Dell asked.

"Yeah, but there's no sign of Campbell. Just a pair of ladies' tennis shoes."

"Maybe Brad Johnson will recognize them."

Shark punched some numbers into the keypad on his phone and instructed the Marine Patrol to pick him up at Palmetto Bay Marina in an hour.

"Where did they find him?" Dell asked.

"Just outside of Brunswick."

"Are they towing his boat back?"

"Yeah."

"It'll take them hours. Why did you tell the Marine Patrol to meet you so soon?" she asked.

"It's better than sitting around here doing nothing. Maybe I can convince them to head on south to meet the Coast Guard boat so I can start questioning him. We need to find out about Campbell as soon as possible."

"Shark, you've just got to accept the fact that she's dead.

Nothing you do is going to bring her back. All you can do now is concentrate on building a strong case against him."

"But what if . . . ?"

"But what if what? If she's not on the boat, then she's in the water. If she's in the water, she's dead. Just pray he had the decency to kill her before he threw her over."

Shark ran his hand through his short salt and pepper hair and looked down at the floor. Finally, he glanced over at Dell. "I know you're right. I just don't want to admit that we failed her."

"Neither do I, but now our focus has to be on the investigation so we can nail his ass. I'll call the team and have them on standby. When the boat gets to the dock, they can go over it."

"Thanks. And there's no need for you to waste your time waiting. You might as well go on home and spend some time with Josh this evening."

Dell chuckled. "Do you really think I'm going to let you on that boat without me there? Fat chance! We'll *both* do the interrogation when we get him back here."

"It's not like I'd be alone with him, although I would sell my soul for the chance. The guys on the marine patrol will be there."

"Those officers are all your buddies. I can see you talking them all into facing starboard and taking a leak, while you hold the perp by his ankles over the port side, until he confesses."

"Starboard and port. Hey, that's pretty good. But did you have to say perp?" he said with a grin.

"At least it got a smile out of you. Can we pick up some sandwiches or a bucket of chicken on the way to the boat? I'm starved and it could be a long night."

"Sure. Maybe I'll even buy you a bag of M&M's for dessert."

As Shark and Dell headed toward the exit, Deputy Sayles hailed them. "A package just came for you, detective." He paused dramatically. "The return address says Cecilia Campbell."

The detectives gaped in disbelief, then rushed over to the desk. Sayles handed Shark a 5×7 manila envelope. He could feel something hard inside. He ripped it open, and four computer disks fell out. A note slithered after them.

> *Detective Morgan,*
> *The enclosed disks contain the research data from Tony's computers. These are the originals. I am planning to give a copy to a newspaper reporter at the* Savannah Morning News *that a friend of mine is introducing me to, and I have a copy.*
> *If something happens to me, please make the public aware of our research. Tony deserved that much, and a lot more. Thanks for your assistance. CC*

Shark's hand shook as he passed the note over to Dell. It was like being visited by someone from the grave. The young, vivacious Cecilia Campbell, was dead. All because he'd been unable to get her to agree to protective custody. He vowed to make sure her killer didn't get away with it; and, even if he had to put his career on the line, he would find a way to honor her last request.

The sky took on a rose color as the sun dipped slowly toward the horizon. Closer and closer it fell, until finally it drowned in the west. Cece hated to think that soon the blanket of darkness would engulf her once again.

Her growing hunger had been replaced by nausea. Yet, her mind continued to create fantasies of food and drink. Steamed lobster with melted butter, shrimp cocktail, warm chocolate chip cookies, her mother's date pudding drizzled with caramel sauce.

She knew her movements were slower. Cold, hunger, and fatigue were all taking their toll.

The air hung heavy with the dampness of an approaching storm. The wind began to pick up. The surf began to churn. Cece prayed that the storm would pass over.

"I'm not sure I can survive another night," she whispered.

She had begun to shiver. Her right shoulder felt as if it had been pulled out of the socket from being dragged behind the cooler in the surf. It took her a long time, but she finally succeeded in working loose the swollen knot around her right wrist. She retied the line to her left wrist and tried to move her shoulder a little.

Is this my night to die? She thought back over her life. *I should have had more fun. I always worked hard, and played little. I took life way too seriously. I'm not sure I ever really learned how to play.*

Cece's biggest regret was that she would never experience the joy of motherhood. She couldn't imagine what it must feel like to hold your child in your arms. To have someone love you unconditionally.

She would never see the ruins of the Acropolis or the Parthenon, something she had longed to see since high school Latin class. She hated the fact that she would never experience the Egyptian pyramids or the Sistine Chapel.

Who besides Dad will mourn me when I'm gone? Sure, I have some acquaintances, but no best friend. Not like Trudy, my confidant for about ten years, until some guy, whose name I can't even remember now, destroyed that friendship. How stupid that seems now in the scheme of things. I should have reached out to her a long time ago. Will I really see a white light when I die? When old St. Peter grabs the tablet with my name on it, how will I measure up? What have I done to make the world a better place?

Cece wracked her brain, but couldn't think of anything significant. Sure she'd given a few bills to a homeless person now and then, but not much else. It was sad to think she had been on this earth for 26 years, and had wasted every one of them. She guessed she deserved to die.

Cece wondered what Hell was like, since she didn't have much on her calling card to get into Heaven. Was it the fire and brimstone like they taught you as a child in Sunday school? Or did some people really get reincarnated and have a second chance? If so, she vowed she would never waste the opportunity again, like she had this time around.

The seas began to build and crash down around her. Salt water stung her already red eyes. Undulating foothills quickly became small mountains.

Cece knew the sun was usually down by six this time of the year, and didn't rise until around seven. Could she really take another twelve or thirteen hours of this? She wanted to believe in her heart that she could, but her body told her differently.

Deputy Russell Mitchell slid the 30-foot marine patrol boat expertly up to the floating dock at Palmetto Bay Marina a little after four. Shark and Dell, laden with Kentucky Fried Chicken and a six-pack of Coke, jumped aboard. Noticing their lightweight jackets he said, "You guys are going to freeze to death out here. And we're supposed to get a storm with fifteen to twenty knot winds. Are you sure you really want to do this?"

"Yeah, I'm sure," Shark said, glancing over at Dell. "I tried to get her to go on home, but she's afraid I'll throw the suspect overboard when you have your back turned."

"Or worse," Dell piped in.

"Well then, you better grab some foul weather gear out of the cabin, or better yet, just stay down there. What time do you expect to rendezvous with the Coast Guard?"

"You tell him, Shark, that way he can throw you overboard instead of me."

Shark shot her a dirty look. "It's going to be awhile. They left Brunswick a little over an hour ago, and they're towing the suspect's boat. I was hoping maybe we could ride on out and meet up with them."

"Damn it, Shark! It's going to take them several hours to get to Braddock's Point. And if you think I'm heading out to sea when we're going to get a storm with high winds, you're sadly mistaken. What the hell were you thinking man? You know better than that."

"Listen Russ, we may have a woman still alive in the water. We've got to talk to this guy as soon as possible."

Russ turned and looked at Dell. "He's delusional. The woman is not alive. He just won't admit it to himself," she said quietly.

"You don't know that for sure. Maybe she jumped overboard. She *could* still be alive."

"Even if she was alive when she went into the water, without a flotation device she wouldn't last more than a few hours. I'm not putting my boat at risk for someone who's already dead. We'll stay here at the dock until I raise them on the radio and they're about thirty minutes out. End of discussion."

"By God, I outrank you and you'll do what I say!"

"Cut the crap, Shark!" Dell yelled. "Quit acting like a bully in the school yard. I'll tell you what—I'll shave my head if Campbell's still alive. Do you think I would say that if I thought there was any chance in hell she wasn't already dead? Russ is the captain of this boat, and we'll do what he says! Sorry about that Russ. Let's go down in the cabin and have something to eat. Maybe that'll help Shark think straighter."

As they munched on chicken in the small cabin, Shark tried to restore his relationship with Russ. "Hey, I'm sorry man. I just feel so frustrated we didn't do more to keep Campbell alive. I want to nail this bastard's ass for the three murders."

"Do you have any physical evidence to tie him to the Kline murder or to the arson?" the deputy asked.

"No physical evidence from the scene, unless we recover the gun he shot Kline with. Hopefully it's still on his boat."

"I wouldn't bet on it. Maybe we should concentrate on the kidnapping/murder of Campbell. At least we'll have Brad Johnson's testimony, which should help," Dell added.

"If you don't have Campbell's body, you may have a little trouble there," Russ said, shaking his head.

Thunder roared overhead and gusty wind blew sheets of rain onto the deck. "Damn, I hope this rain doesn't wash away all the physical evidence on the asshole's boat," Shark muttered.

"Just be glad you're not on the Coast Guard boat towing that baby back. Who knows how long it'll take them? It could be a long night," Russ said, pulling a deck of cards out of one of the storage compartments.

Terminal darkness descended on Cece again. There was no moon and not a single star to be seen. The seas had begun to build over the previous hour. Somersaulting waves crashed down around her. The blowing wind forced the salt water into her already swollen eyes. Cece tried not to swallow more salt water as the deluge began.

The rain created a pinging noise as it struck the cooler lid. The combination of the deadly forces wrung the air from Cece's lungs, and her mind battled with her shivering limbs for the opportunity to breathe. Suddenly, she heard rumbling. Could it be a boat? Then she realized it must be a big wave. Cece listened to its approach. She feared it would crush her.

The wave built to a crescendo, growing louder and louder, until it seemed to consume the very air around her. Cece could feel it rising over her, then momentary silence, before the fist of Neptune struck, and the huge wave washed over her.

Cece was completely engulfed by the rushing frigid water and couldn't breathe. She desperately tried to hold her breath as the crushing wave tossed her about like a piece of flotsam. The cooler was wrenched out of her grasp. It felt like her shoulder was pulled completely out of the socket as the rope attached to the cooler drug her along in its path. Still completely under water, her lungs screamed for air.

Suddenly, her head broke the surface. Sputtering, she spit out the salt water the monstrous wave had forced into her mouth. She opened wide, gulping in precious oxygen. Rainwater filled her mouth and temporarily washed away the taste of salt. Cece broke out in tears, crying like a baby.

Hand over hand she pulled on the rope attached to the cooler and wound it around her arm. Finally, she grabbed onto the handle. She flipped the cooler onto its side, opened the lid, and turned it upside down. She closed her eyes and surfaced inside the chamber of the cooler. The pounding rain sounded like gunshots as it struck the bottom. But at least it protected her from the pelting rain.

Cece had never been so cold. Her pulse was racing. And she could feel her heart pause as if it wasn't going to beat again. Then suddenly it would take off like a racehorse in the final stretch. She slowly became aware of the fact that she had stopped shivering, and knew that was not a good sign. Her reflexes were slower, her fine motor coordination increasingly impaired. She closed her eyes and screamed inside the echoing chamber, "Please God, get me through this night!"

The rain had finally stopped. Shark climbed out onto the deck, pulled his cigarettes out of the yellow rain slicker he had donned, and began to pace. He flicked his lighter and looked at his watch. It was a few minutes after 10. *Surely they have to be getting close.*

Suddenly, he heard the Coast Guard boat calling on channel 16 on the marine radio. There was a lot of static, and he could barely make out the transmission. He raced over and switched to channel 22 as they had instructed. He picked up the microphone and acknowledged their call.

"Beaufort County Marine Patrol, this is Coast Guard Boat 2540. We should be at Braddock's Point in approximately thirty minutes. Will you be there to pick up the suspect?"

"This is Beaufort County Marine Patrol. Affirmative. We will leave immediately."

Shark threw his cigarette overboard and yelled down to Russ, "Let's get this show on the road."

An hour later, they had the drenched, handcuffed suspect aboard. Towing his boat, they limped back toward the marina. Down in the cabin, Shark and Dell attempted to get their prisoner to talk, but he remained mute. Shark wanted to beat him until he gave up where Campbell was, but knew he'd never get the chance, at least not as long as Dell was around.

It wasn't long before Russ, not paying much attention to the NO WAKE ZONE in Broad Creek, slid up to the floating dock and cut the engines. Shark opened the cabin door and roughly pulled the suspect onto the deck. Dell followed closely behind.

"I'm going to leave both boats docked here until daylight," Russ said. "Think I can get a ride back to the office with you guys? I'll come back and drive the boats over to Beaufort in the morning."

"Sure thing," Shark said.

Russ locked the cabin door and pulled the key out of the ignition. He began to shiver. "Damn, I'm freezing. Please tell me we can stop somewhere and get a decent cup of coffee. That squad room stuff is rotting my gut."

They piled in the car, Russ in the back seat with the suspect, whose hands were cuffed behind his back.

Shark stopped at the first convenience store they came to, and Russ and Dell ran inside. She quickly grabbed a large cup and filled it with steaming white chocolate cappuccino, then fixed two more large cups with regular coffee. Russ stood by the front door, watching the car, both hands wrapped around his cup as Dell paid for her purchases.

When they stepped outside, Dell said, "Let me sit in the backseat with our guy. You sit up front with Shark."

"Whatever you say," he said, pulling the passenger door open.

Dell climbed into the back seat and set the bag with her cappuccino and one large coffee between her feet on the floor, while she buckled her seatbelt. She glanced over at their prisoner, but he stared straight ahead. "I bought you some coffee. I'll be glad to give you a sip as soon as it cools off a little. You have to be freezing in those damp clothes." He didn't say anything, just continued to stare straight ahead.

Dell pulled the lid off both coffees and blew on her cappuccino, trying to get it past scalding so she could take a sip. The tantalizing smell wafted throughout the interior of the vehicle.

Shark didn't say anything, just maneuvered the car down William Hilton Parkway. He knew what his partner was trying to do—gain the prisoner's trust. So he guessed that made him the "bad cop." He could handle that.

A few minutes later, when the coffee had cooled sufficiently, Dell picked up the cup and leaned over toward their man. "I'll be glad to hold this for you if you want a sip. It sure helps take away some of the chill."

The man turned his head to look at her, then nodded. She put the cup to his lips, and he took a swig. "Thanks," he said, then looked away quickly.

"You're welcome. I'll give you another drink in a minute." Dell studied his profile. He didn't appear evil, but she knew all too well that looks could be deceiving. She thought of Ted Bundy, one of the worst serial killers of all time. No one would have guessed by his handsome, schoolboy face, that he could murder anyone. She leaned over and gave him another drink.

They made it to the office in record time, traffic being light at that hour. Shark was anxious to start the interrogation.

Chapter Twenty-six

The pounding rain continued for what seemed like hours. It almost lulled Cece to sleep. Her head still inside the cooler, she fought desperately to stay awake, fearful that if she closed her eyes, she'd never awaken.

She slapped her cheeks and took her pulse, for something to do. Her heart rate seemed to have slowed dramatically. Her hands and limbs were growing increasingly stiff and felt leaden. At times she almost forgot to breathe.

Some time later, she suddenly found herself standing in front of a beautiful grand hotel. It looked like a palace one might see in Russia. Gold domes topped the cupolas, spires reached far into the sky, and the façade glittered like diamonds as the warm sun struck the turquoise walls.

The doorman was dressed in a long red coat with gold epaulets and buttons. His black hat, with a visor and thick gold braid, reminded her of a sea captain's. He paid her no mind, as she cautiously approached the wide, intricately-carved front door. Mysteriously, it opened, and she entered a breathtaking lobby. The floor was dark green marble with flecks of gold. White columns were scattered throughout as far as she could see.

To her right was a large oriental vase, at least five-feet tall. On its surface was a piece of circular glass that held a towering arrangement of fresh flowers. The delicate pink orchids were the largest she had ever seen. The yellow roses almost looked artificial, they were so perfectly formed. She crept over and buried her nose in the soft petals. The fragrance filled her nostrils.

Cece glanced up at the large intricate cut glass chandelier. Each piece shimmered from the twinkling light of hundreds of small bulbs. The beauty of it temporarily took her breath away.

Antique-looking sofas and chairs, covered with colorful tapestries, were arranged in small groups. One beautifully carved wooden table held a large assortment of fresh fruit on a silver tray. Rushing over, she grabbed a soft fuzzy peach. She furtively glanced over her shoulder to see if anyone was watching, then bit into the aromatic fruit. Juice dribbled down her chin as she chewed the sun-kissed flesh. She stood frozen to the spot, until all that was left was the pit, which she placed in a large glass ashtray.

Starting to wipe her hands on her jeans, they froze in mid air, as she was startled to find she was wearing a midnight-blue velvet ballgown. Confused, she turned back and picked up a white damask napkin that was lying on the table.

Cece's attention was drawn to the glass display case off to the left that was filled with crowns, tiaras, and heavy silver necklaces that were adorned with diamonds, emeralds and rubies. She studied the stunning delicate Faberge eggs.

Voices drew her focus to a white marble registration counter. A man in a black tuxedo, his arm around the waist of a young woman dressed in a full length mink coat, was handed a gold key.

Cece took a deep breath, then cautiously approached and asked for a room. The handsome young man behind the counter handed her a key, then directed her to the elevator.

As the gold cage ascended, Cece was treated to a panoramic view of the entire lobby. She'd never seen such grandeur.

The elevator stopped on the fifth floor, and Cece opened the door onto a hushed corridor. She stepped delicately in her silver high heels onto a rose-colored carpet, so deep and lush she was tempted to lie down and take a nap.

Instead, she inserted her key into the third door on the right, then entered a plush suite decorated in pale yellow. She was shocked to find her mother, dressed in a black cocktail dress with a beautiful strand of pearls adorning her dainty neck, sipping a glass of white wine at a small dining table laden with covered dishes.

"Mother!" Cece screamed, rushing over to hug her tightly, and give her a kiss.

"Darling, it's about time you got here. I've been waiting for hours. But you always were a fighter, even as a child."

"You look wonderful, Mother, so young and healthy. Even your cheeks are rosy."

"Well, I chose to be thirty again. Remember how I'd lost fifty pounds and my hair hadn't even started turning gray? I always thought that was when I looked my best. Sit down, and I'll pour you a glass of this lovely chardonnay."

Cece dropped slowly onto the fragile-looking white chair, afraid it wouldn't support her weight. She picked up a delicate crystal wineglass and held it steady while her mother filled it with the pale yellow wine.

"To your new adventure," her mother said, then gently touched her glass.

Cece took a sip of the cool wine. It was the best she had ever tasted. "But what do you mean, my new adventure?"

"I mean you're about to start a new chapter in your life."

"A new chapter?"

"Yes, it's time to leave all this nonsense behind and come home again."

Cece didn't say anything, just raised her glass to her lips.

"Quit looking so frightened. Come on, let's eat."

Her mother began to uncover all the dishes on the table. "Here's your lobster. I don't know how you eat that stuff. Me, I prefer the prime rib."

Cece couldn't get enough of the delicacies her mother put in front of her. In addition to the lobster, there was shrimp, steak, mashed potatoes, date pudding, pecan pie, and warm chocolate chip cookies. Finally, she pushed back from the table.

"My word, child, where did you put all that?"

"I have no idea. So, now what?"

"I guess it's about time to go. Let me finish this lovely wine, and we'll be on our way."

Chapter Twenty-seven

It was a little after seven, the morning overcast and the temperature hovering around 52 degrees, when Captain Bill Mackey, his spine ramrod straight as all good marines were taught, made his way across the tarmac at the Marine Corp Air Station Beaufort. He'd just come from the SAR Ready Room where he had received a weather briefing, filed his flight plan, and estimated his fuel consumption and ETA back to base.

This morning he and his crew, consisting of a rescue swimmer, a medical corpsman, co-pilot, and crew chief, would be practicing SARs, search and rescues. The captain had already done a partial preflight check before his briefing, and knew his men would have readied their gear and run through most of their checklists by the time he approached Angel One, the old HH-46 Sea Knight chopper. There were three of the old war hogs on base. Built in 1964 for the Vietnam War, it was surprising that any of them were still in the air.

As he strode purposefully toward the tandem rotor helicopter, his eyes did a quick sweep of the exterior, as any good pilot would. He climbed aboard and briefly glanced around the spartan interior. Meant to transport about 30 men, the back third of the chopper was currently taken up by a large silver cylindrical container, their secondary fuel tank. The walls were lined with sling seats, and the familiar smell of military canvas filled his nostrils. Ropes of multicolored cables were strewn overhead, all the way back to the hydraulic gate at the very back.

Mackey called a good morning to Private Rick Gillette, the rescue swimmer, who was putting on his dry suit. HM3 medical corpsman, Tom Winston, was busy checking the Stokes Litter and the floating backboard. Two IVs hung at the ready. He waved his hand in greeting, then continued assembling his medical equipment. Sergeant Roger Fields, the crew chief, nodded his head in greeting. Responsible for everything that took place in the plane, except for the cockpit, he returned to observing his team closely, as they went through their preparations.

Captain Mackey entered the cramped cockpit and squeezed his tall athletic frame onto the thin orange cushion that attempted to keep his ass from going numb on the hard gray metal seat. He noticed several drops of hydraulic fluid on the floor. He paid little attention to the light petroleum oil smell, since there always seemed to be some of the viscous liquid about. "How's it going?" he called to his co-pilot, Chuck Thompson.

"Pretty good. I should be finished with the load computations by the time you finish the pre-flight check. So we're headed up by Edisto Beach, huh?"

"Yeah. I thought a little change of scenery might help break up the monotony since we've been hanging out in Port Royal Sound a lot lately."

"Sounds like a plan."

As soon as Captain Mackey completed his pre-flight duties, he called to the men in the back on the ICS, internal communication system. "Everybody set back there?"

The crew chief looked around to make sure all the men were strapped in. "Everybody set, sir," Sergeant Fields answered.

"Angel One calling the tower. Requesting permission to takeoff northeast," he called into his radio.

"Cleared for takeoff northeast," the air traffic controller responded.

Mackey grabbed the collective, the stick on the left side which controlled the power to the rotors, then moved the cyclic, the stick between his legs, with his right hand, to set the chopper in motion. Suddenly they were airborne.

The sun began to peek out from behind the gray clouds as they made their way north up the coastline. Lush green foliage and oceanfront homes dotted the landscape, while the twisting Intracoastal Waterway wound its way over sandbars and oyster beds. The charm of the Low Country never ceased to capture the captain's attention.

"So have you figured out where you're going to take your wife for your wedding anniversary next weekend?" Mackey called over to his co-pilot.

"I thought I might treat her to dinner some place nice over on Hilton Head. Give her a break from the cheap Mexican joint we usually end up at. Got any suggestions?"

"I've only been to a couple of restaurants over there. The Oyster Factory was really nice, and it's on the water. The food was good, but pricey. I can't remember the name of the other place. It was some Italian joint."

"My neighbor said the food at Charley's Crab was really good, but cost about as much as a week's worth of groceries. Maybe I should just take her someplace up in Charleston."

"So how long have you and Cindy been married?"

"Ten long years. Only kidding."

"Well, if she's put up with your bull for that long she deserves a nice night out."

"Can't argue with you there. So how's Shane's basketball team doing?"

"They've only had three games so far. They're two and one."

As they approached Edisto Beach, Rick Gillette donned his flippers, mask perched at the ready on his forehead, and moved closer to the side door.

Captain Mackey circled the area at about 200 feet a couple of times, determining the sea conditions and prevailing wind. "Hey, Chuck, do you see that red cooler down there?" he called over to his co-pilot.

"Sure do."

"Let's make that our target."

Captain Thompson called the crew chief and apprised him of their target as Mackey circled again and dropped down to 100 feet. When everyone in the back was ready, he maneuvered the chopper so it was pointing into the wind and descended to 15 feet.

Crew Chief Fields slid open the side door and dropped a phosphorous flare which would put off white smoke for approximately 25 minutes. Co-pilot Thompson radioed the Coast Guard that they had a flare in the water, so if anyone reported seeing the smoke, they would know it was just a training mission.

Captain Mackey circled again and descended to 10 feet. The crew chief tapped the rescue swimmer on the chest one time, which was his signal that he was clear to release his gunner's belt. The medical corpsman pulled it clear behind him.

"You are clear to jump, jump, jump," Mackey said into his ICS.

"Roger, clear jump, jump, jump," the crew chief repeated, then tapped the swimmer on the shoulder three times, which was his signal he was clear to go.

Mask and fins in place, Gillette jumped out feet first and entered the water. As soon as he was out the door, Captain Mackey immediately moved the chopper left 25 feet and ascended to 50 feet to minimize the backwash from the rotors for the swimmer. There was already a mild chop on the water, and he didn't want to slow the private's progress any further.

Once Gillette had almost reached the target, the captain descended to 15 feet. Winston swung the hoist that was above the door and lowered the cable, which had a Rescue STROP attached, into the water. The crew chief stood next to the emergency cable cutter and observed Gillette's progress.

It wasn't long before the strong swimmer reached the overturned cooler. He treaded water and used both hands to grip the slippery red plastic. Flipping it over, he was stunned to find the body of a young female partially submerged. He wondered how she remained afloat, until he saw the rope that was wound around her swollen wrist and attached to the handle of the cooler.

Quickly he checked for respiration. Finding none, he placed two fingers over her carotid artery, and prayed for a pulse. Nothing. He grabbed his knife and quickly cut the rope that attached her to the cooler.

"What the hell! Is that a body?" the co-pilot muttered.

Captain Mackey didn't take time to respond, just concentrated on moving his chopper closer to the rescue swimmer, then hovered in place.

Gillette grasped the body around the neck and began swimming toward the cable, fighting the rotor wash and bubbling surf.

"I'll take her, sir," the crew chief said into his ICS. The captain flipped a button in the cockpit, and transferred control of the aircraft to the crew chief.

"She's all yours, Sergeant."

"All mine, Captain," he repeated back.

Crew Chief Fields maneuvered the chopper to the right slightly, so that the cable was as close to the swimmer as possible. Gillette grabbed the sling attached to the end and rapidly strapped the body inside, then hooked a safety strap around her as well so she wouldn't slide out. Attaching his harness to the STROP, he motioned for the crew to take them up.

Tom Winston quickly winched the two bodies skyward and they were soon at the open door of the chopper. Nine minutes had elapsed from the time Gillette had entered the water.

"Returning control of aircraft to you, Captain," the crew chief said into his headset.

"Resuming control of aircraft," the captain repeated.

The corpsman quickly removed the body from the

STROP and placed her on a litter, while the crew chief retracted the hoist and got the door up.

Gillette began cardiac compressions as Winston grabbed an intubation tray. The crew chief covered the victim with two wool blankets.

Winston expertly placed the endotracheal tube down her throat in a matter of seconds, then attached an Auto Vent 3000 that breathed 12 liters of oxygen into her lungs. As Gillette continued chest compressions, Winston cut away patches of her wetsuit so he could slap electrodes onto her chest and attach a heart monitor. He said a silent prayer as he flipped it on, but found only a straight line.

"Contact the Medical University of South Carolina and tell them we are in route and to have an ambulance meet us at the football field at the Citadel," Captain Mackey called over to his co-pilot. Even though MUSC had a helipad, the 23,000-pound chopper was too heavy for it. They had to use the football field or the field at the baseball stadium.

Thompson dialed up the channel, which was one of 12 that was already pre-programmed into his radio on the stick between his legs. "This is Angel One calling MUSC Trauma Center. Come in."

"Switch to channel twenty-four and then go ahead Angel One," a voice responded.

"We are in route with a young female we recovered at sea. No pulse, no respirations. She is intubated and we are doing CPR. Please have an ambulance stand by at the Citadel football field. ETA eight minutes."

"Copy Angel One. We will have an ambulance standing by."

Next the co-pilot contacted base and relayed what they'd found and where they were headed.

"We will advise the Coast Guard that your training mission turned into a recovery," the air traffic controller radioed back.

One, two, three, four, Gillette counted as they continued to do CPR in the back. Winston expertly slid a scalpel up the inner arm of the wet suit and peeled it back to expose the antecubital area, in front of the elbow. He tied a tourniquet tightly around her upper arm, then slapped her cold lifeless limb.

"ETA two minutes," Captain Mackey called into his ICS.

"ETA two minutes," the crew chief repeated.

"Damn, I can't find a vein," the corpsman muttered as he removed the tourniquet.

Captain Mackey set the chopper down in the middle of the football field. Two paramedics shielded their eyes from the downdraft and blowing debris, as they raced toward the helicopter with their gurney.

Winston hastily removed his equipment; the paramedics attached their ambu bag to the endotracheal tube, and quickly transported their patient to the waiting ambulance. It was only a two-minute ride to the hospital.

Angel One was back in the air before the patient was headed to the trauma center, and Captain Mackey turned toward base. His co-pilot radioed in their ETA.

"Good job, guys," Mackey called back to his crew.

"I still can't believe it," Private Gillette said, shaking his head. "I almost crapped my pants when I turned that cooler over."

"Guess that goes to show you we should always be ready for anything," Winston said, returning the Auto Vent to its proper place.

"Man, I just hope we didn't try and resuscitate someone who could end up being a vegetable if they get her back. We don't have any way to know how long she's been down," Gillette said softly.

"She didn't look like she'd been in the water too long," Winston said as he continued to stow the equipment. "If she's just suffering from hypothermia, and her core body temperature hasn't dropped too low, she may have a chance. The cardinal rule for hypothermia is you're not dead until you're warm and dead."

"So how low can it go and the person still survive and be okay?" the crew chief asked.

"A few kids have survived with body temperatures in the low sixties, but it's a lot higher for adults. And you have to get the person warmed up to at least eighty-six degrees before you can defibrillate and try to restart the heart. But the older the person is, and the longer the amount of time has elapsed, the greater the likelihood of suffering irreparable neurological damage, or dying from aspiration pneumonia. You have to be extremely careful when you try to warm up somebody suffering from hypothermia."

"Why do you reckon she was tied to that cooler?" the crew chief asked.

"Well, it was a pretty effective flotation device. Without it, she would surely have drowned," Gillette said.

"Maybe she was on a sailboat or something, and she knew it was going down, so she tied herself to the cooler," Winston speculated. "Several people have survived, when their boats sank, by floating in large fish coolers."

An hour and 10 minutes after his initial takeoff, Captain Mackey set Angel One down softly on the tarmac, then groaned when he thought of the rescue report he'd have to fill out.

Once they had cleaned, restocked and refueled the chopper, the entire crew headed to the Ready Room for a debriefing. There they would review the entire rescue and discuss what went right, what went wrong, and what they could do better the next time.

Chapter Twenty-eight

Sirens blaring, the paramedics continued CPR on the short ride to the emergency room. They pulled into the covered bay, quickly lowered the wheels on the stretcher, and raced into the entrance to the trauma center.

"Young female recovered at sea. No heartbeat and no respirations," the younger of the paramedics yelled to the triage nurse as they ran down the hall.

"Room three," she shouted as they raced by.

Turning to an RN who was charting at the desk, the triage nurse asked, "Where's Dr. Blankenship?"

"Doing that pelvic exam and rape kit in room six."

"Get him!"

The RN hurried down the hall, knocked briskly on the door and stuck her head inside. "Excuse me, Dr. Blankenship, but we need you in room three, immediately."

The doctor's eyes shot to the doorway and his face forecast clearly his irritation at the interruption. "Two minutes," he said softly. He turned back and rolled one vaginal swab onto a glass slide, and inserted the other one into the proper container. He closed the rape kit and handed it to the female police officer standing in the corner, then ripped off his exam gloves, and threw them into the trashcan. The doctor walked to the head of the bed. "Sarah, you were very brave. I'm all finished," he said, patting the pretty College of Charleston coed on the arm. "I'm going to leave you now with Officer Stewart and Mrs. Delphi," he said, glancing at the rape crisis volunteer who held the victim's hand. "I hope you'll follow through with some counseling at the center."

"Thank you, Doctor," the young girl whispered.

Once out the door, the 50-year-old trauma physician hurried down the hall to room three. As he barreled through the swinging doors he asked, "What've we got?"

"Young female recovered at sea by Angel One," a first-year intern answered as he did chest compressions. "No heartbeat, no respirations."

"How long was she in the water?" he asked, pulling on a fresh set of surgical gloves.

"Unknown."

"Get a core body temperature and let's get a warming blanket in here and get her hooked up," he called out to one of the nurses. "Baker, have you ever done a subclavian cutdown?" he asked the nervous intern.

"No sir," he said, silently mouthing his count as he continued pumping on the patient's chest.

"No time like the present. We've got to get a line in so we can give her some heated saline IV to help warm her body temperature. I'll take over compressions. Tina, let's get her hooked up to a cardiac monitor," he said to the petite RN who was checking the victim's pupils. "Call Respiratory Therapy and have them get her on a respirator. Baker, did you put in the endotracheal tube?"

"No sir. The marine corpsman did that in route."

"Good. Once we get that IV going, draw a CBC and electrolytes, and put in a urinary catheter so we can measure her output."

"Core body temperature seventy-nine degrees," Tina said, shaking her head.

"Damn!" Blankenship said. "She was in the water for awhile. I'm surprised her skin isn't in worse shape."

"She had on a wetsuit," Tina said.

"That would explain it. See how dry and cracked her hands and feet are from the salt water, and how swollen and cracked her lips are. All her mucous membranes will be irritated from the exposure. How you doing with that cutdown, Baker?"

"Almost got it."

"Good. Time is of the essence."

"Do you think she's got a chance? Can we shock her and get her heart started again?" Baker asked as he taped the subclavian line in place.

"Don't get ahead of yourself, Baker. The first thing is to warm her up. Do you remember what the body temperature has to be before you can attempt to restart the heart?" he asked, never one to let a teaching opportunity pass.

"Uh, I'm not sure," Baker said raising his eyes, his forehead wrinkled in concentration.

"What, did you sleep through that lecture?"

"No sir," he said, beginning to blush.

"Eighty-six degrees, Baker. Don't forget it. I'm going to ask you again tomorrow."

"Eighty-six degrees," Baker repeated two times. "You didn't answer my question, sir. Do you think she has a chance?"

"Not much of one. Do we have an ID on her?"

"No. We're calling her Jane Doe until we find out who she is," the RN replied.

A respiratory therapist arrived pushing a small respirator. Within a couple of minutes she had attached it to the endotracheal tube and adjusted all the settings. Each time it aerated the patient's lungs, it made a whooshing sound.

A lab technician quickly drew blood on the Jane Doe before they attached her to a machine that would perform chest compressions.

Dr. Blankenship stood at the foot of the bed surveying the IV that dripped into her vein and the multiple machines that were performing the necessary functions to keep her from becoming brain dead—if she wasn't already.

"What else should we do, sir?" the intern asked.

Blankenship paused for a moment, then turned to him

and said, "There's nothing else we can do until she's warmed up and we try to restart her heart, except pray."

Shark was depressed and frustrated as he pulled up in front of Dell's a little after 8:00 A.M. and tooted the horn. The interrogation hadn't gone well. Their man had refused to talk. He wouldn't even give his name, just remained mute. They hadn't recovered the weapon that had killed the doctor, and there was no one to place him at the arson. Campbell was the only one who could verify that he was the man following her, and she was missing and presumed dead. They had sent his prints off to SLED who would forward them on to AFFIS to see if he was in the Federal Data Bank. Unless they came up with something to hold him on other than the fake IDs, he wouldn't be cooling his heels in the Beaufort County jail for very long.

Dell ambled slowly to the car. Her long face practically reached to her knees. As soon as she opened the car door he asked, "What's the matter?"

"Oh, Josh left this morning for California for a couple of days. It came up suddenly and I didn't know anything about it until I walked in last night, or should I say this morning, and I saw his packed bag by the front door."

"Well as many hours as we're logging, I doubt you'll hardly realize he's gone."

Dell shot him a nasty look. "Short night," Shark said, attempting to change the subject.

"I can't go to bed at three and get up at seven, like I did when I was in college."

"I know what you mean."

"Stop at the Citgo station so I can get a cappuccino. I need caffeine bad. If only I could figure out how to get a hit intravenously, it would be a lot easier."

"Sure," Shark said as he pulled out into traffic.

"So where do we go from here?" Dell asked.

"I don't know. I plan to call Brad Johnson when we get to the office, and arrange for him to go to the jail. See if he can pick our man out of a lineup. If so, we would at least have his statement that he's the person who abducted Campbell from his home."

"But it's awfully hard to prove a murder without a body. Maybe we'll get lucky and find he has an outstanding warrant or something. Guess we won't know until we hear from AFFIS."

"The way our luck's been running, I wouldn't hold my breath."

Ten minutes later, Shark pulled into the convenience store and Dell hopped out. "Want some coffee?" she asked before she closed the door.

"Might as well."

They were almost to the bridge onto Hilton Head when Sheriff Grant contacted them on the radio. "Shark, I got a call from the Coast Guard that Angel One pulled a young female out of the water up by Edisto Beach this morning. Identity unknown. They transported her to MUSC. I just got off the phone with the Medical University and the female is suffering from hypothermia and on life support. Her condition is listed as grave. You and Dell get on up there and check it out. It could be Campbell."

"Yes, sir," Shark said, suddenly wide awake. He barely slowed down as he pulled onto the grassy median and did a quick u-turn.

"Hey, cool it. You trying to get us killed?" Dell said, wiping cappuccino off her blouse. "Even if it is Campbell, didn't you hear him say she's on life support? You know what that means. Even if she survives, she'll probably be a vegetable."

"Shut up, Dell. It's more than we had two minutes ago," Shark said, as he turned on his siren and raced down the highway.

Dr. Blankenship had just finished inserting a chest tube in a red-headed six-year-old boy from an auto accident in which both of his parents had been killed, when Dr. Baker stuck his head around the curtain.

"Excuse me, sir. Jane Doe's body temperature is up to

eighty-seven degrees. I'd like to try and get her heart going."

"Then let's do it," Blankenship said as he peeled off his surgical gown, wadded it up, and dropped it into the linen basket.

As they hurried down the hall he asked the young intern, "Have you shocked anyone yet?"

"Once, sir."

When they entered the room, Blankenship saw the defibrillator pushed close to the bed among the myriad of other equipment. "Okay, folks, let's give it a shot."

The nervous intern applied gel to the metal paddle that would act as a ground and slipped it under the patient's back, then turned on the machine. As he waited for it to become fully charged, he applied conductive gel to the paddles. "I thought I would start at 200."

"Sounds good," Blankenship said.

Tentatively, Baker picked up the paddles, then placed them on the patient's chest. "Everyone clear," he yelled, then he pushed the button on top of the paddle in his right hand and the patient's body convulsed momentarily. Every eye in the room was glued to the heart monitor—but it remained a straight line. Paddles still on the patient's chest, Dr. Baker yelled over to the RN, "Charge to 300."

A couple of seconds later, she said. "Charged to 300."

Baker yelled, "Everyone clear," then pushed the button again. Still, there was no change on the heart monitor.

"Charge to 360," Baker said, knowing it was the highest setting on the machine.

"Charged to 360," the nurse responded.

"Everyone clear," he said looking over his shoulder to make sure no one was touching the bed. "Come on," he said softly as he pushed the button.

The strong electrical current coursed through Jane Doe's body, causing her to almost sit halfway up as her arms flailed about, and her body stiffened before falling limply back to the bed. Baker raised his eyes to the monitor. A small wavy line suddenly appeared.

"She's in ventricular fibrillation," Dr. Blankenship said excitedly. "Cut it back to 200 and shock her again."

"Charge to 200," Baker called out.

"Ready at 200," the nurse said quickly.

Baker hit the button, then yelled, "Yes," as he saw the steady beat progress across the monitor from left to right.

"Normal sinus rhythm," Blankenship said. "Let's get her up to ICU stat. Good job, Baker."

"Thank you, sir. Do you think she'll have a lot of neurological damage?"

"We won't know until she wakes up—if she wakes up at all."

Chapter Twenty-nine

Shark roared to a stop in front of the emergency room at MUSC. He hadn't had much to say on the drive, just concentrated on weaving in and out of traffic. He and Dell raced inside to the information desk. Shark flipped open his wallet as he approached the young female behind the desk who looked like she was barely out of her teens. She was talking on the phone and writing something on a pad. Shark impatiently rolled his eyes and shuffled from one foot to the other. Finally she hung up the phone. "Can I help you?"

"We're detectives from the Beaufort County Sheriff's office. We're here in reference to the young female that Angel One brought in this morning. We may know her identity. Can we see her?"

"They just transported her up to ICU."

"Does that mean her condition has improved?" Dell asked.

"Well, I wouldn't necessarily say that. I understand they shocked her and got her heart going, but she's still unconscious and on a respirator."

"How do we get to ICU?" Shark asked.

"Go down the hall to the elevators on the right. ICU is on the fourth floor."

"Thanks," Shark called over his shoulder as he raced toward the elevators.

Once they reached the fourth floor, Shark rang the buzzer at the double doors that prevented entry to the ICU.

"Yes," a female voice said over the intercom that was just above the keypad on the wall.

"We're from the Beaufort County Sheriff's office. We need to talk to you about the female who was just transferred to your unit. We may know her identity."

"I'll buzz you in," the voice said.

Jayne Hudson, the head nurse, looked up as the detectives hurried down the hall. "So you think you know the identity of my Jane Doe?"

"Possibly. Could we see her please?" Shark asked.

"Right this way." She escorted them two cubicles down, then stood back and let them enter first. Shark and Dell approached the bed slowly, conscious of all the tubes and machines attached to the patient.

Her hair was matted and her eyes swollen almost shut, her lips bulging and cracked, but there was no doubt in their minds that it was Campbell.

Shark cleared his throat, then turned to the nurse. "Her name is Cecilia Campbell. The aunt she lived with died in a fire a few days ago. It was arson, and her boss was murdered the same evening. Miss Campbell was abducted and taken aboard a boat. That's all we know. We really need for her to wake up as soon as possible. We're holding a suspect, but her testimony is critical to our case. What are her chances?"

"Step out in the hall, please," the nurse said softly.

Once they were out of earshot she explained. "Many times unconscious people can still hear what is being said. I didn't want to talk about her condition in the room. Her body temperature was very low and she was suffering from hypothermia when she was plucked out of the water. The doctors warmed up her body temperature and then shocked her heart to get it going again. Sometimes people who suffer from hypothermia recover completely. Other times, they'll have a lot of neurological damage."

"What does that mean exactly?" Dell asked.

"She may never regain consciousness, or if she does, she could have some memory loss, and muscle weakness in her limbs. Aspiration pneumonia is also a frequent complication in cases like this."

"You mentioned memory loss. Would it be temporary or permanent?" Shark inquired.

"It could be either one. We won't know until she wakes up—if she wakes up."

"How soon could that be?" Dell asked.

"It could be a few hours, or a few days. Or never. You're welcome to wait in the lounge. If there's any change in her condition, I'll let you know."

"Thanks," Shark said as he glanced into Campbell's cubicle again. The whoosh of the respirator ran chills up his spine.

Once they were seated in the lounge, Shark pulled out his cell phone and dialed the office. "This is Shark. I need to talk to Sheriff Grant."

A few seconds later, Grant came on the line.

"Well, it's her. But she's in bad shape. They got her heart started but she's still unconscious and on a respirator. The nurse said if she does regain consciousness, she could have memory loss. We're going to hang out here for a while. There's a possibility that she could come to in a few hours. I need you to get in touch with Brad Johnson. His number is on my desk. See if he can get over to the jail and pick our suspect out of a lineup. At least we could charge him with abducting Campbell." Shark listened for a minute, then said, "I'll ask them to do a pelvic and check for sexual assault, but since she was in the water that long, I don't know if it will be helpful. I'll keep you posted."

Lunchtime came and went. Still there was no change in Campbell's condition.

Cece tried to claw her way through the gray mist that seemed to hover all around her. The struggle hardly seemed worth it. But there was something in her throat, choking her and making her gag. If she could only raise her arms and pull whatever it was out of her mouth. But they felt as if there were weights sitting on them. It was just too much effort. Her mouth was so dry. If only she had some water. Cece tried to moisten her lips, but there was something in the way. She couldn't move her tongue. And her chest was moving of its own volition. The darkness mercifully engulfed her again.

Shark paced in the lounge and hall most of the afternoon, while Dell took a nap. He contacted Jazz, and she said she would bring them some dinner when she got out of court. He tried to convince himself that Cece would recover fully and provide them with the information they needed to send their man away for a very long time. Had she jumped overboard? He'd been surprised to find that she hadn't been shot or stabbed. How had she survived for that long in the cold water? Would she remember everything when she woke up? He needed a cigarette. But just as sure as he went outside for one, she'd wake up.

Several hours later, muffled sounds began to invade Cece's consciousness. She tried to concentrate really hard to identify them. Again, she felt as if she were choking. An annoying whooshing noise seemed right next to her ear. As soon as she heard it, her chest would move as if she were taking a deep breath. But she wasn't. Then she noticed an intermittent beeping of some kind. It seemed to have a rhythm to it. A telephone rang insistently in the distance. She felt the gagging sensation again, and thought she was going to vomit. She was afraid if she did, she wouldn't be able to spit it out because of the thing in her mouth. She began to panic. The beeping noise seemed to get faster.

Linda DeWitt, RN, sat at the nurse's station charting on one of her patients, the gun shot wound to the abdomen. Another nurse, Sheila Townsend, who was watching a bank of monitors, called over to her. "You better go check your other patient, Campbell. Her heart rate has picked up quite a bit."

Rising quickly, DeWitt said, "Maybe she's regaining consciousness."

The nurse hurried down the hall and entered the patient's room. She approached the bed and called out, "Miss Campbell, can you hear me?"

Cece tried to respond, but couldn't. A low moan escaped from around the tube in her mouth. She wanted to open her eyes, but hard as she tried, they wouldn't budge.

Suddenly, her left eyelid was pried open and a beam of light painfully pierced her skull. Finally, the brilliant beam was extinguished. "Miss Campbell, you're in the hospital. You've had an accident, but you're going to be all right. You have a tube in your throat. That's why you can't talk, so don't even try."

Cece started gagging. Her pulse began to race and the noise rumbled throughout her head. She wanted to breathe, but couldn't. She was going to die.

"Miss Campbell. You need to calm down. Your heart rate is going up too fast."

At that moment, Dr. Blankenship stuck his head in the cubicle. "How's our patient doing?" he asked as he approached the bed.

"She's just started waking up, but she's fighting her endotracheal tube. Her heart rate is up to one forty-five. Do you want me to pull it?"

"Not yet. I'd like to leave it in until we check her blood gases again in two hours. Let's take her down a little bit. Give her Valium 10 mg. IV."

"Okay, I'll be right back."

Dr. Blankenship reached down and lightly began to stroke Cece's arm. "I know you're frightened, but you're going to be okay. I need to leave that tube in your throat a little longer. The nurse is going to give you a sedative to calm you down a little. I'll look in on you again in a few hours. If things are going well, I'll consider taking it out."

Cece's anxiety began to wane a little at his touch. His voice was comforting and reassuring. The nurse returned and began to inject something into the tube in Cece's arm.

It wasn't long before the powerful sedative stole through her veins. She tried to fight its anesthetizing effects, but warmness washed over her and the gray mist descended again.

Shark was snoring softly, his legs splayed out in front of him, his head resting awkwardly on the back of the chair, when Brad Johnson walked into the lounge a little after 10 P.M. He cautiously approached Dell. She glanced up from the Sandra Brown paperback she'd bought earlier in the gift shop. It took her a moment to place him, having seen him only once.

"Mr. Johnson, what are you doing here?" she asked softly.

"I'm sorry. I just couldn't stay away. After I finished the lineup in Beaufort, I just had to drive up to check on Grace. Uh, I mean Miss Campbell. How's she doing?"

Dell motioned for him to have a seat next to her, then filled him in on what had transpired with Cece's recovery at sea and her first few hours in the emergency room. "A few hours ago she began to come to a little, but she started fighting the tube in her throat, so they had to sedate her. The nurse said they might take her breathing tube out in a little while, after they check her blood or something. But tell me, how did the lineup go? Did you recognize anyone?"

"It was hard at first. The man who came to my house had a mustache and a hat on. None of the men in the lineup did. I thought I recognized one guy after studying them closely, so I asked if they could have him say something. Once he opened his mouth, I knew it was him."

"Great! Thanks for your help. You look exhausted. Why don't you go on home? There's nothing you can do here."

Brad Johnson glanced down at the floor. "Would it be okay if I stayed for a little while? I feel responsible for what happened to her."

Dell reached over and touched his arm. "It's not your

fault. You thought you were doing the right thing. Don't place that burden on your shoulders."

Brad looked at Dell, tears welling up in his eyes. "It's hard not to."

Chapter Thirty

Cece slowly became aware of a band tightening around her arm. It was painful. Someone was calling her name. She wanted to respond, but there seemed to be cobwebs in her brain.

"Cecilia, if you wake up, I can take that tube out of your throat. Dr. Blankenship came by and said your blood gases were doing pretty good. Cecilia, can you hear me?" the nurse said, as she rubbed her knuckles down Cece's breastbone.

Ow! Stop that! Cece couldn't get the words out. She could hear an intercom paging a Dr. Goodman. *Who the hell was that?* Music played softly somewhere close. *What is that smell?* It was as if someone had taken a bath in Ciara perfume. Finally, she pried one eyelid partially open.

"That's good, very good," Nurse DeWitt said as Cece closed her eye again. "You'll feel so much better when you get that ol' thing out of your throat. I'm going to deflate the cuff on it now." Afraid of what was about to happen, Cece opened both eyes widely. She saw the nurse pull a large syringe out of her pocket and attach it to a skinny tube attached to the big tube in her mouth.

Cece tried to ask if it was going to hurt, but all that came out was a muffle.

"This is not going to hurt, dear, just make you gag when I pull it out. And I don't want you to try and talk for a little while afterwards. Your vocal cords are going to be bruised and you won't be able to talk above a whisper for a couple of days, so it's best not to try and talk at all. Just rest those babies for a day or two." Cece watched as she turned some dials on the machine next to her bed, and finally the annoying whooshing noise stopped. "Okay, now on the count of three I am going to pull. Are you ready?"

Outright fear was reflected in Cece's wide eyes as she looked at the nurse. Cece clenched her fists and tensed her entire body. "One, two, three!"

It felt as if someone was trying to pull a boulder out of her throat. It made her gag, and she couldn't get any air. Suddenly, it was out and she was coughing and gasping, tears streaming down her face. Finally, she could take a deep breath.

"You did real good, sweetie. Now remember, don't try and talk. I'll bring you a pad and pencil to use to communicate. There are some detectives here who have been waiting all day to talk to you. Do you feel like seeing anyone?"

Detectives? Confused, Cece looked up at the dark haired nurse, who was fiddling with her IV. *What had happened to her? What kind of accident had she had?*

Nurse DeWitt noticed the lost look on her patient's face. "Don't you remember, hon? You're in MUSC in Charleston. The Angel One helicopter plucked you out of the ocean up by Edisto Beach? How'd you get there anyway?"

Now Cece was really confused. "Oh well, I'd better let the detectives explain all that to you. I'll get you some paper and let them in. You rest for a minute now."

After she left, Cece tried to figure out what in the hell was going on. Someone had plucked her out of the ocean? She thought she must have been in a car accident or something when they had told her she was in the hospital.

How long had she been here? What were her injuries?

Cece moved both her legs and feet to make sure they still worked okay. Had she been in a coma? Did she have a head injury? Was that the reason everything in her mind seemed so fuzzy? Cece noticed her left arm was attached with gauze to some kind of small board, then tied to the bedrail. She figured it was to keep her from moving her arm and inadvertently pulling out the IV that hung on a pole at the head of her bed. *What in the hell happened to her?*

Cece's eyes felt as if they had grains of sand in them. And there were a couple of sore spots on her chest, a burning sensation. *What was that all about?* Her whole body ached. When she tried to take a deep breath, a stabbing pain in her left side almost took her breath away. *Did she have some broken ribs?*

She was thirsty, so thirsty. If only someone would bring her some water, or better yet, a jumbo Diet Coke. Cece ran her tongue across her lips. They felt cracked, and about twice the size they normally were.

The nurse returned and approached Cece's bed, followed by a man and woman. "Here's your pad and pen. Now, remember, try not to talk. I'll be back in a little while to check on you."

Cece reached out with her free arm and grabbed the nurse's wrist. "Water," she pantomimed.

"Sure, honey. I'm sorry I didn't think to offer you some as soon as I took that tube out of your throat. I'll go get a pitcher of ice water for you. Be right back."

When she left, Cece stared at the detectives, who stood at the foot of her bed. They looked familiar. She felt as if she should know them. The man walked up and leaned on the bedrail next to her.

"Hello, Cece. You've had quite a time, but it sounds like you're going to be okay. Do you remember anything about what happened to you?"

Cece stared at the bandage on her right wrist and shook her head no. The man turned his head and looked back at the woman. Cece grabbed the pad off her bedside tray and wrote, "You look familiar. Have we met before? What happened to me?"

"I'm Detective Shark Morgan, and this is my partner,

Dell Hassler. We met out on Dr. Kline's boat one evening. Do you remember that?"

Tony's boat. There was something important about Tony she should remember. But what was it? Cece rolled her eyes and stared up at the ceiling, her forehead wrinkled in concentration.

"Cece, let me tell you what we know, and maybe it will help you remember. Dr. Kline was killed by an intruder in his house on Halloween. His computers, with all his research, were also destroyed. The house you were living in with your Aunt Sophie was burned down. The same person who shot Dr. Kline was trying to kill you too. You went on the run, to Savannah. You called and asked to meet with us at a McDonald's there. When you arrived, he tried to shoot you. You hid at Chandler Hospital. Does any of this ring a bell?"

As he talked, the memories of all that he said swept over her. She remembered now. Tony and Aunt Sophie being dead, the man with the blue eyes trying to kill her. She nodded yes, indicating that she remembered, tears rolling silently down her cheeks.

"We met on Dr. Kline's boat, where you gave us a description of the man. You continued hiding out, I'm not sure where, since you checked in each day by cell phone with me. After a few days you went to Brad Johnson's house, a man you'd met in the hospital waiting room, and in whose briefcase you had hidden some computer disks. You were abducted from there by the murderer, who was posing as a private investigator. He took you aboard a boat at Palmetto Bay Marina on Hilton Head. After that, we don't know what happened until you were rescued at sea."

Cece scribbled furiously. "Things are all confused in my mind. Some of what you said, I remember, like hiding out at a hospital and about Tony being dead. How long have I been here, and what are my injuries? Did you catch the man who killed Tony?"

"You were recovered early yesterday morning. You had probably been in the water about thirty-six hours. You're very lucky to be alive. You were suffering from hypothermia when they found you. You weren't breathing and had no heart beat. They warmed you up and shocked your heart to get it going."

Cece unconsciously reached up and touched the sore places on her chest.

"The doctor said that things may be a little fuzzy for you when you first wake up. You went through quite an ordeal. We have a suspect in custody, but we'll need you to try and identify him when you feel up to it."

Nurse DeWitt returned, blue water pitcher in hand, and approached the bed. She poured a large glass of ice water and placed a straw in the glass, before handing it to Cece. "Here you go. Just drink a little first. If you drink too much it may make you nauseated."

Cece grabbed the glass and placed her swollen lips around the straw. *Oh God, that tastes good.* But when she tried to swallow, she cringed. Her throat felt as if it had been scalded. But she sucked on the straw again anyway. "That's enough for now. Let's make sure that stays down before we have anymore," DeWitt said, placing the glass back on the bedside table.

The nurse turned to the detectives. "About five more minutes, and then let's let her rest for a little while."

"Sure," Shark said, although he didn't like the idea at all. He needed to get the story from Cece—if she could remember it. "Where was I?" he said, turning back to Cece. "Cece, do you remember going to Brad Johnson's house?"

She closed her eyes, her brow wrinkled in concentration. Cece tried to think. She didn't remember going to Johnson's house. But she must have, according to the detective. Why couldn't she remember that? She opened her eyes, looked over at the detectives, and shook her head no.

Shark sighed.

"It's okay, don't worry about it," Dell said, reaching over and squeezing her hand. "What is the last thing that you remember?"

Cece turned her head away from the detectives, and

stared at the blank wall. She rolled her eyes as she tried to remember. She was at the Hyatt Hotel, down on River Street, under a table, sleeping. Someone had come into the room and turned on the lights. She remembered hearing someone whistle, the man who had set up an overhead projector. But that was the last thing she could remember. Everything was just black after that.

Cece picked up the pen and scribbled what little she remembered.

"Well, don't worry about it," Shark said. "I'm sure it'll all come back to you. After all, the doctor said things might be a little foggy when you first woke up. We're going to let you rest now. We'll be back in a little while."

"Would you like another sip of water before we go?" Dell asked. Cece smiled at her gratefully and nodded yes.

The detectives walked out into the hall and turned in the direction of the nurse's station. They approached the counter and saw Nurse DeWitt writing something on a chart. "Excuse me," Shark said. "Is it possible for us to talk to Miss Campbell's doctor?"

"I'm not sure if he's still on duty. Let me see if he's left the hospital."

The nurse picked up the telephone and put a page in for Dr. Blankenship. After she put the phone down she said, "She's doing remarkably well, don't you think?"

"Yes, but she seems only to be able to remember things up to a point about six hours before she was kidnapped. We need her to remember everything," Shark said, the frustration evident in his voice.

The phone rang and the nurse picked it up. "Intensive Care." She listened for a moment, then handed the phone to Shark. "It's Dr. Blankenship."

Shark grabbed the phone and explained the problem with Cece only being able to remember things up to a few hours before her abduction.

"Well, that's really not uncommon, especially if something traumatic happened to her. The subconscious tries to blank out the unpleasant experience."

"Will she ever remember it?" Shark inquired.

"Probably, but it's impossible to predict how soon that may occur. Frequently, the patient may see or hear something that triggers the memory."

"Is it possible she may never remember?" Shark asked.

"Possible, but unlikely. Give her a few days. She just woke up. Once her body is stronger she may remember."

"What about hypnosis? Would that help?"

"I'm not a specialist in that field. Before I would ever consider putting her through that, I would want her to be a lot stronger. I really have to go now. Let's see how she is in twenty-four hours."

"Thank you, doctor." Shark hung up the phone and relayed to Dell what the good doctor had said.

"Well, let's go tell Brad how she's doing and to go on home. Then let's head to Beaufort and get a shower and some sleep and come back tomorrow," Dell said.

"Might as well, I guess," Shark said, rubbing his hand over the stubble on his face.

Chapter Thirty-one

A little after seven, Cece was awakened by the sharp sound of a breakfast tray being slung onto her bedside table. She opened her eyes, momentarily confused, but it didn't take her long to realize where she was.

The smells emanating from the tray drew her attention, especially the coffee. She pushed the control to raise the head of her bed, then poured a cup from the silver container. Cece ripped open the Sweet and Low and the packet of cream with her teeth, since one hand was still tied to the bedrail. She took just a sip, afraid it would be hot. But it was just the right temperature, so she took a good long pull. *Ah, that tastes wonderful.* Her throat still hurt, but not as much as it had. Next, she removed the silver dish cover to find scrambled eggs, toast, and applesauce. She picked up the fork and dug in.

Cece had eaten only about a third of the eggs and a couple of bites of applesauce, before she began to feel a little nauseated. She pushed the tray away from her bed, lay back, and closed her eyes.

She must have drifted off to sleep, because the next thing she knew a nurse she didn't recognize was placing a blood pressure cuff around her arm. "Good morning, my name is Sally Carpenter. I'm your nurse today. I see you managed to eat a little breakfast."

Cece looked at the red-haired, freckle-faced young girl,

and thought she looked like she should still be in high school. The nurse pumped up the cuff, to the point that Cece felt her arm was going to explode, before she gradually reduced the pressure in it. After the young nurse removed the stethoscope from her ears, Cece whispered, "Can you loosen my other arm?"

"Actually, if you can manage to get enough food and liquids down, we may be able to take the IV out completely. Let me call the doctor and see what he thinks. How's that sound?"

"Great," Cece whispered. After the nurse left the room, Cece began to replay in her mind the conversation with the detectives yesterday. Why didn't she remember being in the water? If she had been unconscious when she was plunged into the ocean, how did she survive? Why couldn't she remember anything after sleeping in the conference room?

She closed her eyes and tried to will the memories back. First, she tried to remember leaving the conference room. *Had she eaten breakfast somewhere? Where had she gotten her caffeine fix that morning?*

As hard as she tried, she just couldn't remember. It was as if there was a stone wall there that she couldn't get past. She wasn't sure how long she'd been lost in thought before Nurse Carpenter returned and took out her IV. "I'm going to leave this paper here on your bedside table. It's called an I&O sheet. That stands for input and output. I need you to write down every time you drink something and how much you drank. You have a urinary catheter that will measure your output. We need to make sure that you don't take in a lot more fluid than you put out, so your lungs don't get congested. Think you can remember to write that down for me?"

Cece nodded her head yes, then whispered, "When can I get the catheter out? I feel like I have to pee all the time."

"I know. Let's see how you do the next few hours, and if things are going well, maybe we can get an order to take it out before my shift is over."

"Thanks," Cece whispered. As the nurse started to turn from the bed, Cece reached out and touched her arm. Carpenter turned back. "When can I try talking?"

"I would like you to continue to just whisper for another eight hours or so, then you can try out your vocal cords a little bit."

"Okay."

It was dinnertime when Shark and Dell returned. They were surprised when they entered Cece's room to find her sitting up in bed, her IV gone, and a dinner tray in front of her.

"Hey, you look a whole lot better than when we left a few hours ago. Got anything good on that tray?" Shark asked as he smiled and approached the bed.

"Help yourself," Cece said softly, lowering her fork. "I can't eat anymore."

"Don't tempt him," Dell said chuckling. "Hey, you're talking a little. That's great."

"Yeah, they said I could a little bit, as long as I don't overdo it. It's a lot easier than writing everything down."

"That's for sure," Shark said as he leaned on her bedrail. "So how are you feeling?" he asked.

"Better. I still can't eat very much before I feel stuffed and start to get nauseated."

"Well, it's probably because it's hospital food. Only kidding. Your stomach probably shrunk when you didn't eat anything for a couple of days. That shouldn't last too long."

"Sure, like you would know," Dell said, hitting him on the arm. "Pay no attention to Dr. Morgan here," she said winking at Cece.

Cece could tell the two detectives were close. She wondered if they were married, but only the lady was wearing a wedding ring.

Shark didn't quite know how to bring up the subject of whether Cece had remembered anything, although he was chomping at the bit to know. He was trying to figure out what to say when Cece said, "I've been trying to think all day, but I still can't remember what happened to me. I tried to reconstruct what I might have done after leaving the conference room. But it's all just a blank. I'm sorry."

The detectives were disappointed, but tried not to let it show on their faces. "Hey, don't try to rush things. It might be better if you don't work so hard at it. Just let the memories come on their own," Dell said, smiling down at her.

Cece liked the lady detective. "Thanks, I know it's really important that I remember, especially if you need me to try and identify somebody. You did say you have arrested someone, didn't you? Or did I dream that?"

"No, we do have a man in custody. And it would help us out a lot if you could remember what happened and identify the person. But we've got plenty of time for that, after you get all better," Dell said reassuringly.

Shark thought perhaps if they talked about things that it might jog Cece's memory. He paused for a moment then said, "You'll be happy to know we recovered the disks."

"The backup disks off Tony's computer?" she asked.

"Yes, they were on the table at Brad Johnson's house, next to your purse. We also have your gym bag."

Cece turned her head away and her eyes squinted in concentration. "There's something about the disks, but I can't remember what. Oh damn it! Why can't I remember?"

"We were surprised that the suspect didn't take the disks and destroy them when he abducted you, if that's what he was after the whole time," Shark said, trying to pull the memories out of her.

"There's something about the disks that's important," Cece said softly.

Shark glanced over at Dell. "How do you know?"

Cece paused, her head thrown back in concentration, her eyes closed. "I don't know how I know, I just know."

The door to Cece's room opened abruptly and a young man waltzed into the room. "I'm Dr. Baker. I'm covering for Dr. Blankenship, who's off tonight. Well, it looks like you're going to make a full recovery, Miss Campbell. I wouldn't have bet a plugged nickel on that when they brought you into the emergency room."

"You were there when they brought me in?" Cece asked.

"Yes, I'm the one who shocked you and got your heart started again."

"Thank you," Cece said as she stared at the young man.

"Really, the guys on Angel One are the ones you should be thanking. If they hadn't acted so quickly, things could have turned out a whole lot differently. Now, let me check your heart and lungs," he said, pulling the stethoscope from around his neck. He leaned over and first listened to her heart, then had her sit up while he listened to her back. "Your heart is strong and steady, and there doesn't seem to be any congestion in your lungs. It looks like you're doing pretty good with your intake and output, so I'm going to leave an order for the nurse to remove your catheter after your visitors leave."

"Oh, thank you, doctor. This thing is driving me nuts."

"Okay then, I'll see you in the morning. If things are still looking good, and there's no sign of aspiration pneumonia, we may be able to let you go home." The doctor strode briskly toward the door.

Home, where was that? Cece wondered. Back in Indiana with her father? She hadn't lived with him since she went off to college "Wait, doctor. Did anyone notify my father that I was here?" Cece asked.

He turned and looked at her. "We didn't even know your identity when they brought you in. Not until the detectives identified you. I'm sorry, if we'd known, we would have contacted him," Dr. Baker said. "Would you like me to call him for you?" he asked.

"Thanks, but I'll do it." Cece said.

"I'm sorry. We didn't know who to notify either," Shark said. "Had you told your father what happened to Dr. Kline and to your Aunt Sophie?"

"Yes, I contacted him by e-mail."

"He must be frantic. Are you sure you don't want us to call him?" Dell asked.

"No, if the police call him, it'll scare him to death. I'd better call him myself. Can you ask them to bring me a phone when you leave, or take me to one?"

"Here, use my cell phone," Shark said, reaching into his pocket. "We'll go get a cup of coffee and give you some privacy. We'll be back in a few minutes."

Cece looked at him, a smile playing over her lips. "Thank you," she said.

Shark and Dell walked out into the hall. "Damn that doctor. I thought we were beginning to get somewhere when he came busting into the room. I think she was about to remember something," Shark said crossly.

"I know what you mean. She seemed sure that the disks were important."

"I know. I got that impression too. Do you think talking about it might help her to remember?"

"Well, I don't think it can hurt," Dell said. "Come on, let's go get that coffee."

Chapter Thirty-two

Cece's father answered his phone after the first ring. "Hello."

"Dad, it's me."

"Thank the Lord. Where are you? Are you okay? Why haven't you contacted me?"

"I'm in the hospital. But I'm okay."

"What hospital? Are you hurt? Do you want me to come?"

"I'm at the Medical University in Charleston. No, you don't need to come. I may be released tomorrow."

"What happened, Babe?"

Tears began to slide down Cece's cheeks. A sob caught in her throat. "That's just it, Dad, I don't remember."

"What do you mean you don't remember? Did you have an accident or something?"

"Apparently the man who killed Tony kidnapped me. They found me floating in the ocean."

"In the ocean? Oh my God. Cece did you say kidnapped?"

Cece relayed what little information she knew to her father. "It's really important that I remember what happened. They need me to identify the man they think killed Tony and Aunt Sophie, then abducted me. But I don't remember anything after getting up that morning."

"Babe, listen to me. Maybe it's better if you don't re-

member. It might be too painful for you. Are you sure
you're all right? Why don't you let me fly down and be
with you?"

"No, Dad. When this is all over I'll come home for a
visit."

"A visit? I want you to come back home to live. Where
else are you going to go? I never wanted you to move so
far away in the first place."

Cece had to smile. Some things never changed. "Dad, I
don't want to discuss this now. I have to finish things up
here before I can come home."

"Why? Let the police handle things. You just hop on a
plane and come on home."

"I can't do that, Dad. Not until Tony's and Aunt Sophie's
murderer is put away for good. I'll call you tomorrow after
I get out of here."

"But where will you go?"

"I don't have the faintest idea. But I'll let you know
when I figure it out. I love you." Cece hung up the phone
before her father could protest.

Shark and Dell sat at a small table in the cafeteria and
shared the piece of key lime pie Dell had gotten to go with
her coffee. "I thought you didn't want any," Dell said bat-
ting his fork away. "I get the last bite."

Shark put his fork down and leaned back in his chair.
"Where the hell is Campbell going to go tomorrow if she's
released? Maybe it would be best if she stayed in the hospital a couple more days," Shark said, watching the look
of disappointment on Dell's face as she cleaned every
crumb off the plate.

"Man, I don't know. I feel sorry for her. Her home and
everything she owned destroyed in the fire. Maybe she has
a friend she can stay with," Dell said, pushing her plate
away.

Shark didn't say anything for a minute, just stared down
at the floor. "Maybe if she stayed someplace familiar it
would help jolt her memory."

"And just where might that be?" Dell asked.

"Maybe Ruth Kline would let Cece stay with her for a few days. I imagine she would probably be grateful for the company."

Dell's mouth opened in surprise. "You know, that's not a bad idea. I wonder how Campbell would feel about that?"

"Why don't we check with the widow before we mention anything to Cece. Let me use your cell phone, and I'll give her a call. If that doesn't work out I guess she could use my guest room." Dell dug her phone out of her purse and slid it across the table to Shark. Shark pulled a notebook out of his pocket and looked up Mrs. Kline's number.

Ruth Kline answered on the fourth ring. Shark explained the situation to her and asked if it would be possible for Campbell to stay with her for a few days.

"Thank the Lord she's going to be okay. What an ordeal that child has been through. You mean the poor girl doesn't remember anything?"

"Nothing since the day of the abduction. We're hoping that if she's someplace familiar, it may help her regain her memory."

"Well of course Cece can stay with me, as long as she likes. This house is way too quiet anyway."

"Thank you, Mrs. Kline. We won't know for sure if she'll be released until the doctor sees her in the morning. I'll give you a call as soon as we know something."

"It doesn't matter. I'll be here all day. You tell Cece I'll be expecting her."

Shark hung up. "Now if Campbell just agrees."

"Let's go find out," Dell said, pushing away from the table.

Dell knocked softly and then she and Shark entered Cece's room. She was curled into a fetal position, crying. "Hey, what's the matter?" Dell asked as she approached the bed. "Is everything okay with your dad?"

"Yes, he wants me to come home, but I told him I have to finish things up here first. But I was just lying here thinking I have no place to go tomorrow. I have no home. Poor Aunt Sophie, if it wasn't for me, she would still be alive."

"Cece, you're not to blame for your aunt's death," Shark said. "Don't lay that guilt trip on yourself. You're not the one who burned down her house. Anyway, we think we have a solution. I just got off the phone with Ruth Kline, and she said she would love to have you stay with her for a few days."

Cece wiped her eyes with the back of her hand. "She did? I'm not surprised. She's like that. She always treated me more like a daughter than an employee."

"Well, it'll probably be good for her, too, to have someone around," Dell said.

"I felt so bad I couldn't go to Tony's funeral. It'll give us a chance to talk."

"Once you get settled at Ruth's, we'd like to have you see if you can pick our suspect out of a lineup." Dell shot him a dirty look. "When you feel you're up to it, that is," Shark stammered.

"Even though I can't remember what happened?"

"If nothing else, maybe you can identify him as the man who was following you. Brad Johnson has already picked him out as the person who was at his house. By the way, Johnson was here last night. He came to see how you were doing."

Cece stifled a yawn. "That was nice of him."

"Listen, why don't we go and let you get some rest. We'll be back in the morning," Dell said, patting her arm.

"I am kind of tired."

On the drive to Beaufort, the detectives discussed how Campbell might react when she saw her pursuer.

"Hopefully, it will unlock the key to her memory," Shark said.

"If not, maybe we should think about taking her back to Brad Johnson's house," Dell said, rubbing her chin with her thumb and index finger as if she were playing with a goatee.

"Now that's a thought. Back to where everything started that day."

"Do you think he raped her?" Dell asked softly.

"I don't know," Shark said, glancing over at her. "The doctor said the pelvic exam was inconclusive."

"If so, maybe it's best if she doesn't remember But I would sure as hell like to know how she got in the water. Do you think he threw her overboard, or did she jump?"

"Since she had on a wetsuit and that cooler ticd to her wrist, I'd say she jumped before he had an opportunity to kill her."

"Can you imagine being in the cold water like that for all those hours?"

"Frankly, I can't. I don't know how she survived. I'm not sure I would have."

Chapter Thirty-three

Cece was released from the hospital a little after 11 the next morning. They were hardly out of the city before she surprised the detectives when she said, "I want to go directly to the jail and get the lineup over with."

Shark glanced at her in his rearview mirror. Dell turned in her seat and said, "Whoa. Are you sure about that? Don't you want to settle in at Mrs. Kline's and maybe rest for a little while before you think of tackling that?"

Cece looked out the window momentarily, then turned back and faced Dell, "No, I want to get it over with. And I want to see if it will help me remember."

Dell glanced at Shark. He nodded his head affirmatively. "Okay then, we'll call and get it set up if you're sure."

"The sooner this is all over, the better."

Dell admired the girl's grit. She pulled out her cell phone and dialed the sheriff.

Cece's legs were shaking so badly that she didn't think they were going to support her as she stood before the curtained observation window at the Beaufort County jail. She wasn't sure this was such a good idea after all. But she knew she had to do it.

"Now remember, no one can see you or hear you, so don't worry about that. If you see someone who looks familiar, just tell us which number he is. You can have him step forward, turn sideways so you can get a look at his profile, or speak. Anything that will assist you in making a positive identification. Do you understand?" Dell asked. Cece nodded, afraid that her voice would fail her if she tried to speak. "Okay, let me know when you're ready."

Shark stood, arms crossed, leaning back against the wall. Cece seemed to respond well to Dell. His partner had a comforting voice and a special way with victims that he lacked. He could tell Cece was nervous. She wrung her hands and kept taking deep breaths, like she couldn't get enough oxygen. He wouldn't be surprised if she passed out.

Cece hung her head and closed her eyes, as if she were praying for strength. After a moment she looked at Dell and said, "Okay."

"Just take your time," Dell said, as she opened the curtain.

There were five men in the room facing the observation window. Dell watched as Cece started with the first one, then quickly worked her way down the lineup.

Shark heard Cece gasp. "Number four, that's him. Number four!" Cece took two steps back, as if she was afraid the man would see her.

Dell looked back over her shoulder at Shark. "Are you sure? Do you need him to step forward or say something?"

"No, I'm sure."

Dell quickly closed the curtain and spoke into the intercom. "Okay, Sayles, we're done."

Sayles escorted the men from the room.

Shark slipped a folding chair under Cece's legs, afraid she was about ready to collapse. "You did real good, Cece. Can I get you some water or something?"

Cece shook her head no. "That was him, wasn't it? The man who killed Tony. Now you'll be able to throw him in prison for the rest of his life."

The detectives didn't say anything for a moment. Shark paused, then cleared his throat, and said, "Well, that's not as easy as it sounds. We have no weapon, no physical evidence, and no proof that he was the murderer. All we really have is the fact that he was following you, and Brad Johnson's statement that he abducted you from his home."

Cece was stunned. "And what about Aunt Sophie's murder?"

"We have no physical evidence to tie him to that either, unfortunately."

Cece leapt out of the chair. "Are you saying he's going to get away with it?"

"Let's not jump the gun here. We've sent off samples to the state lab that may verify that you were on his boat. But if you can remember what happened, maybe we can get him for not only kidnapping you, but attempted murder as well. If we can charge him with that, maybe he would be willing to make a deal and turn over on who hired him to hit Dr. Kline."

"And if I don't remember, what can you charge him with?" Cece almost screamed.

"Just kidnapping, unless we find the weapon or some other evidence comes to light."

Cece fell back into the chair, leaned over, her hands supporting her head and stared at the floor. "But I can't remember," she said softly.

"Maybe if we took you back over to Brad Johnson's house, that would help," Dell said, draping an arm around Cece's shoulder.

"Can't you hypnotize me or something?" Cece asked, the desperation apparent in her voice.

"Maybe, but we'd have to get your doctor's permission," Shark said.

"Then call him, I'll do whatever is necessary."

"Let's just take one step at a time. Let's get you on over to Mrs. Kline's. You need to rest. You've had quite a day already," Dell said.

Cece and Ruth relaxed out on the screened porch, a blue afghan thrown over their legs as they sat side by side in the swing, sipping glasses of Fumé Blanc. The sun had already set, and a half moon was visible. The sound of the surf at high tide acted as background music.

"You didn't eat much dinner. Can I get you something to snack on?" Ruth asked.

"No thanks. I'm not very hungry. It seems funny to be here without Tony around."

"I know. I miss him terribly. I used to nag at him about leaving his towel on the bathroom floor, or not putting his socks in the clothes hamper. How petty that seems now."

"I'm sorry I wasn't at the funeral. Was it a nice service?"

"I think so. Actually, I don't remember a lot about it."

"So what will you do now?" Cece asked.

"I've already put the house and Tony's boat up for sale. I never really liked it here much, not like Tony did. My sister wants me to move close to her in upstate New York, but I don't know about that. I'm toying with moving to one of the Caribbean islands, maybe St. John's. What about you, Cece?"

Cece was stunned that Ruth had already put everything up for sale. Especially Tony's boat. How had she made so many important decisions in such a short time? And if she didn't like Hilton Head, why would she think another island would be better? "Dad wants me to move back home. But that's about as likely as my becoming a prima ballerina. I have absolutely no idea what I'm going to do. First, I have to get all this behind me. And it's not over yet. Not until I remember what happened and they can put Tony's murderer away for life."

Ruth gazed out at the ocean. "It's hard to imagine you out there all that time. And to think you don't remember any of it. God works in strange ways. Maybe that's a blessing."

"I keep thinking there's some reason I must have survived. That there must be something I am to do. I don't really believe in God like you do. I wish I did."

"Well, my religion has been my comfort through all this.

Maybe those memories of yours are just so painful that God thinks you just can't handle them right now."

Cece yawned.

"Come on, it's getting cold out here," Ruth said. "Why don't you take a hot shower and climb into bed."

Cece felt that tonight she might finally be able to get a good night's sleep. For the first time since all this had started, she felt safe.

Chapter Thirty-four

A little after 10 the following morning Cece sat in the back seat of the detectives' car as it pulled into a subdivision, Norwood Place, in Savannah. She peered curiously out the back window as Shark parked in the driveway of a brick ranch house. Dell turned around in her seat and asked, "Look familiar?"

"Not in the least," Cece said tentatively.

"You know you don't have to do this," Dell said.

Cece took a deep breath. "Yes, I do."

Shark walked around and opened her car door. As they approached the front door of the house, Brad Johnson came rushing out. "Grace, it's so good to see you. I'm so sorry for everything," he said as he stood, head bowed in front of her.

"It's okay, Brad. I don't blame you."

"If I had just listened to you, none of this would have happened. Grace, I mean Cecilia, can you ever possibly forgive me? I don't think I'll ever get used to calling you Cecilia."

"Only my mother called me that, please, just call me Cece. And don't beat yourself up about this. I may have done the same thing if I'd been in your position."

"We're hoping that possibly being back at your house will help Cece to remember what happened," Shark said.

"I'm sorry, please come in."

Cece slowly approached the front door, not really sure if she was ready for this. But when she walked inside, nothing seemed familiar.

"We were sitting in the kitchen," Brad said, as he headed in that direction.

"Tell me what happened," Cece said softly.

"You had asked me to introduce you to a reporter. You planned to turn over some information to him. Said it would be a big story. And it was only a couple of minutes after we started talking that you jumped up and said you had to use the restroom. He grabbed your wrist, said you weren't going anywhere. You begged me to help you," Brad said, looking down at the floor. "He gave you a shot of something to calm you down, and I helped him get you to the car. That's about it."

Cece closed her eyes, and tried to visualize what Brad had just described. She wanted to get her memory back. No, she *needed* to. "Why didn't I recognize him when I first came in?" Cece asked.

"Because he had a mustache and brown contact lenses in," Shark said.

"And he was wearing an old fishing hat," Brad chimed in.

"So what made me suddenly realize who he was?"

Brad shrugged his shoulders. "I have no idea."

Cece glanced over at Shark, who was leaning against the kitchen counter. "Sorry, nothing."

"Well, it was worth a shot." He turned to Brad, "Thanks for letting us come by this morning."

"I'll do anything to help. What else can I do?"

"Can't think of anything at the moment," Shark said, taking Cece's elbow and leading her towards the front door.

"Cece, wait." Brad approached slowly and stood in front of her. "Would it be okay if I kept in touch with you? I'd kinda like to know how this all turns out. I mean, if you get your memory back and all," he said.

Cece could see the anguish in his eyes. She knew what it was like to feel responsible for someone's misfortune.

She thought of how guilty she felt about Aunt Sophie. "Sure, Brad, that would be fine. I'm staying with Dr. Kline's widow." She rattled off the phone number, then walked on to the car.

There was little conversation as Shark threaded his way through the heavy traffic. They had just crossed the state line back into South Carolina when Cece asked, "Does he know I survived?"

"Who?" Shark asked.

"Garrett, or whatever his name is."

"We just learned this morning that his real name is Harold Whitaker. And no, we haven't sprung that little surprise on him yet," Dell said. "We were waiting to see if you got your memory back. We thought if you did, he might be willing to turn over on whoever hired him."

Cece didn't say anything for at least five minutes, her mind racing with possibilities. She was almost afraid to voice what she was thinking. She cleared her throat. "What if he thought I remembered? Do you think he would tell you then?"

Shark glanced at Dell. "What are you thinking, Cece?" Shark asked.

"I don't know exactly. But maybe if he saw me, he might be willing to come clean."

"That would mean you would have to confront him. Do you think you're up to that?" Dell asked.

"No, but I'm not sure I have a choice. Who knows how long, if ever, it will take me to remember?"

"You would have to waltz in there and play the role of your life. You couldn't appear afraid of him in any way. You'd have to act as if you had the upper hand. That you delighted in the fact that you were going to be able to put him away for life. Act cocky almost," Shark said.

Cece bit down on her lower lip. Could she really do that? The thought of it scared the hell out of her.

"I don't know, Cece. The trauma of confronting him may not be good for you," Dell said, peering back over her shoulder.

"What's the worse that could happen? That I remember everything?"

Dell wasn't sure what to say. Shark looked over at her and curled his lips into a silent shhhhhh.

"Why don't you just think about this a little more? Make sure it's something that you want to do," Shark said, glancing at her wrinkled brow in the rearview mirror.

In the silence that followed, Shark's mind raced with the possibilities. He wondered what Sheriff Grant would say. He wasn't sure he would approve.

Finally, Cece said, "I want to do it, for Tony and Aunt Sophie. I've got to get this over with, so I can put everything behind me. Can we do it now, before I chicken out?"

"Right now?" Dell asked, the surprise evident in her voice.

"Let me think about this for a minute, Cece." Shark said, his mind suddenly in overdrive. Should he call the sheriff? What if he said no? If he didn't ask him, and it didn't turn out well, what would be the repercussions? Maybe if he had her sign a statement that it was her idea and that she was doing it of her own free will. Would that be enough to cover him and Dell? It was worth the risk if it would make old Harold willing to deal. But could she really pull off the bluff?

"Cece, did you ever act in any plays in high school or college?" he asked.

"I was in a couple in high school. Nothing in college. Why?"

"Do you think you could pretend like you were in a play?"

"You mean you would give me lines and stuff to say?"

"No, I don't think we can do that. You know, just kinda act the part of a certain character. For instance, let's say you marched into the interrogation room and said something like, 'I'm going to put you away,' or 'Guess who's back?' You know, something with an attitude. Then maybe tell him you remember everything, and start describing what happened in Johnson's kitchen. I think just the shock

of seeing you still alive may be enough to make him co-
operate. And you wouldn't have to be in there very long.
Not more than a couple of minutes. What do you think?
Think you could do that?"

"Just a couple of minutes?" she whispered.

"That's all," Shark said reassuringly. "And we'd be right
there with you."

Dell gave him a dirty look, but didn't say anything. She
was convinced that this was not a good plan. She pulled
her notepad out of her purse and wrote, "Shouldn't we clear
this upstairs first?"

Shark ignored Dell's note. "Cece, there's just one thing.
We would need you to sign a statement that this was all
your idea, that no one put you up to it. Would you be
willing to do that?"

"Yes, because it *was* my idea."

"Are you sure about this?" Dell asked again.

Cece didn't say anything, just nodded, and began to bite
her fingernails.

Shark pulled his cell phone out of his pocket and dialed
the jail to set things in motion.

It seemed to Cece that only moments had passed before
they were crossing the Broad River Bridge into Beaufort.
A few minutes later they turned off Ribaut Road onto Duke
Street and drew up in front of a three-story stucco building
that almost looked like a school. The jail hadn't changed
any since her visit yesterday.

As soon as Shark cut the engine, Dell jumped out and
opened Cece's door. Cece didn't move, her head bowed
and eyes closed, left fist clenched to her mouth. Dell put a
finger up to her mouth and motioned for Shark to be quiet
as he rounded the back of the car.

*You've got to help me here, Mom. I don't think I can do
this without your help. Give me the strength to pull this off.*

Finally, Cece opened her eyes and looked up at Dell.
"It's okay. We'll be right there with you. I bet you can put
on quite a performance. I admire you. Not very many peo-

ple would have the guts to do what you're about to do. I'm not sure I would. Just remember, you're a survivor."

A half smile played across Cece's lips at the familiar words. *Okay, Mom, I hear you.*

Cece followed the detectives into the building and waited in a folding chair while Shark typed out a statement for her to sign, that she was doing this of her own volition. She didn't even read it when he handed her a clipboard with the paper attached, just signed it quickly and handed it back to him. "He's in interrogation room three. Just follow me," Shark said.

Cece followed him down the hall, Dell bringing up the rear. Shark led her into an empty office next door to where *he* waited. She couldn't call him Harold, it didn't seem to fit him. "Okay, Cece. You just let me know when you're ready," Shark said calmly, although his heart was racing and his palms sweating.

"Can you give me a couple of minutes alone?" Cece asked, her voice trembling.

Dell took both of Cece's hands in hers and squeezed them hard. "Sure. You take as much time as you need. We'll be right outside."

As soon as the door closed behind the detectives, Cece began to pace as best she could in the small confined space. She threw her shoulders back and stood up straighter. She needed to work herself into a rage. This was the man who had murdered Tony in cold blood, and killed her precious Aunt Sophie. The man who had stalked her and tried to kill her. She needed someone to portray. A character who was mean, but cool under fire. And then she had it, Dirty Harry. She could be Dirty Cece.

Cece didn't even pause, just pulled the door open and walked out into the hall. Shark and Dell were shocked at the transformation in her demeanor. But only briefly, because she didn't even look at them, just flung open the door to interrogation room three and marched inside. They rushed in behind her.

Bama had been cooling his heels for almost 20 minutes.

He sat in the hard metal chair, his legs splayed out in front of him, examining his fingernails. Suddenly the door to the room was wrenched open.

"Hello, asshole. Remember me?"

Bama jumped up from the chair so fast he almost turned it over. His mouth hung open to the point that it almost dented his chest.

"You look like you've seen a ghost," Cece said, chuckling. "You should have killed me when you had the chance. Now, I'm in control."

"You don't have any concept of what control really is," Bama sneered. "You're just a lowly female who probably can't even control your lover."

Bama noticed that some of Cece's bravado seemed to have vanished, at least momentarily. But then she came right back at him. "Well I'm still alive, but in case you hadn't noticed, you're stuck in jail. And isn't it surprising that a stupid female could manage to outwit you? You're going to fry. For Tony's murder, Aunt Sophie and Carl's murders, for kidnapping me, for everything," she spewed.

Bama reached up and began to massage his right earlobe with his thumb and index finger, his hate and contempt for her written all over his face. Cece watched as he played with his ear lobe. And then she knew; that's what had tipped her off in Brad's kitchen. That's how she had recognized him, by that nervous habit. Cece advanced toward him, her eyes squinted and forehead wrinkled in concentration. "And I came back for this," she said, spitting in his face.

Bama was shocked. He roared and lunged for her, but Shark shoved him roughly back against the wall as Dell whisked Cece from the room.

"What's the matter, Harold? Did you think she was dead?"

But Bama clammed up and refused to say anything else, no matter how much Shark baited him.

Out in the hall Cece leaned up against the wall, her legs shaking so badly they finally failed to support her. Her back slid down the wall and she put her head on her knees and looked down at the floor.

"You just did one hell of a job in there. Julia Roberts couldn't have done better," Dell said as she squeezed Cece's shoulder. "Come on, let's go back in the office here where you'll have a little privacy."

Dell pulled Cece off the floor and led her next door. She sat her down in the desk chair. "Would you like something to drink or eat?" Dell asked.

Cece shook her head no. "I just want to go back to Tony's and lie down. I feel exhausted."

Dell was all too familiar with how it felt once the adrenaline rush dissipated. It made you feel as if you'd worked 40 hours straight. "Okay, you wait here for just a minute and I'll go leave a message for my partner where we've gone. We can take your formal statement in the morning. I don't think you're up to it right now."

Dell returned and handed Cece a Mountain Dew. "You look like you could use a hit of caffeine." Cece clutched the can gratefully.

There was little conversation on the drive to Hilton Head. Cece seemed lost in her thoughts, and Dell didn't want to intrude. Just as they were crossing the bridge onto the island, Cece turned to Dell and said, "I remembered something, when I was in there talking to him. He has this nervous habit of playing with his ear lobe. That's how I recognized him in Brad's kitchen."

"Hey, that's great Cece. So do you remember everything that happened at Johnson's?"

"A few bits and pieces. I recall struggling and watching this large hypodermic needle come towards me. That's about all."

"Well, it's a start. Maybe things will come back a little at a time. Just don't worry about it. It will come when it comes."

"Thank you for being so kind to me," Cece said, smiling over at Dell.

"Hey, it's my job," Dell said, laughing nervously.

A few minutes later the detective pulled into Port Royal Plantation. Soon she had delivered Cece into the widow's care and was headed to the Hilton Head office. She was anxious to talk to Shark and see if he'd made any headway with their man.

Chapter Thirty-five

After a long nap, Cece and Ruth enjoyed a leisurely dinner, then took a stroll on the beach. The air was cool and the sky overcast. They were bundled up in jackets, Cece wearing one of Tony's. As they made their way down the beach, hermit crabs scattered across the sand. Cece stooped and picked up a starfish that had been stranded by the outgoing tide, and flung it back into the sea.

"That lady detective said you started to remember some things when you talked with that awful man today," Ruth said, glancing at Cece.

"Not much really. He had this nervous habit of pulling on his earlobe. When I saw him do that, I recalled him doing it in Brad's kitchen, and that's what made me recognize him."

"Maybe those memories of yours that are locked away are about to present themselves."

"At times I hope so, but in a way I hope I never remember parts of it."

"The detective said that he beat you up. What a terrible thing for you to have to go through. Just keep all those awful memories locked away and don't even try to remember them. Some things are best forgotten. I'm so glad you're staying here with me, Cece. Otherwise, I don't know how I would bear the silence."

"Well, I appreciate your hospitality, Ruth. I don't know where I would have gone."

"What do you plan to do once all this is over?"

"I have no idea, what about you? Have you decided if you're going to go back to New York?"

"No, I don't think so. I plan to put the furniture in storage and travel around Europe for a while, until I decide where I eventually want to land. As a matter of fact, I'm hoping to leave in just a few days."

Surprised, Cece glanced over at Ruth. "But won't you have to stick around until the trial or whatever is over?"

"Oh, I'll come back whenever they need me. But you know how slow the courts are, it could be a year or longer before there's a trial."

They walked for another 20 minutes, before the cool wind sent them scurrying inside.

Bama lay on his bunk, hands behind his head, his brow wrinkled in deep concentration. He never should have told Campbell who his employer was. *So why hadn't she told the cops? That know-nothing detective had tried to get him to finger who'd hired him. Why didn't he already know? Were they trying to trap him? Why offer him a deal if they already knew who it was? Something wasn't right in Gotham. Why hadn't Campbell told them already? It was almost as if she didn't remember their conversation. Son of a gun, that was it! She must have amnesia or something.*

So as long as he kept his mouth shut, and she didn't remember, it might not be too bad after all. So they had him on kidnapping, but that was about it. Sure beat three counts of murder.

Cece had difficulty falling asleep after taking such a late nap. Tossing and turning for almost an hour, she climbed out of bed and made her way quietly to the library. She browsed through the books and finally headed back to bed with a book of short stories. *Maybe this will put me to sleep.*

As she began to read, she found she couldn't concentrate on the words in front of her. Her mind kept returning to those few minutes in the jail. She had been so frightened. And just being in the same room with him had made her nauseated. She never wanted to be that close to pure evil again. She shook her head and tried to focus again on the words in front of her.

As the hours passed, she remembered more of what had happened in Brad's kitchen, or maybe she was just filling in the spaces from what Brad had told her. But she remembered taking the disks out of her purse, and laying them on the table. She also remembered the Terminator's car, a white Grand Am. But that's all she remembered. Morgan had said he'd taken her aboard a boat at Palmetto Bay Marina.

Cece closed the book and glanced at the clock on the nightstand. Almost two. She yawned, reached over, and turned out the light, then snuggled down into the flannel sheets and positioned her pillow just so. A few minutes later she drifted off.

Screams of terror coming from some place in the house awakened Ruth. She glanced at the clock radio. It was a little after four. She threw back the covers and grabbed her robe as she hurried from the bedroom. She hit the switch in the hall and squinted as the bright light assaulted her pupils. The sounds were emanating from the guestroom.

Ruth cautiously opened the door and peered into the dark room. From the light in the hallway she could see Cece thrashing about on the bed. Her hands were clenched in fists, beating against the sheets. She called Cece's name softly, but got no response. She tentatively made her way across the room. It was obvious Cece was in the throes of a nightmare. She didn't know if she should try and awaken her or not. But the agony of Cece's cries tore at her. She carefully leaned over the bed and touched Cece gently on the shoulder. "Cece," she called a little louder.

Cece thrashed about reliving the beating and her plunge

into the sea. Huge waves were bearing down on her, crushing her. She couldn't breathe. She was going to die. Something was pulling on her shoulder.

"Cece, wake up! It's okay. You're just having a nightmare," Ruth repeated over and over.

Cece was jerked awake, disoriented, and scared. She shrugged off Ruth's touch and scooted to the opposite edge of the bed. Tears streamed down her face. She looked around, confusion apparent in her wide eyes. Cece pulled the covers close around her body. "Oh my God, it was awful. The waves were sucking me down under water. I couldn't breathe."

Ruth sat down on the edge of the bed. "Hey, you're okay, honey."

All kinds of jumbled thoughts raced through Cece's mind. She tried to make some sense of them. She banged her fist against her head, as if trying to blot out the memories. The gun, it was at her temple. Bile rose in her throat. She tried to force it back down. Sweat broke out on her forehead. Cece began to tremble. She was going to be sick. She hastily threw off the covers, hand to her mouth. She barely made it to the bathroom in time.

Ruth called to Cece behind the closed door, "I'll go make you a cup of tea. Maybe that will make you feel better."

Shortly Ruth returned with a steaming mug of Plantation Mint tea and handed it to Cece, who was sitting on the side of the bed.

"Thanks," Cece said wrapping both hands around the mug, then scooting to the far side of the bed, as Ruth sat down on the edge.

"Do you want to talk about it?" Ruth asked softly.

"No," Cece answered emphatically.

Ruth reached out to touch Cece's knee, and Cece immediately pulled them up under her and said, "Don't touch me."

Surprised, Ruth placed her hand back in her lap. "I'm sorry, dear, I was only trying to help. I didn't mean to frighten you."

"I'm okay now. Please, I'd like to be alone."

"Are you sure?" the hurt apparent in Ruth's eyes at Cece's rebuff.

"Yes, thank you for the tea. I'm sorry I woke you."

"Oh hush, don't worry about that," Ruth said as she smiled and rose from the bed. "Just call if you need anything," she said as she closed the door behind her.

Cece breathed a sigh of relief once she was gone.

As Ruth walked down the hall, she wondered what Cece had remembered.

Shark pulled up in front of Dell's right at eight o'clock. But it was almost five minutes before Dell came ambling down the sidewalk, trying to juggle her purse, a newspaper, two cups of coffee, and her bullet-proof vest. Shark rolled down his window and gratefully grabbed one of the coffee cups.

They'd been called out a little before midnight when a deer had collided with a Volkswagon in front of Rose Hill Plantation. The driver had been killed, his lime-green vehicle smashed. They hadn't gotten home until a little after four.

Dell opened the car door, threw her vest into the backseat, placed her coffee cup on the dashboard, and dropped into the passenger seat. "Couldn't we have called Campbell and just told her we would pick her up a little later?"

"The sheriff wasn't real happy yesterday when you whisked her off before we had a chance to get her statement. And you'd better put that vest on before he chews you out."

"Hey, you're lucky I've got my bra on. We're just picking up Campbell, give me a break."

"Yeah, but you know Sheriff Grant said we have to wear them at all times now since you went and got shot last year. You had to screw it up for all of us."

"Well, excuse me," Dell said, grabbing her coffee as Shark put the car into gear. "You think we've got enough time to stop at the bagel place in Bluffton?"

"Depends on the traffic."

Dell picked up the California newspaper that she had found on Josh's luggage by the front door. He had gotten in a few minutes after she had climbed into bed.

Shark was paying attention to the heavy traffic when Dell suddenly screamed, "Oh my God. You're not going to believe this!"

"What?" Shark asked, glancing over at her with alarm.

"Just listen. Maxine Walters Philips, oil baroness, was found dead in her bed by her husband, Devon Philips. She appears to have died of natural causes."

"Devon Philips! You don't think it's the same Devon Philips, Marissa DeSilva's first husband, do you?"

"Let me finish reading this. How many Devon Philips can there be anyway?"

"Hundreds? I don't know how common Devon is as names go." Shark thought back to the murder case of Marcus DeSilva they had worked on last October, when Dell had been convinced that Marissa, a suspect in her third husband's murder, was a black widow since her previous wealthy husband had died after a short time in an equestrian accident. But her first husband, Devon Philips, whom she had married and divorced while in college, was still alive, and therefore didn't fit the pattern. Dell had feverishly tried to connect Marissa and Devon as co-conspirators in Marcus' murder. The case had strained his relationship with Dell because he had been attracted to Marissa, and he had let it cloud his judgment about her. Thankfully, he and Dell were well past it now.

"It's the same Devon Philips. It says here he owns three restaurants in San Francisco. And it looks like they had been married less than a year. Sounds very suspicious to me. Remember how his first wife died in a boating accident on their honeymoon? Sounds like a pattern. I bet he murdered both of them," Dell said excitedly.

"You mean his second wife don't you? Marissa was his first."

"You knew what I meant."

"The same kind of pattern that made you think Marissa had something to do with Marcus' death?" Shark chided.

They had found the real murderer, and much to Dell's chagrin, he had not been linked to Marissa at all. "Does it say how old she was?"

"Fifty-nine. A lot older than Philips—just like his last wife. This afternoon, we should call the police out there and tell them what we know."

"We don't *know* anything."

"Yeah, but at least I could save them some time digging through his past. I'll call them when we get to the office."

"I'm sure they'll do a thorough investigation if it's indicated, with or without your help."

Shark wondered where Marissa was and what she was doing. The last he had heard from her she was traveling around Spain, and that had been almost a year ago. "What kind of bagels do you want?" Shark asked as he pulled into the Bagel Shoppe parking lot in Bluffton.

Chapter Thirty-six

Cece dressed and threw her meager belongings into her gym bag. When she couldn't get back to sleep after her nightmare, she had decided on a short-term plan. She was going to ask the detectives to take her to the bank, after she gave her statement this morning, so she could draw some money out of her account. She desperately needed to buy some clothes, so she could throw the ones she'd worn for so many days now into the closest dumpster. And was her car still at the Savannah airport, or had they impounded it? How much longer would she have to stay on the island? She was feeling an urgent need to go home and see her father. And then what? Would she ever return to this beautiful island she had grown to love?

Her mind was filled with too many questions and not enough answers as she made her way to the dining room.

"There you are, dear. You're looking better this morning. Sit down and have some coffee," Ruth said as a buzzer sounded in the kitchen. "I made some blueberry muffins. Sounds like they're ready to take out of the oven," she called over her shoulder.

Cece filled her cup from the white insulated thermos that Ruth always poured the coffee into as soon as it had finished brewing. Tony had told her Ruth was convinced it kept the coffee hotter and from getting bitter.

Ruth came in carrying a basket covered with a blue cloth

napkin and placed it in the center of the table. "Those smell wonderful," Cece said as she reached for one.

"Well eat up, dear. You need to put some meat back on those bones. You're all dressed," Ruth said, glancing down at her own bathrobe.

"Yeah, I need to go to the bank and buy some clothes, once I find out where my car is."

"Oh, that's too bad. I was hoping that maybe you would want to go to the gym with me this morning. I haven't been since Tony died. I guess it's time I got out of this house and started doing something. My trainer called and asked if I was coming back. If not, he said he wanted to fill my time slot with someone else."

Cece's hand froze with a piece of muffin halfway to her mouth. Stu, the trainer, there was something important about Stu she should remember. Cece wracked her brain trying to remember. She was back on the boat. *"Can you at least tell me why I have to die?"* she had asked her captor. He had paused, then said, *"I guess you at least deserve that much, since you'll be taking that information with you to the grave."* And then he had told her how he and Stu had been cellmates, and that Stu and Ruth were having an affair. He had even laughed when he talked about how Stu and Ruth used to meet when she was supposed to be at quilting conventions.

Cece looked up at Ruth, the fear apparent in her eyes.

"I wondered how much you remembered last night. You know, don't you?"

"What do you mean, know what?" Cece said, looking away.

"Cece, come on."

"Yes," Cece whispered, raising her eyes and staring at Ruth. "But I just realized it. Why Ruth? Why did Tony and Aunt Sophie have to die?"

"Because I hate this island, and Tony loved it so much. Once he bought that stupid boat, it became his damned mistress. I knew he would never leave. We got married when we were in high school. People change, *I changed*.

All Tony cared about was his work, golf and fishing. And I hate all those things. He never wanted to do anything with me, not that there's anything to do on this stupid island. And I found someone who makes me feel young and desirable again. And who wants to travel and do the things I want to do. You only go around once, so I plan to make the most of it. But I must admit I do feel bad about your aunt. I didn't know Bama was going to do that."

"But why not just divorce Tony?"

"Because if he could prove I was having an affair, I would get hardly anything. And working is certainly not on my agenda. We plan to live in Paris or Rome, and that takes money."

Ruth reached into the pocket of her bathrobe and pulled out a small revolver and pointed it at Cece. "Well, it's really unfortunate you got your memory back, and that old Bama had such a big mouth. I always kind of liked you. I'm sorry about this."

Cece's mouth was so dry she didn't think she could speak. Finally, she managed to get out, "So, you're going to kill me now too? Do you know how to use that gun?"

"Oh yes. Tony used to take me target shooting."

Cece reached over for her coffee cup, trying to stall for time. She glanced up at the wall clock. "So how are you going to explain shooting me?" Cece inquired.

"I'm not sure yet, but I'll think of something. Maybe you had a terrible nightmare and went crazy and attacked me. I don't have all the details worked out."

They both jumped when the loud doorbell pierced the silence. "Don't make a sound," Ruth said softly.

"It's all over Ruth. Put down the gun."

"It's not over until I say it's over. Now shut up," she hissed.

The doorbell rang insistently again.

"You reckon they've gone for a walk on the beach or something?" Dell asked.

"Beats me."

Dell glanced down at her watch. "It's ten after. Campbell knew we were planning to pick her up at nine."

Cece knew she had to do something. If the detectives left she would die. She slowly placed her hands in her lap, grabbed the edge of the tablecloth, then yanked and dove for the floor. Hot coffee spilled into Ruth's lap and she fired.

Dell's finger was about to press the buzzer again when the glass in the front picture window exploded, followed by the unmistakable retort of a gunshot. "I'll take the back," she yelled as she drew her weapon.

Shark used the butt of his gun to shatter the glass pane in the front door, then reached inside and unlocked it. He crept into the foyer and yelled, "Cece, are you all right?"

"Yes," she yelled from under the dining room table. "It's her. She's the one."

Shark peered around the doorway and saw Ruth, gun pointed in his direction, standing by the table. He saw Dell attempting to open the backdoor, but it was locked.

"Put the gun down slowly on the table, Mrs. Kline."

"I don't think I can do that, Detective."

Shark walked into the room, his gun gripped in both hands and trained on Ruth. "Cece, I want you to crawl out from under the table and go unlock the back door for Dell." Cece whimpered, then slowly rose, her eyes darting back and forth between the two of them. As soon as she had taken two steps back, she ran into the kitchen.

"Well, well, Detective. You'll have to admit it was a good plan. With my husband and Cece both dead, you would have been convinced it had something to do with their research. If that stupid oaf hadn't told her, I don't think you would ever have figured it out."

"You may be right. But we'll never know now. I think it's time you put down your gun. My partner is coming in the back door."

Ruth's shoulders fell dejectedly. She took a deep breath. "I don't think so. You see, I'd never make it in prison." Ruth reached over with her left hand and cocked the gun.

"Ruth," Shark pleaded, "don't make me shoot you."

"But I don't have the nerve to do it myself. So go ahead, do it."

Shark could see Dell creeping in slowly from the kitchen, both hands extended in a shooter's stance, her pistol never wavering. "Put the gun down *now*, Mrs. Kline," Dell said authoritatively.

Tears began to stream down the widow's face. She shook her head no. Dell came into her peripheral vision. "Mrs. Kline, we can work this out. Just put the gun down," Dell said more calmly. Shark could hear Cece crying in the kitchen.

"Please, Ruth!" Cece yelled. "Hasn't there been enough dying?"

But it was as if she hadn't heard Cece. She stared into Shark's eyes, then turned her head and looked at Dell. Then she knew what to do, she knew what would push his button. She wrapped her left hand around the grip of the pistol and supported her right hand.

It was as if her arms were leaden with heavy weights, and everything seemed to happen in slow motion. She whispered softly, "I'm sorry," as she moved the gun away from Shark, pointed it at Dell, and fired.

"No!" Shark screamed, fear erupting in him like a geyser, as he let loose with two quick shots. Cece sobbed loudly in the kitchen.

"Dell, Dell, are you all right?" Shark pleaded, his eyes never leaving the widow, who was sprawled back in the chair, the gun still in her hand.

After what seemed like days to Shark, Dell said, "Hell no, I'm not all right. She shot me in the arm."

"Just in the arm? Are you sure?"

"What do you mean *just in the arm?* It hurts like hell. How come I'm always the one to get shot?"

And then Shark sighed with relief. He knew his partner was going to be okay. "Cece, call 911 for an ambulance!" he yelled as he approached the widow and removed the gun from Mrs. Kline's hand.

"You think your arm hurts, just wait until Sheriff Grant finds out you're not wearing your vest."

"Oh crap, come on, help me get it on before the ambulance gets here."

"No way, Jose."

Dell examined her wound and saw that the bullet had just grazed her. She ran her hand through her hair as she leaned against the wall.

Shark began to smile.

"What are you laughing at?" Dell asked.

"When I saw you run your hand through your hair, I remembered something. Didn't you say that if Campbell was still alive you would shave your head?"

All the color drained from Dell's face. "You wouldn't!"

Epilogue

Cece pulled into the driveway of a small ranch house on Highway 17, about halfway between Savannah and Hardeville, and parked behind the familiar white pickup truck. She opened the car door, shucked out of her white lab coat, and threw it onto the passenger seat. It had been a busy day in the laboratory at Chandler Hospital. She was so happy she had finally talked her father into moving to South Carolina.

Cece walked around the side yard and approached the healthy looking garden in the back. She bent down and plucked two ruby-red tomatoes off the vine. She brought them to her nose and inhaled their sweet aroma. It was still close to 90 and the humidity hung heavy in the air. Cece wiped the sweat off her brow with the back of her hand. She sauntered toward the back door, noticing the riotous colors of the Vinca in the flowerbed.

Cece walked up the steps and entered the kitchen door. "Dad, your garden looks wonderful, and something smells scrumptious."

Then she stopped dead in her tracks. Her father, his back to her, was busy at the stove, but Brad Johnson sat in her seat at the dinner table. She didn't say anything, her mouth hanging open in surprise. "Uh, your dad was kind enough to invite me to dinner," Brad said, rising out of his chair. Cece glanced at her father, but he kept his back to her.

"The poor man could turn gray waiting on an invitation from you," her father grumbled.

Brad approached Cece. He drank in the sight of her. She was finally beginning to gain a little of the weight back she had lost.

"Where's your car?" she asked.

"In the garage. Your dad wanted to surprise you."

"Well, he did that all right."

Brad reached out and took Cece's free hand in both of his. "I'll go if you want me to." Cece looked at him and could see the hope written all over his face. He had called her frequently, but she had always declined his invitations. She needed to heal first. Maybe it was time to put everything behind her.

"No, it's okay if you stay," she said, smiling up at him.

He pulled her into his arms and gave her a big hug. "Thank you."

"It's about time," her father mumbled under his breath. Maybe he'd get to have some grandkids running around this place some day after all. "Oh, by the way, Stone Phillips from "Dateline" called. He wants to set up an appointment to talk to you."

Surprised, Cece said, "That's strange. I never contacted 'Dateline'."

"Well, somebody must have," her father said. "It's about time the public learns about all those side effects the damn cell phones can cause."

"Dad!" Cece shrieked, as she and Brad started laughing.